DATE DUE

| 1994 | 1999 |
|------|------|

# The Painted Lady

*Also by Stephen F. Wilcox:*

THE DRY WHITE TEAR
THE ST. LAWRENCE RUN
THE TWENTY-ACRE PLOT
ALL THE DEAD HEROES
THE NIMBY FACTOR

# THE
# PAINTED
# LADY

## A HACKSHAW MYSTERY

# STEPHEN F. WILCOX

**St. Martin's Press    New York**

Library of Congress Cataloging-in-Publication Data

Wilcox, Stephen F.
    The painted lady / Stephen F. Wilcox.
        p.   cm.
    ISBN 0-312-10520-7
    1. Hackshaw, Elias (Fictitious character)—Fiction.
    2. Journalists—New York (State)—Fiction.   I. Title.
PS3573.I419P35   1994
813'.54—dc20                                                    93-43489
                                                                CIP

First edition: February 1994
10 9 8 7 6 5 4 3 2 1

To the memory of my sister, Shirley
Lenhardt, whose laughter still echoes in
the quiet times.

You've got to go along to get along.

That's the first thing you need to know about small town life. Oh, we talk a good game—about rugged individualism and e pluribus unum and all the rest—but it's mostly bunk. The truth is, small town folks don't like change, and they don't like strangers, and, more often than you'd expect, they don't even like each other.

The second thing you need to know about small towns is this: everybody comes from one. You, me, the mayor of New York, and the queen of England. Everybody.

Because, after all, a city is just a collection of insular neighborhoods divided according to race or religion or culture or money. And suburbs—well, your typical suburb is basically a city neighborhood with good schools and riding mowers. And neighborhoods are simply small towns, rubbing shoulders with other neighborhoods and flinching at the friction.

The point is, when you take some of the small out of a

small town—when it gets a little more crowded, a little less homogenized, a little unsure of itself—you begin to see tiny cracks in the civilized veneer.

And when that happens, believe you me, the results can be murder.

It began, fittingly, amid the worst humiliation of my life. Mid-June. The Port Erie Volunteer Firemen's Carnival. You know—candied apples, Ferris wheels, simple games of chance.

And, of course, the dunking stool.

"Whatsamatter, Hacka-shaw, you not havin' a good time uppa there?"

"Uppa yours, Fettuccine."

"Is *Finapolia*, you . . . you . . ."

The stammering fool was a little Neapolitan who, since arriving on our shores a decade ago, had operated a shoe repair shop next to the barber on Port Erie's main street. The other fool was me.

"*Bafa-coulo!*" He hooked a thumbnail under his upper choppers and snapped off an Italian salute of some kind.

I wiped my watery eyes with a nonexistent sleeve and retorted, "Yo mama."

Admittedly not my finest hour, sitting there in my swim trunks like a beached flounder, exchanging sophomoric insults with a miniature Mussolini wannabe. But can you blame me? It was bad enough I'd let myself get trapped into participating in such a gross indignity in the first place; don't ask me to suffer the mockery of stunted cobblers in the bargain.

A victim of my own altruism is what I was. I mean, you try to do something nice for people and where does it get you? It was my sister Ruth who deserved most of the blame. She was the one who first put me up to writing a prosaic piece on community spirit, as a way to shame a few more Port Eriens into volunteering as cashiers and ticket takers and hot dog chefs for the firemen's annual extortion fest. Little did I realize how my own words would boomerang back at me a week later when dear Mrs. Cooper of the Port Erie Ladies Auxiliary showed up at the office in search of "celebrity" dunkees for the carnival's favorite cash cow.

In case you were brought up in China or Manhattan or some equally backward place, I should explain that the dunking stool is a diabolical concept, probably of Puritan origin, in which a witless soul sits on a high platform suspended over a tank of water. The platform is a two-piece job rigged with a piano hinge, with a trip wire connected to a metal arm that extends out to one side. On the end of the arm is a round metal target the size of a pie plate, usually painted with a red and white bull's-eye. If you haven't guessed by now, participants pay a dollar for the privilege of firing three baseballs at the target; a solid hit plunges the hapless dunkee into the aforementioned tank of fetid $H_2O$. Not my idea of a good time from either perspective, but try explaining that to my beloved sister.

"It's for a good cause, Elias," she had cajoled me at the time. "Besides, you yourself wrote how imperative it is for citizens to give of themselves for the betterment of the community."

She was hissing at me, partly out of pique and partly because Mrs. Cooper was hovering anxiously just out of earshot on the far side of our compact newsroom.

"In the first place, Ruthie," I explained patiently, leaning backward in my creaky swivel chair, "that whole spiel was your idea. I only wrote the damn thing because you're my only living relative, cousins excepted. And because we needed to fill a four-inch hole in our layout."

"And because I happen to be the publisher of this newspaper. Let's not forget that little detail."

3

As if she'd ever let me. The newspaper in question is a slim suburban weekly called, at my sister's insistence, the *Triton Advertiser*. The "Triton" bit is an allegedly witty play on tritown—as in Kirkville, Port Erie, and Chilton, the three small western New York townships that make up our circulation area. I've been the editor in chief for the paper ever since Ruth talked her husband, Ron Barrence, into bankrolling the enterprise as an adjunct to the printing shop he operates in Chilton. But don't let the lofty title fool you; the pen may be mightier than the sword, but the mightiest pen of all is the one that signs the checks.

"In the second place," I went on, ignoring Ruth's bullying, "I was exhorting people to volunteer in their own communities. I live in Kirkville, in case you've forgotten that little detail."

"In case *you've* forgotten, Elias, Port Erie provides forty percent of our readership. If looking hypocritical doesn't bother you, think of the public relations disaster we face when word gets around you refused to participate in the town's biggest annual charitable event."

"Not to worry, Sis," I said airily. "If SAT scores count for anything, Port Eriens have short memories."

All that sally earned me was more vituperation from my sibling, who was soon joined deskside by the earnest Mrs. Cooper. Together they performed the classic good cop–bad cop routine, with yours truly as the beleaguered collar:

"You're absolutely perfect for this, Hackshaw. . . ."

"You owe me this, Elias, after the scene you created at last month's Chil-Kirk PTA meeting. . . ."

"You're well known and, shall we say, controversial enough to have legions of detractors who would love a chance for a little payback. . . ."

"Just because you're my little brother doesn't give you a free ride around here, you know. . . ."

4

"All in good fun, of course, Hackshaw. . . ."

Well, they went on that way for what seemed like an hour, yammering at me in stereophonic sound until finally, with every last drop of free will pestered out of me, I promised to give up a Saturday afternoon to become a sitting duck for the damn Port Erie Volunteer Firemen's Carnival.

And it was even worse than I'd imagined.

"You shoulda brung you water wings, Hacka-shaw."

"And you should've brought an interpreter, you miserable mincing miser—"

Just then a burly townie, his right arm as wicked as his grin, sent a fastball caroming off the pie plate, plunging me back into the wet stuff and setting off another laughing fit by the vindictive shoe elf.

Finapolia had sworn a vendetta against me ever since I'd innocently misspelled his name in my Ramblings column awhile back. It came out "Fanapoli," which apparently is some sort of grave Sicilian insult on the man or his hometown or both. Another argument against good deeds—I'd only mentioned him in my column in the first place to give that hole-in-the-wall shop of his a little free publicity.

Okay, there may have been some barter involved, too, as in noncash payment for resoling my Dexters—but that isn't the point. The point is, I was a captive audience, condemned to spend the afternoon alternately listening to little Luigi's bilingual insults and, all too frequently, dropping butt first into a tank of freezing, chlorine-laced water. Most annoying was the fact Finapolia hadn't parted with a penny for his amusement. For the past hour he'd contented himself with standing off to one side, gleefully watching others try to put me into the soup and squealing like a La Scala tenor every time someone succeeded. The parsimony wasn't exactly a news flash. He still had the first dollar he ever made and failed to declare, framed and hung on the wall behind his work table. (I once suggested it would be more appropriate to mount it under the table, but Luigi failed to see the humor.)

Let's face it, you make a few enemies along the way when you're in the journalism game. Quite a few. Which is why Mrs. Cooper was so desperate to sign me up in the first place; I was making a fortune for the firemen.

Not that I was the only celebrity dunkee on the roster. Mr. van Lunt, Port Erie's junior high school principal, who had preceded me on the platform, was a big favorite with the Clearasil crowd. But he'd had it easy by comparison. Most of the budding couch potatoes taking aim at him had no idea what to do with a baseball absent uniforms, organized league play, and a clutch of overnurturing parents in the bleachers. Also, the kiddies were conserving most of their dollars for the Belgian waffle concession. My admirers, on the other hand, were old enough to remember sandlots and backyard games of catch with their dads, yet spry enough to whang balls off the bull's-eye with disspiriting regularity.

"Jeez, Hack," someone called out when I resurfaced, "you look like a big old lake trout I hooked off Sandy Point the other week. Only that was a keeper."

This was contributed by Fritz Kohl, a local who strung phone lines for Rochester Tel when he wasn't out on Lake Ontario tormenting fish from his twenty-foot cruiser. As far as I could recall, I'd never written anything particularly derogatory about Kohl, but there he was, third in line for a chance to punish me. Just another example of that puckish German sense of humor, I suppose.

Anyway, that's when I decided enough was enough.

"Hey, man," the oaf with the cannon arm shouted. "Get your ass back up there—I still got two balls left."

"We should all be so fortunate."

"Yeah, Hacka-shaw, where you think you goin'?"

I had climbed out of the tank by then, but instead of

returning to the platform, I had snatched my towel from one of the ladder's middle rungs and was vigorously wiping off.

"I think I goin' home," I said to Finapolia and anyone else who wanted to know. Cries of protest rang out from little Luigi and Fritz Kohl and the blustery townie and the half dozen others in the line. The racket must've carried all the way to the over-under booth, because Mrs. Cooper came running quicker than you can say drip-dry.

"Wait, Hackshaw! You can't leave yet!"

"Watch me."

"But you're our best draw—"

"Flattery will get you nowhere."

"What am I supposed to tell all these people in line?"

"How about 'Get a life'?" I said as I squeegeed a quart of water from my hair.

Mrs. C. was distraught. "Think of all the contributions you're bringing in for a new medivan—the ambulance volunteers desperately need a new vehicle."

"So add the cost to the next property assessments."

"You know very well that's impossible," she lectured. "The voters have already rejected the latest school budget and now the town's operating budget is under attack too."

That's another thing. People want everything under the sun, so long as they don't have to pay for it. You have to trick and wheedle the money out of them with carnivals and raffles and bake sales so they think they're getting something extra out of the deal.

"Maybe if you tried handing out Kewpie dolls along with the tax bills," I suggested, still toweling.

"Just stay until four, Hackshaw. Then everyone will drift over to the tug-of-war contest at the mud pit. *Please* do this for me." Her eyes were suddenly damper than my enthusiasm. Women never play fair.

I exhaled a curse.

7

* * *

"Um, excuse me. Are you Mr. Hackshaw?"

"Who wants to—oh!" I stared openly for a long moment, then had the presence of mind to finish zipping my jeans. "Yes, ma'am, that would be me. Absolutely."

I was standing inside an ancient camping trailer the size and shape of a giant kidney bean, to which I had retreated at the stroke of four o'clock. The trailer, provided by one of the firemen as a changing room for us celebrity volunteers, was parked on a square of lawn that ran behind the dunking platform. The rounded metal door was too battered to shut properly, so I'd left it cracked open a few inches while I slipped into my civvies. My unexpected caller had nudged it open a few inches more and was staring up at me skeptically from a patch of trampled grass that served as the trailer's stoop.

"My name is Hester DelGado, Mr. Hackshaw—"

"Most folks just call me Hackshaw. Or Hack, as unfortunate as that sounds in my case."

Her thin, dark eyebrows rose into question marks.

I hastened to explain. "Given my occupation, I mean. I'm a newspaperman, y'see. In the news game a hack is—" I realized I was babbling and broke off abruptly, but she pretended not to notice; well-bred, apparently.

"I understand you also do restoration work on old houses? As a sideline?"

"Indeed I do." I stepped down out of the ratty camper and eagerly shook the hand she was offering.

She was lovely, this Hester DelGado, but then, aren't they all? Somewhere in her mid-thirties, I'd guess. Her hair was russet and long and thick and flowed in soft waves from the top of her head to a point just above her impressive breasts. Her eyes, under languid blue-shadowed lids, were midnight black, direct and knowing in a way that sets off warning bells in the heads of sane men and a tingle in the groin for the rest of us. She was wearing blood red lipstick and dashes of rouge on each high cheek and a pair of jeans that looked a lot better on her than mine did on me. Along with large hoop earrings and paired bracelets jangling at each wrist and half a dozen gaudy rings on her slender fingers, she wore around her neck a gold chain with an ice blue tear-shaped crystal attached. Strapped under her left arm was a black leather shoulder bag large enough for all of her cosmetics and probably the camping trailer as well. With her top-heavy figure teetering above a pair of spike heels, she looked ready to tip over at any moment but serene in the knowledge that there'd be any number of eager males to break the fall if she did.

"I've only moved to Port Erie recently," she said. "And I'm in the process of fixing up an old Victorian." Then she mentioned a Virginia Street address, and a light came on in my waterlogged brain.

"Ah!" I nodded. "So *you're* the painted lady."

2

"If you mean my house, yes," Hester DelGado said through an uncertain grin. "I bought the old Mott place in May."

"You've kept busy, judging from what I can see on a drive by."

The Mott house, as it's been known ever since Philbin Mott had it built back in the 1850s, is a large Italianate, complete with a cupola—or belvedere, if you like—centered atop its low-hipped roof. Mott was said to be a successful banker in his day, but he's been dead for a hundred years so I guess there's no point holding a grudge.

In recent decades his once-grand estate had deteriorated considerably; a subsequent owner, probably back in the thirties, had covered the original clapboards with god-awful asphalt shingles, and the spacious grounds that once surrounded the house had been subdivided into building lots sometime after the Second World War. But most of the house's decorative touches—the broad cornices and heavy bracketing, the ornate front porch and hooded windows—

10

remained undisturbed, if neglected. All the old manse really needed was someone with good sense and ambition—and deep pockets—to buy it and return it to its former glory.

My interest in its fate comes honestly. I dabble in architectural restoration when I'm not covering school board meetings and church socials for the *Advertiser*. Partly I do it out of necessity, to supplement my income—those checks Sister Ruth signs define the phrase *working poor*. But mainly I do it for purely selfish reasons: I'm a soft touch for elegant Victorian buildings and the history and craftsmanship they represent, and I do my humble best to see that they enjoy a long and dignified old age.

So you can imagine my joy when, a couple of weeks earlier, while driving out to the west end of Virginia Street on my way to an assignment for the paper, I discovered that all of that disgusting asphalt had been torn off in favor of a fresh, polychromatic paint job. Now, I will admit that the new color scheme threw me off a bit; the body of the house had been done in what designers call dusty rose—pink, to the rest of us—with lavender and maroon and taupe used to accent the otherwise white trim. A little overstated for an Italianate, in my opinion, but a huge improvement nonetheless. Overnight, it seemed, the dowager had been transformed into a vivacious painted lady.

I remember thinking at the time that some yuppie couple must have moved here from the city with plans to convert the Mott house to yet another bed and breakfast. We've had a glut of those in recent years, bless their preservationist hearts. Now I found myself hoping I was at least half wrong—that the alluring creature standing before me might be unfettered with a significant other.

So I decided to go straight to the meat of the matter. "Um, would that be Mrs. or Miss DelGado, by the way?"

"It's Miss, but I prefer Ms.," she said, adding invitingly, "Hester to my friends."

"Well, like I said, Hester, you've done wonders with the place in just a few weeks."

"Thanks. It's been a challenge, and there's still lots to do. In fact"—she frowned at her wristwatch—"I have to get back to meet with a plumbing contractor at five. But first things first." She slipped the leather bag off her shoulder and fished around inside it, pulling out a tired cigar box, the contents of which rang like sleigh bells when she handed it to me. "I heard you had a good reputation—when it comes to salvage and restoration work—and I . . . well, I wondered if you could tell me what these are."

I couldn't fail to note the qualifier: "when it comes to salvage and restoration work." Obviously, whomever she'd spoken with was less flattering when it came to other aspects of my reputation. It also was obvious that this was a test, to determine if what she'd been told about my expertise was true. But fair enough. I flipped open the lid and, instead of petrified panatelas, found some two dozen pieces of tarnished brass staring up at me. They were shaped like the letter C, about half an inch wide with a narrow cutout, like an elongated keyhole, running lengthwise along the curving metal.

"Hmm. Sash cups," I said, raising my gaze. "Which corner of the attic did you find these in?"

"It was the basement, actually. The workmen ran across them when they were removing the old furnace." Her voice had the slightest trace of an accent that could've been Madrid or San Juan or even East Los Angeles, for that matter. "What exactly are sash cups, Mr. Hackshaw?"

"They were used to hold the cords in place on double-hung windows. You know—those little ropes you see running vertically on either side of the windows." Seeing as how this was an audition of sorts, I felt the need to elaborate. I pointed out the little keyhole cutouts and explained how a knotted cord or chain is fitted through the groove and how the whole works slips into channels cut into the sash's stiles. Then all you need is a pair of little pulleys up near the top of the jam and a couple of cast-iron weights at the other end of the cords, dangling free in hidden cavities behind the window casing, and you're in business—a window sash that, at least in theory, slides up and down effortlessly. In practice, years of warping and rotted cords and paint buildup render many an old double-hung inoperable.

"Mmm, I see—I think," Hester said when I finished showing off. "But I don't believe I have any of those kind of windows left in the house. I guess a previous owner must've had them replaced."

"Happens a lot with these cantankerous weight-and-pulley systems," I said neutrally. They're simple enough to fix if you have a few hand tools and some new nylon cord and lots of time to putter, but most folks don't bother these days, preferring to exchange their old windows for thermal replacement units. And it's hard to argue with them. Aesthetics aside, modern windows are easier to operate and much more energy efficient. But here's a tip: if you replace your old sashes, don't forget to remove the weights and insulate the cavities behind the jams. Those empty spaces account for at least half of your heat loss.

I tried handing the cigar box back to Hester, but she shook her head.

"Keep them if you want. Maybe you can find a use for them, or sell them for scrap or something."

"Well, if you don't want them—" I did happen to know of an architectural salvage firm in Rochester that probably would give me half a dollar each for the sash cups, then resell them to fresh-faced do-it-yourselfers for a 200 percent markup.

"The last thing I need is more boxes of junk around the place," she told me. "In fact, that's one of the reasons I sought you out. I have all these odd bits and pieces of the house squirreled away everywhere—the basement, the garage, the attic. Old doors and window frames, shutters, doorknobs, heating grates—and things I can't even identify, like those sash thingamabobs. I don't know how much of it, if any, I need to save. Or if I should just put everything out at the curb."

"Christ, don't do that!" Not until I had a chance to come by with my Jeep and a flatbed trailer. "I mean, you never can tell what you might need to complete your renovation plans."

"Exactly what I was thinking," Hester said, the easy smile now in full flower. "I'd like to hire you to oversee a few restoration-type repairs I've got in mind. At the same time, I thought you could sort through all the old materials and set aside anything we can reuse. The rest you can toss or haul away—whatever you see fit. If any of the stuff has salvage value, maybe we can figure it in as part of your payment for the restoration work."

"Sounds good." Then the Oriental rug merchant in me decided to hedge his bets. "You understand, there's not a lot of margin in reselling old house parts. I mean, I may be able to find someone to take a few of the items, but—"

She flapped her bejeweled fingers dismissively. "Whatever you think is fair. I'm sure you'll do the right thing, Mr. Hackshaw."

"Naturally," I assured her, grinning lobe to lobe. Now don't go jumping to conclusions. I wasn't planning to cheat her or anything like that. It's just that, when dealing with a beautiful woman on any subject, I've found it's better to reduce their expectations at the outset. "And it's just plain Hackshaw, remember?"

"Hackshaw it is, then." She shook back her dark red hair, causing the sun to glint off the gold hoops in her ears, and glanced at her watch again. "I have to get home and meet the plumber, but I'd like to set up a time for you to come by, the sooner the better. Would Monday be all right?"

"Why not tomorrow?"

"On Sunday?" My eagerness seemed to put her off a bit; suddenly I was a potential ax killer trying to get a foot in her door. Or maybe she was recalling certain other facets of my checkered reputation. Whatever, I hurried into the breach with a perfectly plausible explanation.

"If I'm not mistaken, trash pickup is Monday morning over your way," I said. "If I can cull out the obvious junk tomorrow, we can have it gone by the next day. You wouldn't want a pile of debris sitting out at the curb for a week," I added. "An eyesore like that wouldn't do anything to endear you to your new neighbors."

She rolled those sensuous eyes around in their blue-shadowed sockets. "God, that's the last thing I need—more hassles with the neighbors." Before I could ask her what she meant, Hester checked her watch a third time—it was still there—and said, "Tomorrow would be fine, but not too early; I like to laze around on Sunday mornings. Maybe you could make it around one o'clock; stay for dinner later, too, if you like." She hefted the bag higher on her shoulder and began backpedaling, surefooted as a mountain goat, on those precariously high heels. "Gotta run now, Hackshaw. See you tomorrow afternoon, okay?"

"You bet." I watched her disappear around the far end of the dunking platform, enjoying the rotation of her hips as she went and thinking maybe this day hadn't been a complete waste after all. Then, with a sigh, I reached back into the trailer, snatched my gym bag from the grimy linoleum floor, and set off for the tug-of-war pit, relishing the opportunity to see others dragged through the mud for a change.

But I didn't get more than fifty feet down the midway

before I was accosted by an older couple. The Murrays, Vern and Doris; a pair of local retirees who lived in a tidy postwar Cape Cod, also over on Virginia Street, coincidentally. Or not so coincidentally, as it turned out.

"Well, just the fella we've been wanting to see. How you doin', Hackshaw?" Vern Murray asked in a tone that implied he didn't give a damn how I was doing. He squinted disapprovingly at the top of my head. "Your hair looks a little damp there."

"Muggy day."

"Hmmph." He glanced around, apparently checking the air for visible evidence of moistness. Finding no suspended droplets, he said, "You think this is humidity, you oughta try St. Pete sometime."

Like many of our seniors, the Murrays had bought a winter home in Florida the minute Vern's biological clock struck sixty-two. I think it's a state law or something.

"Here's the thing, Hackshaw," he went on. "Me and the missus think you should write up an essay in that paper of yours, pushing the politicians to do something about the deer and raccoon problem once and for all."

The missus bobbed her head in assent. She was a short, plump woman—a little gray partridge in contrast to her husband, who was lean and leathery and beaky as a vulture.

"You think so, huh?" One of the hazards of being a newsman is that everyone assumes you're interested in hearing their opinions.

"Darn right we think so. Having all our shrubs eaten up and our garbage drug all over creation is bad enough, now we've got these animals runnin' through the yard any hour of the day or night, destroying our property like, well, like a plague of locusts."

"Uh-huh." The local deer contingent, and to a lesser extent the raccoons, had been a hot topic in Port Erie for

16

several years. The west end of the village proper bordered a small county park and a somewhat larger pine woods held in trust by the state. Both were prime habitat for the indigenous fauna—so prime, in fact, that the woods had become over-populated. Which meant that the animals were forced to come into town to forage for food, prompting some folks to advocate a controlled hunt to thin out their numbers. I'd heard the Murrays' thoughts on the subject at many a town board meeting, but there didn't seem to be any way to avoid hearing them again, so I said, "Our furry friends have been up to some new mischief?"

"There's nothing funny about it, Hackshaw. The other morning a big buck came tearing across our front yard and charged one of our deer statuettes. Just knocked it flat—I saw it with my own eyes from the breezeway. And something's been gnawing the yarn off Dorie's sheep, too. I'll bet you dollars to donuts it's those raccoons."

"Doris has sheep?"

"Not actual sheep, for pity's sake." The missus decided to handle this part herself. "Lawn ornaments. You know— plywood cutouts with the features painted on and everything? I've got a mother and her three little lambs."

"In other words," I said deadpan, "the real wildlife are interfering with the fake wildlife."

"That about sums it up," Vern said.

"Well, I'll give some thought to an editorial." When St. Pete freezes over.

I laid on my best public relations smile—the one Ruth likes me to wear whenever dealing with subscribers—and began to inch away, but the Murrays weren't through with me yet. I should've suspected as much, judging by the sly appraisal I'd been getting from Doris. You know the look—the sort a female puts on whenever she's about to say something catty, usually about some other female.

17

She immediately confirmed my suspicion. "Wasn't that the DelGado woman we saw you talking to?"

"As a matter of fact, it was. She's looking for someone to do some renovation work on her place."

Doris sniffed. "I'll bet that isn't all she's looking for."

"There's something else you oughta be investigating, Hackshaw," Vern instructed, poking the air between us with a knobby index finger. "Funny things been going on over to the Mott house ever since that hippie moved in."

I barely managed to contain a laugh. "I thought she seemed very nice."

"You would," Doris said dryly.

"She's trying to turn the place into a flophouse, Hackshaw. Got a bunch of young hellions moving in. Next it'll be dope addicts, if it isn't already. Why, we've already had one attempted break-in at our house, and I'd bet it was one of those pregnant runaways of hers—"

"Pregnant runaways?"

Doris nodded grimly. "Two or three so far. Renting 'em rooms, as best we can figure."

"And if that's not bad enough," Vern interjected, "have you seen what she's done to that place?"

"You mean the fresh paint job? I'd say it looks great—"

"You would."

"Hell, Hackshaw." Vern fairly expectorated the words. "It looks like a damn French whorehouse."

"Now, how would you know that, Vernon? Oh, I forgot. You did a hitch in Paris during the war, didn't you, you old fox."

Hearing that crack, Doris abruptly switched her little blue laser beams from me to her husband, who was choking out a vehement denial. It seemed like the right time to exit gracefully, which is what I did.

3

I managed to make it over to Hester DelGado's place on time Sunday afternoon, no thanks to a Saturday night poker marathon that had started out in the party room of the Kirkville Legion Hall before moving in the wee hours to my carriage house apartment—an idea that had seemed much brighter when I suggested it at midnight than it did when the game finally broke up some five hours later. I woke up at noon to a mild headache and a living room littered with empty beer cans and overflowing ashtrays and crushed potato chips. But just as I was about to promise God never to do such a thing again, I remembered I'd finished thirty bucks to the good, which left me feeling much better about the whole thing.

At any rate, I was reasonably flush, if short on sleep and patience, when I turned off Port Erie's main drag onto Virginia Street a few minutes before one o'clock. The sight of the place, as I slowly drove up the block, was enough to chase away the last of my cobwebs. To appreciate the impact the house had, imagine a huge pink wedding cake with four or five complementing colors as part of the elaborate icing. And centered high up on its low-hipped roof, rather than a giant bride and groom, was a tall, glassy cupola done up in progressively darker shades of mauve with taupe accents.

It took a little getting used to, as I've said, but it's really only the shock of deprivation at work, like a coal miner emerging into sunlight. The surrounding homes were nice enough—typical postwar capes and ranches mostly, neat and tidy on the whole, with a brick front here and a jalousied breezeway there to break up the uniformity. But in comparison with the Mott house—well, let's just say it dominated the block the way a queen dominates a roomful of commoners.

Virginia Street wasn't much different from a lot of other streets in a lot of other older upstate villages. It was still woody and wild back in the mid-nineteenth century, when places like the Mott house were built. Spacious homes surrounded by acres of lawn, these were the residences of local merchants and doctors and bankers and their families. Back around the Great Depression, when family size and expectations began to shrink, middle-class "mansions" like these fell out of favor, many of them converted to professional offices or cut up into apartments, their superfluous acreage gradually subdivided into building lots for smaller, less ornate, but admittedly much more affordable homes for the families of returning war veterans like Vern Murray.

The real tragedy of these grand old dames isn't that they've been displaced by modernity, but that so many of the ones that endure have been mistreated and misunderstood, the craftsmanship and architectural heritage they represent so often remuddled away or simply overlooked. Just a block farther up on Virginia, for example, sat another sprawling Victorian, this one a combination of the Gothic Revival and Italianate styles that were popular just before the Civil War. It was now sectioned up into apartments, but that wasn't my gripe. It was larger than the Mott house, and it had at least as much elaboration in its turned balusters and hooded windows and gable ornaments. But you'd never notice any of that exquisite detail on a drive by because the place was painted white from sill to cornice, a bland vanilla scheme that I'm sure would've horrified both the builders and the original owners of the house. Because contrary to popular belief, polychromatic Victorians—so-called painted ladies—aren't an aberration dreamed up in the last twenty years by effete urban gentrifiers with too much time on their hands. If you were to scratch paint samples off that white elephant down the block, you'd most likely discover that a hundred years ago it was done up in half a dozen cheery colors, each one intended to bring out the intricate geometry of a dormer's gingerbread trimwork or the satirical grin of a hand-carved gargoyle.

Now, I'm not saying you shouldn't paint your house all white or all brown if you want to, or cover it with vinyl siding, or do any other damn thing that pleases you. All I'm suggesting is that if low maintenance and low profile are your goal, don't buy yourself a Victorian.

But, as zealots often will, I've allowed myself to drift away from the subject at hand.

My window was rolled down on that warm Sunday afternoon and, as I drove slowly up the driveway, I inhaled deeply. The air was redolent with the smell of fresh paint and glazing putty, an intoxicating mix for an old house maven like me.

And speaking of intoxicating . . .

I parked my vintage Jeep Cherokee in the shade of the porte cochere and continued on foot toward the back of the house, inspecting the new paint job as I went, putting one foot in front of the other without the slightest regard for where I was stepping.

"*Watch yerself—*"

I was suddenly and viciously yanked backward by the

collar. Only then did I notice, between gasps for air, that I'd been about to step off into an open cellar bulkhead.

"Jesus!"

"Amen, brother." My savior, if you'll pardon the expression, unhanded my shirt and nodded agreement. "He was smilin' down at you just now, Hack, that's for sure."

Step Garris, of all people.

"What're you doing here, Step?"

"Haulin' trash up through that there cellar door. Lucky for the both of us I was on my way back down just now, 'stead of comin' up them steps loaded down with whatnot. You'da landed right on me." Then he laughed, a short, harsh bark imbued with the unpleasant odor of stale whiskey.

Every community has at least one. A drifter in spirit who somehow never manages to make it much farther than the edge of town. The sort who punishes himself by night with the demon rum and by day with the Ten Commandments; who fervently believes the Apollo moon landings were faked and professional wrestling isn't.

Not that I didn't like the guy. I did, basically. But like fried foods and bluegrass music, he was better taken in small doses. He was somewhere around fifty, medium height and rangy, with an unruly lion's mane of curly gray hair and a bushy black beard. As far as I could remember, Step hadn't held down a steady job since the Port Erie car wash had automated, forcing him to retire his chamois.

"So you're doing a few odd jobs for, uh, Ms. DelGado?"

"Better'n that, Hack." He thrust his chest out. "She's got me on what she calls retainers. Like cuttin' the grass and haulin' the trash and fixin' up them old storms." He pointed to a row of recently primed and puttied storm windows that were propped up against the side of the garage—the source of the fresh renovation smells I'd picked up on earlier. "Anythin' needs doin', she calls me, I come runnin'."

"Uh-huh." Just then the screen door of the service porch swung out with a squeal and the lady of the house stepped through.

"Hackshaw," she said, her smile as warm as the day. "I'm glad you could come by."

"Me too."

I probably stared a little too long this time, too, but who could blame me? Yesterday's tight jeans and pullover had been replaced by a long, pleated skirt and a paisley blouse. Some of the jangly jewelry was different and so was her hair, pulled back behind her ears with the aid of a pair of blue barrettes. But the carefully made-up china doll's face and the ice blue stone resting on the swell of her breasts and the curve of her hips were exactly as I remembered. In other words, like her wedding cake of a house, she looked good enough to eat.

"I see you already know my new handyman."

"Around here, everybody knows everybody."

"Something else I'll have to get used to," she said. "When I stopped to think how much junk there is tucked away in this old place, I thought it would be good if you had another pair of hands to help you, so I called Step."

"Good thing you did." I pointed down into the bulkhead opening. "He just spared me a broken leg—and you a nasty lawsuit." I grinned to let her know I was only kidding, but it went right past her.

"God, that's all I need right now, more legal hassles."

"Troubles?"

"Mmm." She looked from me to Step and back, then heaved a mighty sigh and said, "Let's save the gory details for later, over dinner—you are planning on staying for Sunday dinner?" I assured her I was. "Good. Now, while Step deals with the obvious trash in the basement, how about if you and I start at the top, in the attic? On the way up I'll give you the

23

minitour of the house and maybe point out some of the work I've got in mind."

I clambered up the sagging steps and fell in behind her as she led the way from the service porch into a smallish kitchen that had undergone its last remodeling back when Lucy and Desi were still married. A young woman stood awkwardly in front of the sink, angling her protruding belly to one side as she languidly ran water over a colander filled with pea pods. She looked up and favored me with a weak smile.

"Hackshaw, this is Jennifer," Hester said, barely breaking stride. "She's . . . staying with me."

I managed a nod and a quick smile of my own before Hester's undertow pulled me straight on through the adjoining butler's pantry and out into the dining room. It was, as the realtors say, a great space—cross-beamed ceiling, half-paneled walls of golden oak, a big built-in sideboard with leaded glass doors on top, and an angled bay window looking out over what remained of the side yard.

"Take a look at this." Hester was standing in the doorway between the dining room and the central hall, straining to pull out one of the pocket doors. I hurried to give her a hand, the heavy door rattling and wobbling as it rolled along its hidden overhead track.

"This could use some adjustment, not to mention a few drops of oil," I said.

"I know, but it's the bottom that really concerns me."

I glanced down, then nodded in recognition. There was a gap of almost two inches between the door and the hardwood floor. The shag carpet syndrome.

"Almost every door in the house is like that, including all the bedroom doors upstairs."

"I gather there was thick wall-to-wall carpeting throughout the place when you bought it?"

She grimaced. "A dirty old orange thing, matted down

24

like a wet dog. God, it was gross. I've recently had most of the floors refinished—the bedrooms I'm having recarpeted. But now I'm stuck with all these chopped-off doors."

Another unfortunate but common remuddling in old houses, thanks to the shag carpet craze of the 1960s. Combine one of those furry monstrosities with a half-inch-thick pad and you have a problem—no swing clearance for your doors. Of course, your friendly carpet installer had a simple solution. *For a nominal charge of just two bucks a door, lady, I'll run out to the truck and get my circular saw . . .*

Hester said, "Is there anything you can do, I mean short of replacing all these doors? I don't even want to think about how much that would cost—I doubt my budget could stand it."

I uttered the perfunctory sympathies, having heard similar laments from scores of yuppy rehabbers over the years. But in this case I suspected the poor-mouthing was more than a negotiating ploy. Grand as the dining room itself was, the furnishings were strictly garage sale quality—much like my own place. The table was depression-era oak, very substantial but badly in need of refinishing, as were the mismatched chairs gathered around it. Down at the other end of the room, flanking a triple window that looked onto the front porch, was an informal home office setup consisting of an assemble-it-yourself particleboard desk and a cheap pine bookcase, its shelves swaybacked from the weight of several dozen books and catalogs.

Obviously Hester DelGado was pouring whatever resources she had into rehabilitating her wonderful old house and deferring other purchases in the meantime. It was a noble sacrifice, to my way of thinking, which is why I felt obligated to provide her with good professional advice at rock-bottom rates. The fact that she was sexy and single was only a minor consideration.

"We'll just have to be creative," I said as I mulled over the problem. "Do you have any old, original doors in with the other extra house parts?"

"Yeah, there's one or two stored in the garage loft, left over from when the kitchen was remodeled, probably."

"Great. They should be the same type of wood and the same thickness as the rest of the doors in the house. I know a stair mechanic who's also a whiz with doors. He's very reasonable, and anyway, he owes me a favor." I tapped the pocket door's stile. "He can cut strips off the spare doors and use them to patch the others. Once they've been sanded and refinished, the repair job will barely show."

"Wow, that is *such* a relief to hear." Then, to my surprise, she took my hand in both of hers and squeezed gently. "Y'know something, Hackshaw? I think you're just the man I've been looking for."

Well, if I'd known then what I know now, I might've seen the artifice at work behind those smoldering dark eyes and saved myself a lot of grief.

But then again, probably not.

4

The girl, Jennifer, set a bowl of candied yams on the dining room table with a thud, then massaged her swollen belly plaintively and headed back toward the kitchen.

I looked up from the canned ham I was carving. "You're not joining us?"

"Uh-uh. I've got . . . like, a date."

"Hmmph. A date," Hester said. "Returning to the scene of the crime, you mean." At my quizzical look she added, "Having dinner over at the home of the boy who got her pregnant."

"We've got a lot to talk about," Jennifer said defensively. "Bobby's not so bad, if you'd give him a chance."

"You gave him a chance and look where it got you."

"That's just not—oh, *shit*." With that the girl waddled off through the butler's pantry.

"Don't mind her," Hester said as she poured the ice water. "She's got the third-trimester blues."

The truth is, I was relieved. Expectant women always

make me nervous, for some reason. Besides, I'd just spent three sweaty hours hauling junk down from the attic and up from the cellar, the whole time having to listen to Step Garris's views on the Warren Commission conspiracy, so I was looking forward to a quiet, relaxing meal. If I had to spend it one-on-one with the delicious Hester DelGado, all the better.

I placed a ham slice on Hester's plate while she dished some yams and pea pods onto mine. "Well, at least it sounds like she and this Bobby are trying to work things out."

"Bobby's mother is more like it. Bobby couldn't care less about Jennifer or the baby. Too young and full of life to settle down, he says." She shook her head. "To put it bluntly, he's an asshole. Mom is the one who's arranging things with the adoption agency and seeing to it Jennifer eats right and does all the prenatal stuff—probably half hoping her little Robert will eventually come around and do the right thing. She's even paying for Jen's room and board here, not that it amounts to much. I'm not in this to make a killing."

"Of course not."

The "this" Hester was referring to was her plan to use the Mott house as a kind of boarding–cum–halfway house for what she termed "young women at risk." Girls in trouble—pregnant, abused, delinquent—whose own families had turned their backs. The way she explained it to me on our earlier minitour, she had always wanted to own a gracious Victorian in a small town setting, and the Mott house had been available at a good price. The problem was, it was too large for one person to live in alone and too expensive to renovate and maintain without some additional income. But she didn't want to cut it up into tiny apartments—that would alter the character of the house too much, she said, and I agreed—nor was she interested in operating a bed and breakfast.

"There're already too many B and B's around," she had

told me. "And anyway, I didn't think catering to tourists was what I wanted to do." But she still had this large house to contend with—four big bedrooms on the second floor, with two more in the old servants' quarters in the attic—so she had come up with the idea of providing a safe haven for the Jennifers of this world. That way she could better handle the upkeep on the Mott house and at the same time "do something useful."

So far she had taken in two boarders, Jennifer and another girl I hadn't yet met. She figured she could handle up to five or six at a time, and she expected to build up to that number gradually as word of her efforts filtered out to various county social services agencies.

I hadn't yet had the heart to tell her that word of her plans was already getting out, and that the word wasn't good. I was thinking, of course, of the Murrays and the bitching I'd had to listen to at the firemen's carnival the previous day. If they were any barometer, I suspected that Hester's neighbors were going to like her halfway house idea even less than they liked the colorful paint job.

I snuck a glance out the side bay window; the Murrays' tidy white cape sat across the street, two doors down. From my vantage point I could just make out part of the attached garage and a sliver of the yard, including Vern's precious deer statuette. Then I looked across the table at Hester, who was concentrating on her meal.

*Beautiful or not, Hackshaw, don't get involved. Other people's troubles are just that—other people's.*

But in addition to being hopeless around an attractive woman, I'm also a newspaperman by profession and inclination. Endlessly nosy, in other words. So I fortified myself with a sip of ice water and took the plunge.

"Yesterday at the carnival you mentioned problems with your neighbors," I said. "And potential legal hassles?"

"God, where should I start?" She started by waggling her fork. "Well, first, when the painters began work on the house a few weeks ago? This middle-aged harpy who lives next door, Mrs. Mobley,"—I didn't recognize the name; probably not a subscriber—"she comes tearing across the lawn like a bull terrier." Her voice went into a grating whine. " 'Oh, my God, you're not painting it *pink!* That's just so *lurid!*' Then the next day, when the guys started putting on some of the trim colors, she's back again with these two from across the street, some skinny old guy and his fat little wife."

"Vern and Doris Murray?"

"Yeah, the Murrays. A couple of real winners. Anyway, all three of them start in on me, how I'm ruining the character of their street, if you can believe it. Christ."

"How did you handle it?"

"Well, I tried to reason with them at first. I explained how Victorian restorations were helping to revitalize neighborhoods all over the country, from Boston to San Francisco. I said they should give it a chance, they'd get used to the colors—might even like them eventually." She closed her eyes for a moment and shook her head. "So this Mrs. Mobley says, real snotty, 'It's up to you to conform to neighborhood standards, not the other way around.' And then the old guy—Vern?—he tells me if I like 'fag' colors so much I should move to San Francisco."

I must've let a smile seep out, because Hester said heatedly, "It isn't funny, Hackshaw!"

"No, of course it isn't." Just typical. I can't tell you how many times I've run into similar problems on other painted ladies I've been involved with.

Hester took out some of her anger on a Parker House roll, masticating it into oblivion before saying, "And that was just the tip of the iceberg, headachewise. A couple days later this guy from the town code enforcement office shows up on my doorstep and hands me a ticket for not having a permit for the work on the house."

I frowned. "Since when do you need a permit to paint your house?"

"That's what I said. Turns out I got shafted on a technicality. Because we were 'altering the structure'—taking off those crappy asphalt shingles so we could paint the original siding—the town claims we weren't just maintaining the house, we were making 'substantive changes to the facade.' And that requires a permit." She sighed. "The guy was polite about it, but it still ended up costing me a hundred-dollar fine."

I'd never known the Port Erie zoning people to be such sticklers, and I told Hester so.

"Yeah, well, I think I'm being singled out for special attention. Wait'll you hear what happened a couple of weeks ago. That old coot, Vern, shows up on my doorstep with a town patrolman and practically accuses me of breaking into his house."

"You're kidding."

"I wish." She tried for a wry grin, but it didn't take. "It seems that while good old Vern and the wife were away that afternoon, somebody kicked in one of their basement windows. I guess the burglar didn't get in, or at least nothing was taken, but that didn't stop the Murrays from making a big stink—"

"But why bother you about it?"

She threw up her arms. "Oh, I'm the new bad apple in the neighborhood, right? Bringing in 'undesirables' to rape and pillage. Anything goes wrong around here, it's got to be that DelGado woman's fault. Anyway, the cop didn't really push it, just asked a few routine questions and left. But as far as the Murrays are concerned, I'm still harboring master criminals over here."

31

"Sure. Like some seriously pregnant teenage girl was trying to steal their furnace. Boy," I said. "Welcome to friendly little Port Erie, huh?"

"I'm not through yet."

"There's more?"

"Oh, yeah." She took a sip from her water glass. "Last week Sue, my second boarder, was moving her things in? So who's out on her porch, watching the whole time with some other sour-faced biddy? Mrs. Mobley. A little while later she calls me and wants to know what's with all these pregnant girls moving in—so I told her." She shrugged. "I figured I had nothing to hide, I'd be up-front about it. I don't have to tell you how she took the news."

"Blew her top?"

"Mmm. Popped the curlers right out of her hair—and I was beginning to think they were surgical implants." This time she did allow herself a brief smile, but it didn't mask the anger in her eyes. "Here's the kicker, Hackshaw. A few days ago I find out that Vern Murray has been circulating a petition around the neighborhood. He wants the town council to boot me out or shut me down or some damn thing. God, I'll tell you, I believe in peaceful coexistence, but sometimes I just wish I could think up some way to get back at that jerk—something that'd really piss him off."

"Try putting a salt lick in your front yard."

"A salt . . . ?" She laughed. "He must be one of these Bambi haters I've been hearing about. You know, that might not be a bad idea—"

"Yes, it would. I was joking, Hester."

"I know, I know. But still . . ."

Just then the sound of a heavy door slamming echoed from the foyer and, moments later, a girl came striding into the dining room. Like Jennifer, she was wearing a flowing maternity top above a pair of terrycloth shorts, but unlike

Jennifer, this one didn't have the telltale bulge. Apparently still some months away from singing the third-trimester blues, which might also explain her cocksure grin.

"Hi, all."

"You're late," Hester said, mildly irritated. "I told you we'd be eating around four-thirty today."

"Hey, no problem. I'll just take some stuff out to the terrace to catch some rays. As long as that moron handyman isn't still hanging around back there."

"Step isn't a moron. And he went home an hour ago."

"Good." She started piling rolls and slabs of ham onto a napkin. Eating for two, as they say, not that it showed. She appeared to be a little older than the other girl, and prettier, too, if you discount the snippy attitude. Long honey blond hair, a good build, and frank blue eyes that, just then, were aimed at me. "Who're you?"

"Hackshaw."

Hester hurried in with belated introductions. "This is my other boarder, Sue Krevin." To the girl she said, "Hackshaw's helping me with some restoration work. You'll probably be seeing him around a lot the next few weeks."

She was underwhelmed. "Whoopie," she said before abruptly heading back out toward the foyer with her make-shift dinner balanced on one palm.

We both watched her disappear toward the back of the house, whereupon Hester said, "It's going to be a long six months with that one."

We went back to our meal after the interruption, the subject of Hester's cold war with her neighbors now displaced with chatter about all the junk we'd hauled to the curb and the sorry state of Hester's butchered doors and a half dozen other small but tricky repairs that the house needed. When our plates were empty she suggested we adjourn to the parlor for dessert.

33

"Chocolate cake and iced tea, compliments of Sara Lee and Lipton's," she said. "I don't cook, I thaw."

I made all the appropriate remarks about the splendid meal—as if anyone could screw up a canned ham—and followed my hostess into the parlor. It was a large, nearly square room with tall windows and high ceilings and crown moldings, but the centerpiece was the fireplace with its lovely hand-carved oak surround.

Hester went to a stack of stereo equipment in the corner and fiddled with the controls for a moment, causing a cascade of pseudo-symphonic slush to gush from a pair of small speakers placed on either side of the front bay window. Turning back to me, she gestured toward a shopworn sofa buried under an avalanche of those little embroidered throw pillows women are so fond of. "Make yourself at home, Hackshaw. I'll be back with the dessert in a minute."

I took the throw pillows at their word and threw three or four of them behind the sofa to clear out a place to sit. Then, trying to ignore the annoying mood music, I browsed through a pile of books on the coffee table—titles like *The Crystal Handbook* and *Holistic Life Cycles*. I was reading the dust jacket on a Carlos Castaneda tome when Hester came in with the tray of defrosted delicacies. Apparently my foot was tapping—from anticipation and impatience, I assure you, but Hester misinterpreted.

"That's Yanni," she said with a nod toward the stereo.

"Ah." Like I knew a yanni from a yam.

"I love his music. It's so . . . emotive."

"Mmm." Rather than elaborate, I busied myself by making space on the coffee table. Hester set down the tray and cozied in next to me on the sofa. Just then the first synthesized tune was replaced by another just like it and I had to ask, "Uh, do any of these numbers have lyrics?"

She gave me that patient look people give other people's

unruly children. "Everything doesn't have to have lyrics, Hackshaw. I mean, when you think about it, there are no words to describe core emotions, things like sensuality and joy and romantic love."

Those sounded suspiciously like words to me, but under the circumstances I decided not to debate the point. Hester had her arm stretched along the ridge of the sofa now, her left thigh so close to my right I could feel her body heat. Frankly, I got caught staring again, momentarily mesmerized by the liquid motion of her breasts as they seemingly floated inside the flimsy blouse. Thank God she misinterpreted my intentions this time, too.

"I see you're fascinated by my Herkimer diamond," she said. She scooped the blue stone from its resting place on her bosom and held it out, suspended from its gold chain. "I could sense its power drawing you."

"Yes. Very pretty. Quartz, isn't it?"

"Mmm, mined here in the state, over in Herkimer County. Some people insist the purest energy comes from clear crystals, like the Mt. Idas from down in Arkansas. But I've always felt a special connectiveness with my little blue Herk."

"Well . . . to each his own, I guess." I tried to feign interest in the conversation, but it wasn't easy, since I had no idea what she was talking about.

Hester let the rock drop to her chest. "Do you know anything about New Agers, Hackshaw?"

"Not really." Except that I didn't care for their music.

"Actually, it involves a whole range of different disciplines, all grouped under one big umbrella. You mention New Age and most people think of the mystical aspects, like crystal healing and channeling and the rest. Of course, I'm into some of that myself, but it's really the underlying philosophy of the movement that ultimately attracts me." She shifted her body,

35

crooking her leg so that her knee was now pressing against my leg. "What it is—it's the empowerment I get from living in the moment, you know? Like I can feel myself growing, moving away from the Personal Self toward the Planetary Self."

A warning bell usually goes off in my brain whenever people start talking in capital letters, but something was jamming my radar this time. Probably the rich lavender scent of Hester's perfume.

"But I won't bore you with a lot of jargon, Hackshaw. All I'm really trying to say is that I'm a very intuitive person and, well, I know we only met yesterday, but already I sense a special kinship with you. Almost like a destiny thing—you know what I mean?"

"I do—I feel it myself."

"You have a rare intuitiveness yourself. Like the way you relate to this old house, and how you really *listened* to my problems. I mean, I feel this current between us."

"Exactly." Actually, our bodies were so close now you couldn't fit a current or anything else between us.

"Which is why I have no qualms about asking for your advice . . ."

"Ask away, dear heart."

". . . and maybe a small favor, too."

5

If you think Mondays are bad where you are, you should try starting your week with our receptionist, Mrs. Hobarth, staring you in the face. To fully appreciate the old battle ax, think retired motor vehicle department clerk. Now think proselytizing Bible thumper. And now throw in teetotaling, puritanical bigot, with the whole package cleverly disguised to look just like somebody's sweet granny.

As you may have gathered, we don't mix well. Which is why I had my head down, eyes glued to the vinyl tile floor, as I hurried into the *Advertiser*'s small reception area.

"Well—a fine good morning to you, too, Hackshaw."

"Huh?" I glanced to my left, then did a double take. As luck would have it, Mrs. H. wasn't behind her battered knee-hole desk. Instead I found myself looking at Alan Harvey, our summer intern, on loan from the local college's journalism program.

The fact is, Alan was probably the reason Mrs. Hobarth wasn't in, just as he was the reason she'd missed so many days of work that summer. She loathed the kid, for all the predictable reasons. His age—nineteen—his clothes, his language, his hair, but mostly for what she perceived to be his life-style. Alan happened to be very, well, flamboyant in his mannerisms. And that made him, to use Mrs. Hobarth's term, a sodomizer.

"Sorry. I thought you were Mrs. H."

"Puh-leeze." He rolled his eyes. "I've been called lots of nasty things—mostly by her—but being confused with that woman—" He shuddered.

"I take it she called in sick again."

"Mmm. She came in this morning but then remembered she had a doctor's appointment the minute Ruth sent me out here to work on organizing the classified ad files."

"If it's any consolation, she can't stand me, either."

"Well, judging by the sort of people she *does* like, that's probably high praise for both of us."

I'm not sure if Alan actually was gay or merely artistic. I do know he wanted to be a film critic someday, so maybe he was just trying to pad his bona fides. He wore little stickpin earrings in both ears—perhaps he hadn't yet made up his own mind—and his clothes tended toward tight T-shirts and baggy, colorful paratrooper pants. His longish brown hair normally hung straight down, with an unruly forelock draped over one eye like a pirate's patch. Today, however, the hair was different, pulled back from his face so severely I could count the bones in his forehead. He noticed me noticing and affected a speculative little frown. Maybe a moue.

"My new 'do." He turned his head, revealing a tiny sprout of hair fixed with a rubber band high up on the back of his skull. "What do you think, Hackshaw. Is it me?"

"Indubitably." Did you ever wonder why they call them pony tails, when they make you look like a horse's ass? "Any messages?"

"There were, but Ruth took them all back to the office with her."

"Uh, anything I should know about in advance?"

"I don't think—oh!" He did that coy look Mrs. H. hated so. "You did get a call from a woman—named Hester? A hint of hispanic, if I'm any judge of accents. Anyway, she wants you to call her when you have a mo."

"Hmm. Okay, thanks, Alan."

"*De nada.*"

I moved down a short corridor toward our small newsroom in back, my mind lingering on Hester's call, hoping she wasn't going to make a nuisance of herself. It's what they do, you know—use their feminine wiles to lull you into a lobotomized trance. Then, when your resistance has sunk to absolute zero, they jerk the carrot away and show you there's a stick at the other end, just to prove that nothing pleasurable in this life comes without strings attached.

But maybe I'm overreacting. I mean, it's not like it was a really big favor. All Hester wanted me to do was to research the Port Erie zoning statutes for her, find out where she stood legally regarding this unofficial halfway house of hers. Like, if Vern Murray's petition convinced the town council to come after her, did that mean she'd be out of business before she even got started? Or might there be something in the codes—a loophole, a grandfather clause, anything that she could cite as a precedent—that would provide her with legal recourse?

And there just might be. With all the heavy breathing I was doing at the time, I'd forgotten to mention old Mrs. Finney. You see, for fifty-odd years Mrs. Finney and her husband had owned the Mott house, raising four or five kids in the process. If memory served, Mr. Finney had passed away sometime in the late 1960s, shortly after the last of the children had completed college and moved out of state to begin a career. That left Mrs. Finney on her own in that big old place. She refused to sell it and move, of course—all women are stubborn that way and old women are the worst—so, as much to stave off loneliness as anything else, she had taken to renting out the spare bedrooms.

As far as I knew, she'd never gotten the proper approvals—it was one of those deals where everybody knew what she was up to but decided to turn a blind eye because the old girl was so nice and such a good neighbor and all the rest. The important thing is, town officials had let her run an informal boarding house for nearly two decades, right up until a couple of years ago, when she died. The house had sat empty since then, while her children fought among themselves over who was to get what from her estate. And now Hester DelGado had bought the place and was planning to use it in essentially the same way it had been used for the previous twenty years.

So Hester just might have her precedent after all. I planned to tell her about all of this once I'd had a chance to double-check the facts. There was no sense getting her hopes up prematurely, and, okay, I figured I'd score more points with her if she thought I had to go out and work a little to uncover the Finney story. Where does it say men can't have wiles, too?

If I haven't already mentioned it, the *Advertiser* office was in a squarish cinderblock building tacked on to one end of a homely shopping strip in Chilton Center. The other half of our cheerless bunker was taken up by a printing shop owned by Ruth's husband Ron, who helped bankroll the newspaper as a way to keep both his presses and his wife busy. With my arrival the newsroom now accommodated the entire full-time editorial staff—all three of us. Ruth, our constantly besieged publisher, was hunched over the phone, absently running her fingers through her short brown hair. Liz Fleegle, who helped with layout chores and wrote a society column called Triton Talk, was staring transfixed at a sheet of three-ply copy paper

40

rolled into her typewriter, her long, red-tipped fingers poised above the keyboard like talons, ready to lock on to a frothy adjective as soon as she could think of one. I waved a generic good morning and sank down behind my own crowded desk.

The moment she was off the phone, Sis greeted me in her routine fashion. "There you are, Elias—late, as usual."

I glanced at the big Elgin on the back wall; it was barely ten o'clock. "I always come in around this time."

"And everyone else is always in by nine."

"Funny, but I don't recall seeing 'everyone else' covering the Chilton pure waters hearings the other night until almost midnight. Or, for that matter, getting turned into a prune at the firemen's carnival on Saturday." Ruth was good to work for, as bosses go, but she had yet to grasp the concept of flextime.

"You're right. I'm being hypercritical this morning." She hopped out from behind her desk. "It's just that we've got tons of copy to deal with this week, and I wanted to have Alan run some errands when he finished the filing, but that turned out to be a mistake on my part—organizing the classified ads files, I mean—because Mrs. Hobarth had a hissy fit and took off again."

"But the really bad news is she'll be back tomorrow."

The old bat had threatened to quit two or three times, and that's just since Alan came aboard. Unfortunately, it was just talk. Without this job, she'd have to stay home all day, and nobody could spend the whole day alone with Mrs. Hobarth—not even Mrs. Hobarth. Working at the *Advertiser* gave her a purpose in life, she said; she called us her "ministry." And Ruth couldn't afford to get rid of her, either. It wasn't a complex job—answering the phone and taking classified ads—but it did call for someone who could read and write and do simple math, and who was willing to do it for minimum wage.

"The problem is," Ruth was saying, "I was going to send Alan over to Port Erie later to pick up ad copy from Harv Stedman at the ShopWise and also stop by the town hall to get some additional information on the Canal Days Festival. But now Alan's covering for Mrs. Hobarth, and I have that Jaycee's luncheon this afternoon . . ."

"Would you like me to handle the Port Erie errands?"

She blinked. "Well . . . yes. That's what I was thinking. You wouldn't mind?"

"Anything to ease your burden, dear."

"That's sweet, Elias. I know how you hate doing gofer work." She also knows how I hate being called Elias, but I can't cure her of it. "Now, all you have to do is pick up the ShopWise ad—and I know there's a handout ready on the Canal Days Festival, but you might want to do a quick interview with Corrine Brooks to get a good quote or two. You know how popular the festival is with our readers."

"I certainly do." Personally I think this explosion of festivals we've suffered in recent years is a conspiracy dreamed up by hot dog vendors. Canal Days is supposed to be "a celebration of the pioneer spirit," according to the organizers, but what it really is is an excuse for Port Erie's merchants to stage a mammoth sidewalk sale, in competition with legions of itinerant silk-screen T-shirt hawkers and the usual cadre of artsy-craftsy types selling homemade jewelry and patchwork quilts. All in all I suppose it's a harmless way to kill off a weekend, if you're into that sort of thing. The highlight of the three-day event is the Great Port Erie Raft Race, a flotilla of homely human-powered craft cobbled together from inner tubes and packing crates and any other buoyant materials the participants can come up with. The object is to race one mile down the Erie Canal—usually in a state of advanced inebriation—in hopes of winning a small trophy put up by the Port Erie Ace Hardware store.

42

"Oh, and while you're over there," Ruth said, "you'd better stop in to see Birdy Wade. He called this morning and asked to talk to you."

"Talk to me?" Bertram Wade, better known as Birdy, was Port Erie's chief of police. "Why's he want to talk to me?"

"I think he wants us to hear his side on the town budget crisis," Ruth said. "Some of the residents are agitating to have his department abolished."

"I know. I covered the last budget hearing, remember?"

"He also has this mini–crime spree to contend with. Maybe he has some public safety tips he wants to get out."

"There's a crime spree in Port Erie?"

"They've had a whole series of minor break-ins and vandalism." She rested a fist on her hip. "Really, Elias, I'd expect you to be up to speed on something like that."

"I'm only one man. Woodward at least had Bernstein."

It was at this point that Liz Fleegle finally looked up from her typewriter, bleary-eyed, and said, "Oh, morning, Hackshaw. What's another word for 'posh'?"

"Overpriced."

"Thanks for nothing."

She returned her glare to her copy while Ruth headed out front to badger Alan for a change. I dug into the pile of press releases and church newsletters and town hall bulletins that had landed on my desk over the past week and began separating the wheat from the chaff. Following my usual pattern, I tossed a healthy number into the waste basket and divided the rest into three smaller piles: timely items for the events calendar, tidbits for Liz's treacly social notes column, and, last, a few community news factoids I might be able to work into my own column, Ramblings. After an hour or so I turned to the phone messages Ruth had stuck under my phone. It just so happened that Hester's message was on top, so I decided to

43

call her first. The number she'd left with Alan wasn't a Port Erie exchange, but that wasn't surprising; she'd told me she worked four days a week at a specialty shop in Rochester's East End district.

"Now and Zen. How can I help you?"

The soft Latin shadings of her voice were an immediate giveaway. For that matter, so was the name of the shop.

"Hi, Hester. It's Hackshaw."

"Oh, great—you got my message. Can you hold a sec? I'm with a customer." There was a click, and the next thing I knew, I was listening to canned music. Not New Age this time, but Old Age—a labored string arrangement of an Elton John song. Two minutes of uneasy listening later, Hester came back on the line. "Sorry. Some of these people can take all day choosing herbal teas."

"Now and Zen is a tea shop?"

"More like an alternative general store for the conscious-ness-minded. Books, meditation tapes, holistic health foods—stuff like that. Anyway, the reason I called your office this morning is I thought you should know there was another incident in the neighborhood last night."

"An incident?"

She sighed. "A town cop showed up at the house at eight, just before I left for work. I guess some kids spray painted graffiti on somebody's garage down the block."

"He wasn't accusing your girls . . . ?"

"No, not directly. He just asked if we'd seen or heard anything unusual. But I'm sure the Murrays and their friends will try to blame it on me. I just thought you should know about it before you go and do any poking around on that other thing we talked about, in case you wanted to change your mind or anything. I mean, I don't expect you to bring any heat down on yourself just because you and I have this mutual attraction thing going . . ."

"Nonsense," I heard myself say. "That's a noble thing you're trying to do for those girls. I'd be glad to do anything I can to help you." I couldn't help it. My brain was so distracted by that "mutual attraction" carrot she was dangling, I completely forgot about the damn stick.

"God, that's so good to hear. Because you know what? I was thinking, after that cop left, how much I could use some good publicity to counter all this negativism. And then I thought, hey, Hackshaw isn't just a renovation contractor, he's got his own newspaper."

"Uh, well, it isn't really *my* newspaper—"

"So, what I was thinking, maybe you could do a little article about the Mott house? Like tell people about all the restoration work I've been doing, and at the same time work in a good word or two about my plans for the place? So—what do you think, Hackshaw?"

I think I'm an idiot.

6

Hester DelGado wasn't the only one looking for a little free publicity in the *Advertiser* that week. Or so I discovered when, in midafternoon, I was able to get away from my desk and drive over to Port Erie.

First there was Harv Stedman at the ShopWise supermarket. He wanted me to plug his new self-serve frozen yogurt machines in my Ramblings column. And since Harv places a full-page ad with us nearly every week, I didn't see how I could flat-out refuse.

Next I swung by Port Erie's old town hall, an imposing cut-stone Romanesque building. In it were the offices of the town clerk, the mayor, the zoning bureau, and, in a new addition in back, a community center that doubled as a meeting hall. Corrine Brooks, who was one of the organizers for the Canal Days Festival, also happened to be the town clerk's assistant and the person who collected the fees for building permits. An expert on local codes, in other words, and yet another supplicant I couldn't readily turn down.

I'd been interviewing her for about ten minutes, doggedly gathering a few good quotes for our article, as Ruth had requested, when Corrine made her pitch.

"Now, all the details are in the press packet I prepared, Hackshaw," she told me as she nudged her tortoiseshell glasses back up the bridge of her nose. "But if you have any questions, feel free to call me, either here or at home. Unless Marvin answers," she added, pinking up a tad.

"And what should I do if Marvin answers?" Her husband; a maintenance crew foreman for the town highway department.

"Well . . . just hang up, I guess, and try back later."

I stared across the service counter. "For Christ's sake, Corrine, it's been fifteen years since you and I—"

"Sixteen," she answered—too quickly, she realized. "Approximately. Anyway, Marvin is very touchy about my old flames." The eyelids fluttered behind the bifocals. "You have to admit, Hackshaw, we did burn rather brightly for a while there."

I didn't have to admit any such thing. Three times we'd gone out. Three times, back before she was even engaged to Marvin, when we were both young and stupid. How stupid I was only just realizing.

"Fine, Corrine. I won't need to call you at home, but if I do and Marvin answers, I'll hang up. Okay?"

"Actually, I didn't intend to get into all this with you today, but since you brought it up—"

Since I brought it up. You see how they think?

"—I wanted to do something special for Marvin's fortieth birthday next Saturday and I thought, for old time's sake, maybe I could get you to sort of salute him in your column. We're having a big party at the Beef 'N' Brew, with a band and everything . . ."

I didn't bother to ask what any of that had to do with

three crummy dates during the Carter administration, I just let her chatter away until she got it out of her system. Then I said I'd try to work something into Ramblings, space permitting. Then, before she could follow through on her threat to give me a big hug, I brought the conversation around to the town zoning codes.

"You want to look at the code book?" Corrine asked, her bureaucrat's antenna suddenly on alert.

"If I might."

"Hmm." She reached both hands under the counter and brought up the book, heavy as a Bible and twice as confusing. "You aren't going to write something that'll embarrass the mayor again, are you? He still hasn't forgotten that editorial you did on his public profanity initiative."

"Nothing like that. I just want to review the zoning restrictions for residential neighborhoods." I flipped open the code book and casually added, "Speaking of old times, Corrine, do you remember much about the late Mrs. Finney?"

After making my escape from the old town hall, I drove a mile and a quarter south of the village to the so-called town hall annex, a sprawling single-story concrete block affair with a fake mansard roof, set back two hundred feet from the road in what had been a cornfield. The building originally had been intended to house only the highway department, which would've been fine. But then Port Erie's town council took a look at the crowded village quarters of the police department and the public library and, rather than renovate and add on to either one, decided to move both of them out to the hinterlands as well.

It was a lousy idea, as I and a few others had pointed out at the time. I mean, one of the reasons folks move to a place like Port Erie is for the quaint small town atmosphere—Main Street America, circa 1890. But when you remove essential institutions from a town's traditional center—the library, the post office, the high school—you take away yet another reason for residents to congregate there. Which means you diminish a community's cohesiveness and create more problems for village merchants, who're already trying to compete with all the shopping strips that have sprung up out on the fringes.

But the majority on the council had won the debate by falling back on four simple words that seem to thrill commuter-crazy suburbanites but send shudders through preservationists everywhere: acres of free parking. The annex, constructed out on a country road a mile from the nearest sidewalk or streetlight, is just another sorry example of community planning aimed at automobiles instead of people.

All but a tiny fraction of those acres were empty when I pulled into the new complex just after three that afternoon. I made my way through a set of smoky glass doors and across a common lobby to the door marked PORT ERIE POLICE DEPARTMENT. The door opened into a large room overly bright with fluorescent ceiling lights. I stepped up to a long counter and was about to announce my intentions to the radio dispatcher seated behind it when I noticed the police chief and one of his patrolmen. They were standing beside a desk inside a small office cubicle separated from the main room by a half-glass partition. Just about the time I spotted the chief, he spotted me and motioned for me to come ahead.

"Thanks for stopping by, Hackshaw," Birdy Wade said as we shook hands. He was a stocky, gray, balding man just this side of sixty. Two things he wore seemingly in perpetuity were his tan double-knit police uniform and a sad-eyed expression. In contrast, his companion, also dressed in double knits, was tall and sturdy and intense and not much past twenty-one.

"I can wait if I'm interrupting anything important."

"Nah, we were just finishing up," Birdy said. "You remember Ricky."

"Sure." I'd written about Ricky Reimer enough times, when he was lugging around a football or running track for the Port Erie High Spartans a few years back. "I thought you were still playing ball over at Brockport State."

His slate eyes shifted away for a second. "I was, but I dropped out to go into law enforcement." He looked at Birdy. "You sure you don't want me to stay, Chief?"

"Waste of manpower. You best get back out on patrol."

For a former star jock he moved awfully slow, pausing to scrutinize me again before shuffling out the door.

"Good kid, but he thinks he's my personal bodyguard." He ran the palm of his hand back over his receding hairline and exhaled. "I suppose you've already guessed why I wanted to see you. You know about the town's budget crisis, and how some folks want to fix it by abolishing my department?"

"I covered the last council meeting. Liveliest I've seen since the mayor tried to pass a leash law on cats."

The crux of the problem was a half million–dollar shortfall in the town's tax revenues projected for the upcoming fiscal year. Port Erie's largest employer, a tool and die company that used to have a lot of defense-related contracts, had announced in the spring its intention to "consolidate" its local operation with a plant down in Tennessee. Combine that news with the recent bankruptcy of a shopping strip on the north side of town and you're left with two big vacant commercial properties on the market with no takers in sight and several dozen locals out of work. The upshot is a smaller tax base and more delinquencies, which means you have to cut services or raise taxes or both. Sound familiar?

"I was hoping you'd see fit to hear what I have to say on the subject and write it up for the *Advertiser*."

"I don't see why not." After all, this was at least as newsworthy as Marvin Brooks's fortieth birthday party.

"Our operating budget is just over $600,000 a year," he said as he settled in behind his desk. "Out of that we pay the salaries of myself, eight patrol officers, and six support personnel, along with liability insurance, health costs, equipment, and vehicles. People act like it's a king's ransom, but it's a shoestring operation. Believe me, nobody's getting rich working for the Port Erie PD."

I had by then taken out my notepad and pen and was seated in a chair. I'd heard Birdy's defense of his department before, and for the most part I was sympathetic. But the other side had its argument, too.

"What about those who say the town can get along just fine without its own force—that the sheriff's road patrol can handle all three shifts, just like it does for almost everybody else?" The majority of the townships in the county, including Kirkville and Chilton, didn't have local departments. They relied on the sheriff's patrol around the clock—in fact, even Port Erie used it for the graveyard shift, from 1:00 to 8:00 A.M.

"That's comparing apples to oranges, Hackshaw. First off, most of those other towns are either smaller in population than we are or spread out more—just a lot of big subdivisions tied together with shopping centers, like in Chilton. In areas like those you can get away with having a patrol unit cruise through two or three times per shift. Our situation's different. More than half of Port Erie's population is bunched in a ten-square-block area in the village—small yards, service alleys, narrow little side streets meandering around. Under those conditions, an officer has to know what to look for. He has to be able and willing to climb out of his unit every so often and check out an area on foot. And the sheriff's people don't have the familiarity with our town or the inclination to do it."

51

I didn't doubt his characterization of the sheriff's road patrol, but the rest of the chief's argument sounded as self-serving as Harv Stedman's frozen yogurt machines. Sure, the terrain in Port Erie was different from Chilton, but it wasn't exactly Beirut. Geography aside, the real question was whether having your own town police was a necessity or a luxury. But when I posed that very same question to Birdy Wade, he had a ready answer.

"Of course crime is relatively low in Port Erie, Hackshaw. Because my department does a good job. You'd think people could figure that out, but no. They get in a panic about this damn recession we're in and the first thing they wanna do is dump the police. Hell, they oughta be talking about expanding the department, not eliminating it. Especially with the upsurge in activity we've had recently."

"I don't remember any dramatic increase showing up in our weekly police blotter," I said.

"You remember that stolen car three weeks ago?"

"Yeah."

"Well, we had another one taken on Saturday. Swiped it right out of the Zwicki's driveway."

"Still, two stolen cars in a month—"

"Used to be we'd have maybe two in a year." He pitched forward. "And that's only part of the story. We've had an epidemic of petty crime and vandalism in town just in the last few weeks—shoplifting, headstones knocked down in the cemetery, windows smashed, attempted break-ins at half a dozen houses, graffiti turning up all over the place."

"Well, that's unfortunate, but it's summertime, Chief. The kids are out of school, and with the Northside Shopping Center closed, there aren't as many summer jobs—"

"This isn't just kid stuff—there's too much of it going on to dismiss it as high school high jinks. And there's something else." His voice suddenly lowered. "We're talking occult, Hackshaw."

"We are?"

"Devil worship. Satanic rituals. I kept this stuff out of the weekly press notice the first two times it happened, for fear of riling people up over nothing. But now it's happened again, and I figure it's better to go public than to let word leak out through the rumor mill."

A cynic might say it was also a good way to sway opinion on the budget issue, but I didn't. Political analysis is fine for the *Washington Post*, but I'd take a juicy devil worship story any day.

"What exactly did happen, Chief?" I asked, pen poised.

"Well, I mentioned the graveyard desecrations."

My pen drooped. "That's a typical drunken prank—"

"Seen as an isolated incident, sure. But there's more." He shifted in his chair. "The first time was maybe ten days ago. Wesley Stanhouse, the owner of that rest home out on Virginia Street?" I nodded recognition and Birdy continued, "He ran across somebody defacing the side of his place in the middle of the night with a can of red spray paint. He ran 'em off before they could do much, but he says he saw somebody dressed all in black. Then about a week ago, we caught a call from the Joneses, over on Martha Street. Somebody painted this weird thing on the side of their garage in the middle of the night, again using red spray paint—a picture of a goat with horns."

"They come that way, Birdy."

"They don't come with wings."

"A goat with wings?"

He lifted his desk blotter a couple of inches and pulled out a photo. "I had one of my men take a Polaroid before Jonesy painted the thing over."

It wasn't much more than an outline, and the head was

twice as large as the body, but I suppose it did look like a goat with wings.

"In Satanic circles they call that a Baphomet—a medieval personification of the devil," Birdy said. I must've looked impressed, because he added, "Or so I was told this morning by Professor Blednau."

"He'd know, I guess." Blednau was Port Erie's town historian and head of the history department at the college in Chilton, a pleasant, enthusiastic man who seemed to know about everything except how to use a hairbrush.

The chief pulled a second photo from underneath the blotter and handed it to me—an inverted five-point star, also apparently spray painted onto the side of a building.

"A pentagram," I said.

Birdy nodded grimly. "That turned up on the side of the Costanza's garage this morning, over on Virginia Street. After seeing it I decided to show both photos to the professor to find out if this crap meant what I thought it did. And he confirmed it: it looks like we have some kind of satanic cult on our hands."

Normally I would've challenged his leap of logic; three isolated acts of boogeyman graffiti don't necessarily mean the Antichrist is among us. But I was distracted by something else he'd said: the Costanzas, over on Virginia Street. This had to be the incident Hester was telling me about earlier, the one that had brought the police back to her door. The retirement home Birdy had mentioned was also on Virginia, and the other thing—the winged goat—that had happened on Martha Street, which paralleled Virginia one block to the south.

Birdy, reading into my frown of concentration, said, "Pretty unsettling, huh?"

"Mmm." I slid the photos across his desk. "Are you sure you want me to put all this in the paper, Chief? I mean, maybe your first instinct was right. Maybe it's better not to rile people up over what still might be a few kids acting out some Stephen King fantasy."

He stared at me, puzzled, as well he might be. How often does a newsie back away from a story like that? About as often as he meets a woman like Hester DelGado, I suspect.

"I'm only thinking of your reputation, Birdy. If this really does turn out to be a prank—"

"I'm telling you, it's no prank! There's a pattern here, and a purpose—I can feel it in my gut." He shook his head. "I appreciate your concern, but . . . Lookit, can I tell you something strictly off the record?"

"Okay." I slipped the pen back into my shirt pocket.

"We think we've already got a line on who might be behind this stuff. There's this new woman in town, bought the old Mott place. . . ."

7

Jackie Plummer was staring.

Not that icy glare she uses when I've done some little thing to irk her, but that other expression she has—the one with female intuition written all over it.

"What?" I asked, my fork suspended halfway to my mouth.

"You're in another world tonight. Haven't heard a word I've said for the last ten minutes. I even made a salacious reference to my boudoir and it went right past you." Now the hazel eyes narrowed into calculating slits. "You're totally preoccupied, fidgety, hardly eating—what's her name, Hackshaw?"

"Give me some credit, Jackie. You think I'd sit at your table and gobble down this wonderful, uh, casserole thing"— what the hell had she called it?—"all the while mooning about another woman?"

"Yes, because you're completely hopeless that way."

I wasn't about to argue with her, and not only because

she was right. Jackie was the closest thing I had to a significant other. We were friends, allies, confidants, and even bedmates, although that last part happened so infrequently these days we might just as well be married. But we weren't. And that's how we both preferred it, free to lead our own lives, to see other people when we wanted. At least that was the party line we both espoused. In truth it doesn't always play out that way. I myself hardly ever utter a disparaging word about the parade of middle-aged preening fops she dates, but Jackie immediately goes off the deep end if I so much as look at another woman.

So you can understand why I had no intention of admitting that, yes, I was distracted by thoughts of Hester DelGado. But who wouldn't be, after what I'd learned that afternoon?

First off, there was my little confab with Corrine Brooks and her code book. As I'd assumed, Hester's portion of Virginia Street, along with the surrounding blocks, were zoned R-1, single-family residential use only. There were exceptions—a few large old places that had been converted to apartments, like the white elephant down the street from the Mott house, and the retirement home where the initial red-paint vandalism had occurred. The place was called Silvertrees and it took up most of a block at the west end of the street. But these were all what the bureaucrats called nonconforming uses; each of the converted properties had at one time or another received a variance approval from the zoning board.

What that means is that Hester, in order to rent out rooms to pregnant teens or anyone else, would be required to seek a variance herself, which would mean prior notification of the neighbors, followed by a public hearing. Which, given the attitude of folks like the Murrays and factoring in the dynamics of local politics, would almost certainly mean no zoning change and no halfway house for Hester.

On the plus side, the talkative Corrine confirmed my

recollection of Mrs. Finney's illegal boarding house; it *had* existed, and town officials had known about it but let it slide. So there was a precedent for Hester to pursue, either with the town council or, if all else failed, in court.

But more troubling was what I'd heard from Birdy Wade. This "satanic cult" scare of his was probably nothing—just kids, as I'd tried to tell the chief—but it had the potential to grow from nothing to something in a hurry when you consider all the wild cards. You had Hester DelGado, a self-proclaimed New Age devotee, and her pink wedding cake of a house, both of whom stood out in staid Port Erie like a belly dancer at a revival meeting. Then there was her halfway house plan, which had prompted the predictable outrage among the neighbors. Obviously, the table was set for a confrontation. Now add in the Port Erie PD's problems with the budget cutters, Birdy Wade's near desperation to prove his department's worth, and the recent increase in petty crime in town—in particular the aforementioned devilish doodles on various west side buildings, all within shouting distance of the Mott house.

Under the circumstances, it wasn't surprising that word of the "strange" new woman on Virginia Street had reached Birdy or that he would lend a sympathetic ear to Hester's critics. He needed a sacrificial lamb to lay before the town council and Vern Murray's petition drive had provided him with one. Satan worshiper or scapegoat, either way Hester DelGado was in for a hell of a time.

But the question that kept pecking away at me was what, if anything, I should do about all this.

I suppose I could write up the flattering article Hester asked me for—that wouldn't take much doing. But as for getting any more deeply involved, well, the absolute last thing I needed was to get tangled up in a zoning dispute in Port Erie or to tick off the chief of police. Still, it really wasn't fair the way the locals were teaming up on poor Hester, when she was only trying to do some good. And I *was* in her employ, in a manner of speaking—that required a degree of loyalty on my part, certainly. And she was on her own in a strange town, this beautiful eccentric with the ruby lips and the shapely—

"You're doing it again," Jackie said, peeved.

"Hmm? Oh, sorry."

"I was just saying, that's probably why you didn't come by Saturday night."

"I had a conflict—the firemen's carnival."

"That was Saturday afternoon. You couldn't make Saturday night because you had a date with your new enchantress. Or there was a card game somewhere in the universe."

"A poker game," I admitted, deciding that truth was the lesser indiscretion. "I needed to unwind after that stressful dunking stool episode."

"Mmm-hmm," she said around a mouthful of whatever it was we were eating. A swallow was followed by a grin. "I'm sorry I had a conflict with the Artisans Guild show—I might've taken a few tosses at you myself."

"Your absence was appreciated in this case."

The Artisans Guild stuff had to do with Jackie's profession. She was a potter, with her own little gallery right there in the front parlor of her Kirkville Queen Anne and a studio in the converted carriage house in back. What had begun as a housewife's hobby had by necessity grown into a full-fledged business some ten years ago, when her then husband walked out on her. I only wish newspaper work and scavenging paid half as well.

"Well," Jackie said. "Whatever the reason, you do seem to be in a funk of some kind. You've barely touched your chicken divan."

I tried shrugging it off. "Monday blahs. You know, post-weekend depression." The chunks of broccoli in the casserole had something to do with it, too, but to criticize Jackie's cooking would've been almost as foolhardy as mentioning Hester DelGado.

But she wouldn't let it go. "I've never seen you depressed about anything that didn't have to do with a woman or a decaying old property. Is that it, Hackshaw? You've found yourself another Larkspur?"

Larkspur referred to a glorious but neglected minimansion I'd had a hand in saving from the wrecker's ball the previous fall. The depression part came in because, although we were ultimately successful in having the house relocated and renovated for use by the Kirkville Historical Society, I'd lost out on handling any part of the actual renovation due to the vindictiveness of a few powerful local political types. Journalism is hell sometimes.

"No, I haven't fixated on another Larkspur." I drummed my fingers on the table, fiddled with my spoon a moment, drummed a little more—all while Jackie interrogated me with that bemused stare. "Well, I guess, in a way . . . I mean, I've just picked up some renovation work on the Mott house over in Port Erie." The moment it was out of my mouth, I regretted having mentioned even that much.

"The Mott house. That big Italianate with the cupola, over near the retirement home?"

I nodded. "It's no big deal; the owner just needs some tricky restoration done and she doesn't have much of a budget to work with—"

"She?" Her eyebrows shot upward.

"Well—yeah, the owner. She happens to be a she."

Jackie plunked her fork down. "Wait a minute, the Mott house? With the new pink paint job—"

"Technically I think it's called sunset rose."

"So! Now the truth comes out."

"No, it doesn't. I mean—what do you mean?" I was so

flustered I inadvertently stuck a chunk of broccoli in my mouth. "Mmm, this is tasty. Chicken divan, you said?"

"Don't try and change the subject, Hackshaw. I passed by the Mott house last week on my way over to Silvertrees; I saw a woman in stiletto heels in the front yard, ordering some workmen around."

"How is your dear mother, by the way?" Jackie's mom lived at Silvertrees. "Still a crossword fan, I imagine."

"Long, dark red hair, a pair of jeans that showed every nook and cranny—"

"I didn't know your mother wore jeans."

"Oh, shut up, Hackshaw." She was shaking her head. "God, every woman's nightmare: a four with boobs."

"It isn't what you—a four with boobs, Gracie?"

She sighed. "A size four with overdeveloped breasts—the type men want to protect and sodomize at the same time."

"That isn't fair, Jackie. Hester's a very decent—"

"Hester, huh? What's her last name?"

"DelGado."

"Hmm. Hester DelGado. Doesn't ring any bells."

"Why would it?"

"I just thought she looked vaguely familiar that day I drove by. Can't place the name, though."

"She's new to Port Erie. Or so I understand. I really don't know anything about her, except she's hired me to oversee some work on the Mott house."

Jackie began picking at her food again. Impaling it might be a better word. "You don't owe me any explanations, Hackshaw. You're a free agent, just like me. And she's very attractive, in an obvious sort of way."

"I suppose so, but I haven't—"

The fork hit the plate again. "You know what really frosts me? That you'd accept my dinner invitation and then sit here and daydream about another woman! That's so damned disrespectful!"

"Look, my . . . inattentiveness or whatever you want to call it has nothing to do with Hester's chest, okay? I could explain everything if you'd give me half a chance."

Jackie decided to call my bluff. Without another word, she leaned back and crossed her arms and waited. I, meanwhile, did a lightning-fast mental inventory of all my options, searching for the best angle to come at her. Then it occurred to me. Go directly for the soft underbelly—her obligatory liberalism on all subjects involving underdogs and/or women's rights issues.

I blurted out my opening gambit all in one breath. "Ms. DelGado wants to open a haven for troubled young women at the Mott house, but her neighbors and the Port Erie authorities are trying to run her out of town."

"Really?"

"It's a potentially ugly situation." Now that I had the high ground, I scrambled to keep it. First I told her about the two pregnant girls Hester had already taken in, and the neighbors' negative reaction. Then I explained about the recent acts of vandalism in the area, and the police department's budget crisis, and the chief's satanic cult theory, and how he was preparing to lay the blame on Hester's doorstep. I may have embellished a little here and there, just to get my point across, but people expect that. I even went so far as to pull a pen from my pocket and sketch out Birdy's winged goat on a napkin. By the time I'd passed the drawing across to Jackie, the only boobs she was steamed about were the ones who lived in Port Erie.

"Imagine those narrow-minded idiots ganging up on a woman like that. It's pathetic." She squinted at the sketch. "What'd you call this thing?"

"A Baphomet, according to Professor Blednau—symbol-

62

izes the devil, he says. They also found a pentagram sprayed onto a different garage."

"Hmmph. Kid stuff." She tossed aside the napkin and rested both elbows on the table. "Don't think you've fooled me, Hackshaw. If this Hester DelGado were an ugly old hag, you wouldn't think twice about her dilemma." I started to protest but she cut me off. "But ulterior motives aside, this is a question of social equity. There's a crying need for shelters for young women in trouble."

"That's exactly what I plan to say in my article."

"You're going to do an article? I think that's great—that you're willing to take a public stand in the *Advertiser*." She was actually smiling again, which is why I didn't mention that the whole thing was Hester's idea. I figured it was better to ride this crest of approbation for all it was worth; maybe even as far as Jackie's aforementioned boudoir. But then I heard the rapid clop of footwear descending the stairs.

"Hi, Hack." Jackie's sixteen-year-old daughter swept into the dinette.

"Hi, Krista. I, uh, thought you were over at the youth center tonight."

"Yeah. Organizational meeting for our Earth Day walka-thon. Starts at eight." She cherrypicked a piece of broccoli from her mother's plate and popped it into her mouth. "I won't be back till almost eleven, if that's what you two are worried about."

Jackie blushed. "Hackshaw and I are just friends . . ."

"Sure, Mom." Krista picked up my napkin doodle. "Hey, bitchin'. *Goat Outa Hell*."

We both stared at the girl, but Jackie, being the mother, recovered first. "You recognize that thing?"

"Sure. I've seen the video." More blank stares from the adults in the room. "For the new Death Squad release. The CD's called *Goat Outa Hell*, okay? And the video opens with a shot of this winged goat, like a cartoon, breathing fire and slobbering green stuff all over Razor."

"Razor?"

"The band's drummer." The way she rolled her eyes, you'd think I'd asked who Elvis was.

"Well, Hackshaw, there's your answer," Jackie said. "It's obviously the handiwork of some teenage metal fans and not some rampaging Manson family."

"Mmm, it looks that way," I said. "Now, if I could convince Birdy Wade of that."

Later, after the dishes were stacked in the machine and we'd adjourned to the couch for coffee, I forgot all about Birdy Wade and evil winged goats. I even forgot about Hester for a moment there.

Regrettably, Jackie didn't.

I leaned in close enough to smell the fresh shampoo scent of her short chestnut hair. "That was funny, the way Krista just *assumed* you and I were planning to—you know."

"It wasn't funny."

My hand lighted on her knee. "I didn't mean funny ha-ha, sweetie—"

"It wasn't accurate, either." She checked her watch. "If you're finished with your coffee, I think you'd better run along. Some of us have to get up in the morning."

"But, uh, I thought you and I would . . ."

She pushed my hand away. "Think again, Hackshaw."

"Aw, that's dirty pool, Jackie. You get a man all worked up with talk of your boudoir and everything, and then turn him out into the night? What am I supposed to do with all this pent-up sexual energy you've generated?"

La Plummer stuck her nose in the air. "I suggest you go home and get a grip on yourself," she said. "Literally."

The trouble with women is they always know exactly what they want at any given moment, but it doesn't last.

Jackie Plummer, to pick a name out of the air. When I'd arrived at her house Monday night, she was as eager as I was for some earnest groping. It was obvious in her bearing, in her clothes—a summery cotton shift she *knew* reminded me of Kim Basinger in *Nadine*—even in the way she'd chided me about passing up her earlier invitation for Saturday night.

Oh, she was game, all right. And I was certainly ready to do my part.

But then Hester DelGado's name came up and suddenly Jackie was into her woman scorned mode, even though I was totally innocent. (Despite Jimmy Carter, I don't think lusting in the heart counts.)

So with both hormones and ego raging, I wasn't in the cheeriest mood when I arrived at the paper Tuesday. And the work load I found waiting didn't improve matters.

To begin with, Mrs. Hobarth was back at her reception

desk, greeting me first thing with a sour expression, a cutting remark, and a fresh fistful of flyers and press releases. Then I found out that Alan Harvey, our ambiguous intern, was off on "an assignment"—at least that's how Ruth put it. I don't consider a day spent watching movie previews at the South Chilton Cineplex as work, especially not when it means I'm the one who gets stuck sorting through a stack of lame press releases. But Ruth insisted that Alan deserved the chance to gain a little experience toward his goal of becoming a film critic, and I couldn't really argue; the kid *had* been working like a slave, and since we don't pay our college interns anything, I guess the least we can do is let them have the occasional perk.

Ruth's other in-lieu-of-good-morning comment didn't sit too well either. "We're running very tight for space this week, Elias, and the events calendar is absolutely huge, so you'll need a close edit on your Ramblings column—and try to keep any stand-alone articles to a minimum."

Just what I needed to hear, what with Hester's Mott house piece and Birdy Wade's unholy crime spree and Corrine Brooks's husband's fortieth birthday bash and Harv Stedman's shiny new self-service frozen yogurt machines, and on and on; everybody in our circulation area, it seemed, had picked that week to blow their own horn.

I mumbled something unpleasant to my sister, who wasn't listening anyway, and rolled up my sleeves. No matter what anyone tells you, there's an art to all this, much like reducing half a ton of cow innards to a package of edible sausages. Corrine and Harv were easy—one line each tagged onto the end of my column. Hester and Birdy were a different story. Make that two different stories. Much as I would've liked to, I couldn't completely ignore the Port Erie police chief's dire warnings about devil worshipers; it smacked too much of real news. And Hester's prenatal boarding house?

True, I hadn't promised her anything that week, but if I waited until the next edition, it might come too late to do her any good. Besides, I'd gone and told Jackie about my noble intentions. If I didn't follow through, she'd think I'd made the whole thing up and I'd be on her least-wanted list for the duration.

I'd just have to manage somehow, I decided glumly. Give Birdy Wade a two-graph lead in the weekly police blotter—not too prominent but enough to say I'd done something. Maybe find a hole for Hester by dumping the piece on the Kirkville Summer Theater auditions or cutting a few inches' worth of sugary adjectives from Liz Fleegle's Triton Talk column. I was about to congratulate myself on my ingenuity when my wandering fingers chanced across the press packet Corrine had given me on the blessed Port Erie Canal Days Festival.

"Son of a . . . Somebody just shoot me now," I announced to the newsroom, but there were surprisingly few takers.

The whole thing came to a head around four that afternoon. After working up the lengthy piece on Canal Days—the promotional photos alone took up a half page—I'd spent several more hours chained to my desk, answering calls or making some of my own, including trying to line up various tradesmen for the Mott house job. Whenever I caught a busy signal or was put on hold, I took a moment to finesse Birdy's satan scare into the police blotter or tighten up my column or scan another press release in search of timely items for that week's events calendar. I was engaged in the latter when I finally lost it. The triggering mechanism was a piece of PR puffery sent over by the local hamburger franchise. It seems they wanted the world—or at least the part of the world that reads the *Advertiser*—to know that the paper sacks they used for their burgers now consisted of "fifty percent post-consumer content."

"Christ on a crutch!" I exploded, balling up the offending release and firing it—appropriately, I thought—in the general direction of the blue recycling box we keep in one corner. The others cast disapproving glances my way, then went back to what they were doing, having seen this sort of thing before.

I know what you're thinking. Yes, it's annoying that so many jargon-spewing business types and bureaucrats are muddying up the English language, but it's nothing to blow your top about, Hackshaw.

Damned easy for you to say—you're not the one who spends endless days and weeks sifting through such hyperinflated crap. I mean, why couldn't they just say their new bags were half made from recycled paper? Better yet, why can't these suddenly eco-minded companies stop mailing out self-congratulatory press releases in the first place? Think of all the paper *that* would save.

But I know what you're thinking again, and this time you're right. Some bonehead copywriter's jibberish wasn't the real reason for my frustration. It was everything else: Jackie Plummer's mental cruelty, the unconscionable work load piling up on my desk, the whole Hester DelGado–Birdy Wade devils-in-the-woodpile thing over in Port Erie. Sometimes I think the only sane way to deal with pressing problems is to ignore them—sort of like the national debt.

Which is how I came to be digging through my pants pocket in search of my own meager cash supply—fixated on a cold beer and a juicy burger at Norb's Nook and simultaneously regretting my hasty decision to stop at the bank that morning and pay off my overdue utilities bills—when my phone rang. *Maybe I could convince Norb to extend my tab another few days,* I was thinking absently as I picked up.

"*Triton Advertiser,* Hackshaw speaking."

"This is Wesley Stanhouse."

Neither the name nor the haughty voice registered immediately. But then it did. "Oh. Stanhouse, right." The one who owned Silvertrees, the retirement home over Hester's way. I was hoping for coincidence, but it wasn't.

"The reason I'm calling," he said in his prep school drawl, "I remember the fine editorial you wrote last year regarding the plan to move the Port Erie library and police out to the new annex?"

"Uh-huh." I remembered, too. He'd been one of a handful of village property owners and merchants who, like me, had opposed the plan. In Stanhouse's case it was concern for the old folks who live at Silvertrees, most of whom don't drive anymore and thus are dependent on local services staying within walking—or walker—distance. "Too bad the editorial didn't cut any ice with the town council."

"Yes, we've had to reschedule our van shuttle service just to see that our residents can get out to the library once a week. Terribly inconvenient." He cleared his throat. "At any rate, knowing how you feel about preservation and planning issues and the like, Mr. Hackshaw, I felt—that is, my residents and I and several of our neighbors felt—that you should be aware of a, um, situation that's come up here on Virginia Street."

"A 'situation'?" I already knew, of course, but that was none of his business.

"I wasn't aware of the problem myself until some of the homeowners came to me with a petition recently." Vern Murray and company. You learn to be wary of retirees with time on their hands and small yards; they'll always find something to do. "You're familiar with the Mott house?"

"Uh-huh." A preemptive strike was called for. "I see the new owner has really spruced up the place."

"Well—yes. If you like that sort of thing." He cleared his throat again; all of that crisp enunciation must be hell on the vocal cords. "The thing is, this new owner you speak of—a woman named DelGado—she has it in mind to use the house as some sort of shelter for, um, unwed mothers or some such. Now, the other property owners have asked me to be their representative on this controversy. Naturally, we oppose the idea—"

"Why 'naturally'?"

"Why?" I could feel him frowning through the phone wire. "Because it's inappropriate for the neighborhood."

"I don't see the problem. There're already several converted apartment houses in the area, not to mention your place. You must have—what, three dozen oldsters rooming over at Silvertrees?"

"Thirty-four *residents*," he stressed, taking umbrage at my characterization. "Occupying twenty-eight individual living suites, each with their own kitchenette facilities. Silvertrees isn't a boarding house, Mr. Hackshaw. Of course, we provide luncheon and evening meals in our dining hall, but we cater to self-sufficient seniors capable of caring for themselves with limited assistance—"

"I've seen your brochure. Exactly what is your problem with the Mott house?" When my stomach begins to growl, the rest of me tends to follow suit.

"I've already said, it's inappropriate. This is a quiet, stable middle-class neighborhood that enjoys a comfortable mix. In addition to Silvertrees' resident population, there are many older couples living on the street, along with families with young children. Bringing in these pregnant teenagers is simply too disruptive." His carefully modulated voice dropped down to a between-you-and-me level. "Rumor has it this DelGado woman plans to bring in runaways as well—family court rejects, Mr. Hackshaw."

"Heavens."

"Yes. And we're already beginning to reap the results in

increased problems on the street. My own property—the dining hall at Silvertrees—was defaced with spray paint recently—"

"By one of, uh, Ms. DelGado's girls?"

"Well, I can't say so uncategorically." He did the throat thing again. "I scared off the vandal—all I saw was a shadowy figure dressed in dark clothing. But it certainly could've been a girl. I'll say this, we never had incidents like this before that woman started bringing juvenile delinquents into the Mott house."

I let him go on for another couple of minutes, telling me what I already knew about the Murrays' kicked-in basement window and the Joneses' garage graffiti and so on. When he broke for breath I said, "What is it you'd like me to do about all this, Stanhouse?" Like I couldn't guess.

"Bring the problem to the public's attention. As I said, the other property owners and I have a petition, which we plan to present to the zoning people and the town council. But the regular meeting isn't for another two weeks, and we'd like to see quicker action—we're calling for a special session to be held as soon as possible. Now, we thought that if your paper could publicize our concerns—"

"I'd be happy to."

"You would?"

"Certainly." Silver lining time. I'd been worrying how I was going to slip my pro-Hester piece past Ruth without her making a fuss; she's unreasonably distrustful that way. Now I had a solid reason, not only for covering the story but for covering it that week, tight news hole or not.

"That's excellent, Mr. Hackshaw."

"You understand, I can't just report your take on all this. I'll have to interview this Ms. DelGado and let her give her side of the dispute, too. Wouldn't want anyone to accuse me of press bias."

"I do understand. All we ask is that our fellow Port Eriens be made aware of the situation."

"That's the idea." The intercom button on the phone started to flash. I remembered to thank Stanhouse for calling before hanging up on him, then I punched the blinking red button.

"Yeah?"

Mrs. Hobarth's eternally judgmental voice answered, "There's some *woman* out here for you."

"Well, send her back. Please."

"I'm not supposed to send anyone back to the newsroom unaccompanied—your sister's rule—and I was just about to close up and go. It's almost four-thirty."

I checked the wall clock; it was twenty after, in fact, but Mrs. H. was retired civil service, so there was no point in arguing. "I'll be right out," I said wearily.

As it turned out, the old crow had inadvertently done me a favor. You see, it was Hester waiting for me in the reception area. If Mrs. Hobarth had allowed her into the newsroom, introductions would've been expected and, for obvious reasons, I didn't want Ruth to meet Hester until after we'd published the Mott house piece.

"I got off work a little early today," she said. "And since I had an errand to do over this way, I decided to swing by afterward and see if you've come up with a game plan on the renovation work. I don't want to interrupt—"

Mrs. H. was scrutinizing us from the coat rack, torn between sticking around to eavesdrop or cheating her time card out of five minutes.

"I was about to head out for an early dinner," I said. "Haven't had a bite all day. Would you like to . . . ?"

"I'd love to."

9

You expect these New Age types to be big on whole grains and tofu junk, don't you? I figured Hester would take one look at Norb's chalkboard menu and settle for a cautious chef salad and maybe a glass of mineral water.

Not even close.

"Wow." She gulped down the last bite of a double char-burger with cheddar cheese. "This hot sauce is really spicy—just the way I like it. Wonder how they make it?"

"I've never had the courage to ask. More ale?"

"Mmm. Split it with you."

I poured the remnants from a pitcher of Genny Cream, topping off her glass and half filling mine. We were seated at a booth in the Nook's front diner section. The rear half of the building contained the knotty pine taproom and a niche used for a coin-operated pool table and video games. Our booth straddled one of the windows, affording us an unobstructed view of the cars and pickups and panel trucks whizzing by out on Buffalo Road, mostly locals shuttling between Chilton and

Kirkville. The heaviest traffic—commuters to and from Rochester and large freight haulers—stuck to the new (ten years past) expressway to the south.

Normally I would've picked a table closer to the bar, but that was out. Buddy McCabe and the regular gang had reacted predictably when Hester and I entered from the rear parking lot. Not that I blamed them—she did look scrumptious in her flowery print dress and high heels.

"So," she said. "This stair guy you mentioned—you'll be bringing him by soon to check out my doors?"

"Stair mechanic, right. Probably on Thursday or Friday. He's tied up tomorrow." And so was I, Wednesday being final-copy day at the paper. "I'm still trying to line up a plasterer to give us a quote on the ceilings and I've got some-one in mind to repoint the chimneys, but I haven't had a chance to call him." I took a swig of ale. "I did touch base with an electrician to handle the upgrades you said you wanted. He can come by for an estimate early next week, if you're sure you want to go in that direction. I mean, it's your budget, but . . ."

Ever since our initial walk-through on Sunday I'd been trying to convince her that having the Mott house rewired was overkill. The evidence in the basement's electrical panel told me that the place had been updated sometime in the sixties, including grounded cable, circuit breakers, and two hundred–amp service, which seemed adequate even for a place that size. But Hester had insisted that she wanted lots more wall recep-tacles installed and a doubling of the service to four hundred amps. Given the number of hair dryers and stereos a houseful of young women were apt to employ, I supposed the extra capacity couldn't hurt. It just seemed to me that there were higher priorities at the moment.

Hester finished nibbling a cottage fry. "I know you think I'm nuts, but I want to handle all the mechanical upgrades and

74

structural problems first. If I run short of funds I'll just have to hold off awhile on new bathroom fixtures and wallpapering and all that."

In theory I didn't think she was nuts at all. Handling an old house's mechanical and structural problems first was exactly how it should be done—assuming there *is* a problem in the first place. But I decided not to press the point; it was her dime, so to speak. Which raised a second concern that'd been nagging me.

"Uh, now that you mention it, Hester, we still haven't discussed an overall budget for the job." I hate to bring up money with a beautiful woman, but since they never do—

"I'd prefer just to handle whatever comes up and pay as I go," she said. "Like, you bring in someone to do the doors, say, and we pay him whatever he needs to get started—a third, maybe, and the rest when the job's done. Naturally, since you're acting as general contractor, I'd pay you and you'd pay the other guy. Minus your ten percent, or whatever. Does that sound okay?"

"Sure." Especially the 10 percent part. But I still couldn't help but worry. Like about how much all of this was going to cost her, a single woman with a four-days-a-week clerking job and an iffy plan to rent out rooms for extra income. And like what would happen if she *couldn't* pay—she'd end up owing me a bundle. Don't jump to conclusions, it wasn't my end I was thinking about. But as general contractor, I'd be the one who owed all those others. Have you ever tried to explain negative cash flow to a guy wielding a claw hammer?

"That reminds me." As if reading my mind—they can do that, you know—Hester reached for her handbag and pulled out an envelope with my name inked across the front. Inside was a check, made out to me, for twenty-five hundred dollars. "Is that enough to get things started?" she asked, fetchingly tentative.

"Uh, yeah. It should do nicely." Now I was embarrassed for doubting her in the first place. Maybe she'd had an inheritance or a big divorce settlement or something. "I didn't mean to bug you about money matters—"

"No, it's better to be totally up-front with that stuff. Business before pleasure, don't you think?" As a matter of fact, I didn't think, but before I could say so she pushed a few gold bracelets clear of her wrist and checked her watch. "God, where does the time go? Look, I need to get home to make a couple calls—"

"So soon?" My frown drooped to my shoelaces. We'd been together for only an hour and I'd wasted the whole time discussing her butchered doors and cracked ceilings like some damn professional. And here she was, sliding out of the booth and gathering up her purse, no doubt rushing off to rendezvous with a boyfriend she hadn't gotten around to mentioning and leaving me with my long face and a dinner tab I couldn't cover. (She'd insisted on separate cars but, as usual, the concept of separate checks hadn't come up.) "I was hoping we could . . ." But I decided I didn't want to say out loud what I was hoping we could, so I let the sentence die out.

But Hester was a continual surprise to me, as women often are.

"I was thinking, Hackshaw, if you don't have plans, maybe you'd like to swing by later tonight. For drinks or something. I've got a new Yanni CD we can listen to."

"I'll come anyway."

"Okay, no mood music," she said, laughing. "We'll create our own ambience. Just give me a couple hours to clear the decks before you come by."

I walked her to the Nook's back entrance, through a gauntlet of covetous stares from the male patrons lined up along the taproom's L-shaped bar. At least they were salivating in silence, but that didn't last. As soon as Hester was safely out the door, the abuse rained down like mortar rounds.

"Jesus, Hackshaw, you got broads fallin' all over you."

Someone snickered. "Only the clumsy ones."

"Christ, you could hang your hat on a rack like that."

"Man, I'd chase a laundry truck ten miles just to swipe a pair of her panties—"

"C'mon, boys. Give her a break. She's a fine lady—"

"Knowin' you, that ain't no lady, it's somebody's wife."

"No kiddin', Hacky, what sorta line do you use on these babes, anyway?"

"I tell 'em they could do worse than a guy like me, Dutch. Then I show 'em a picture of you."

Buddy, the Nook's bartender and keeper of the peace, chuckled as he reflexively drew me a glass of ale. "Y'know, Hack, if you were gettin' half as much as these rednecks think, you couldn't hold down a steady job." Then he grinned, a brilliant white crescent on a field of ebony. "I forgot—you don't have a steady job, do you."

"Oh, that's witty." Like the rest of them, Buddy figured all those words in the newspaper just showed up of their own volition. "Anyway," I said, pushing the dinner bill across the bar, "if you'll add this to my tab—"

He snatched my glass away. "Uh-uh. Norb says your cuffs are frayed, man. No tickee, no washee. Sorry."

He didn't look it. And we were actually friends.

"Maybe you should show him this." I was holding up Hester's check. Buddy read off the sum, then put my ale back on the bar.

"You just opened yourself a new line of credit, Hack. Just be sure you don't forget us after you deposit that thing, right?"

"Oh, ye of little faith—"

"So. That must be the redhead Jimbo was telling me about, from over in Port Erie?"

"That would be her. Hester DelGado. And despite all the leering, I'm only handling some renovation work for her." Jimbo Clark, Hester had told me, was the contractor who'd done up her painted lady. "That reminds me, if he comes in, tell him thanks for the recommendation."

"The way he tells it, you oughta thank the lady. Jimbo says she's the one who brought your name up first."

"Really?" Now, that was interesting. "I guess she must've heard about me elsewhere."

"And decided to hire you anyway. Go figure."

Some things are just inevitable. Hester and me, for example. From the moment I'd laid eyes on her outside the little camper trailer at the firemen's carnival, I'd pictured us entwined in a big four-poster in a warm room lighted only by the moon glow flowing through the window sheers.

More wishful thinking than precognition, you might say. But it wasn't.

"God, Hackshaw."

"Mmm."

"Now I know what they mean when they say timing is everything."

"Mmm-hmm."

"Especially the second time. Like a long, hot bath . . ."

"Mmm." They like to talk after, for some reason. Probably because women are emotional creatures whereas men are, well, rutting pigs, basically.

We went on like that awhile longer, one of us chatty, the other barely capable of monosyllables. Then she came up on one elbow, that moon glow I mentioned washing over her exposed left breast.

"Don't get me wrong, honeybear—"

"Hmm?"

"—but it's probably better if you don't stay the night. I mean, with the girls in the house and everything."

"Oh. Right." Like we could teach those two anything. I wriggled myself upright against the mound of pillows. "Just give me a minute to regain my sea legs."

"There's no rush, Hackshaw. I'm only saying, given my situation, we need to be a little discreet." The breast heaved—mesmerizing. "That's all I need, for the neighbors to see a man leaving here first thing in the morning."

It was already nearly two in the morning and my Jeep had been sitting in the driveway since eight, so I doubted we'd be fooling anyone. Still, she had a point. No sense adding fuel to the fire. I hadn't planned to bring up Wesley Stanhouse, even though his phone call had been nibbling away at the corners of my mind all evening, but then Hester opened the topic herself.

"I feel like I'm under siege or something, the way these people watch everything—driving by real slow, staring, pointing." Her long, red nails combed through her hair. "It's like being on trial, only you don't get to testify in your own defense, you know? That's why I'm so eager to have you run a story in your paper, Hackshaw. If I can have a chance to tell my side—the effort I'm putting into restoring the place, my idea to give at-risk young women a place to pull themselves together—people'd have to respect that, wouldn't they?"

It was more a plea than a question. Naive, too. God, family, and country is what most folks say when you ask them about their priorities. Hardly anyone ever mentions property values. And that's why public opinion polls are pointless: people lie.

But all I said was, "It couldn't hurt, dearheart."

"I don't want to push, but . . . do you know yet if you'll be doing the article this week?"

"With any luck." That's when I gave in and told her about Stanhouse and the move to pressure the town council, and how I'd promised *him* I'd give the controversy some coverage. "It legitimizes the story, you see."

Her bare feet found mine under the sheet. "But you won't be taking their side, will you?"

"I don't take sides," I said piously, shifting slightly to take better advantage of the movement of her calf along my thigh. "I'll simply present both cases—the selfless young woman with a social conscience versus a pack of knee-jerk xenophobes—and let our readers reach their own conclusions."

Don't start. I know, journalists are supposed to be paragons of objectivity. And probably some of them are—I don't claim to know everybody in this business. But some things are more important, if you ask me. Like sticking up for an underdog, leveling the playing field. If the *Triton Advertiser* didn't give Hester a break, who would? Her neighbors? The vote-counting Port Erie Town Council? The council-appointed zoning board?

It was a stacked deck going in. All I was hoping to do was reshuffle the cards a bit. Honestly, I'd do the exact same thing if Hester were some aged crone with halitosis. I just wouldn't enjoy it as much.

Anyway, if you don't like it, start your own damn paper.

Hester still wasn't sanguine. "And what if your readers' conclusions are the same as the Murrays and this Stanhouse and the others? I'll be dead before I start."

"You might have another option," I said, patting her leg. "See, there was this old woman who used to own this place before you. . . ."

She listened attentively as I filled her in on Mrs. Finney's illegal boarding house. When I wound down she said, "Well, that's promising, anyway. I guess."

Her reaction was disappointing and I let her know it.

"Oh, I don't mean to sound ungrateful, Hackshaw. I know you went to a lot of trouble to dig that up—"

"All in a day's work."

"I'm just tired, is all. Tired of worrying about it, tired just thinking about a legal hassle over this place." Then she sighed and playfully poked me in the ribs. "And at the moment, just plain tired, lover man."

Which was my final exit cue. We swapped a few sweet nothings while I rounded up my clothes, then exchanged a fervent kiss and promises of more. Then I convinced her, with little protest, that I could find my own way out.

The stairs were newly carpeted with an Oriental-design runner. That's one reason the girl didn't hear me coming. The other reason was her single-minded concentration on her task, which, I saw as I drew even with the broad dining room doorway, was to rifle the drawers of Hester's flimsy desk.

"Lose something?"

"*Whaa—shit!*" The few bits of paper she was holding jumped out of her hand and floated to the floor like autumn leaves. "God, you scared me. What're you doing here, anyway?"

"I asked you first." We were both whispering. "You're Sue Kramer, right?"

"Krevin. Sue Krevin."

The pretty blond one who looked first trimester. She ran a hand nervously down the side of her shapeless cotton nightgown but said nothing more.

I stepped into the room. "Must be awfully tough to read with just the moonlight coming in. Let me see if I can find a light switch somewhere—"

"Don't bother, I was just leaving."

"Then I guess you found what you were after?"

"No, but it's no big deal." She looked down at the scattered papers and knelt. "I was just looking for a pen and paper," she explained as she gathered up the mess.

"At two A.M.?"

She rose abruptly and began shoveling what appeared to be a handful of invoices and envelopes back into the drawer.

"I couldn't sleep, okay? Maybe you and Miss Congeniality were noisier than you think. And maybe now you're through banging her headboard, we can all get some rest."

Her lips curled into a mocking grin. I couldn't read her eyes in the gloom. Her housekeeping done, she moved past me and on into the foyer, tossing over her shoulder, "Nighty-night—honeybear."

Curiosity has always been my undoing. Without that fatal flaw I probably never would've gotten into newspapering in the first place; probably would've contented myself with remodeling work and scavenging old house parts. But fate dealt me the cards and I was stuck with them.

I looked inside the desk drawer, in other words.

And found nothing much. Bills from various tradesmen mostly—Jimbo Clark's painting outfit, a floor refinisher, a heating and cooling contractor—some stamped paid, others apparently still outstanding. And one odd notation, scribbled on the back of what appeared to be a written estimate for a security system for the Mott house.

"Check with Janus," the note said, in a hand that matched the writing on the check Hester had given me earlier.

So I searched the drawer a second time. And found a newish address book inside. Using the moonlight to advantage, I thumbed through it quickly—and there it was again. Janus. Followed by a phone number with a Rochester exchange, and nothing else.

And all I could come up with was, "Hmm."

 10

Despite everything, I was on a natural high for the next twenty-four hours.

Wednesday was, as always, a hectic day at the paper, what with last-minute ad copy coming in and fact-checking duties and headline writing and misplaced photo art and a dozen other small aggravations that, taken cumulatively, are the tiny acorns from which mighty ulcers grow. Add in the Mott house piece, which I first had to write and then shoe-horn into an impossibly crowded news hole, and you had an exhausting marathon of effort that didn't end until near midnight, when Ruth and I proofed the final item and jigsawed it into the layout and turned the pasteup over to Ron, who would spend Thursday morning's earliest hours running the entire production through his press.

Deadline fever, we call it, and it's normally enough to discourage a Dale Carnegie grad. But not me. Not that particular Wednesday.

Isn't love grand?

Don't misunderstand, I wasn't ready to pick out a china pattern or anything. But there was definitely a spring in my step that hadn't been there pre-Hester, when I was still smarting from Jackie Plummer's rejections, and which wasn't even diminished after the fact by the debilitating work load or Ruth's barbed criticisms of my editorial decision making vis-à-vis my Mott house article. Even my own back-burner doubts about the strange goings-on over on Virginia Street weren't enough to shake the grin off my face.

In retrospect I suppose I should've been more suspicious of Sue Krevin. I hadn't believed her, of course; even in the afterglow of lovemaking I wasn't dumb enough to swallow that line about looking for writing materials at two o'clock in the morning. It's just that, with everything else on my plate, the girl's snooping or petty thievery or whatever didn't seem important.

It was well after the witching hour when I finally made it home to my crib, a small, sloped-ceiling apartment above a three-bay carriage house on Kirkville's north side. I own the place, along with the handsome stick Victorian out front. It's a long story, but the gist is, I can't afford to live in the main house, so I rent it out and make do with the former servants' quarters above the garage.

Anyway, I began shedding clothing on my way across the living room and was dead asleep by the time my head hit the pillow.

Unfortunate choice of words.

I'm not sure just how many synthetic chirps there were before my brain noticed the intrusion. I do know I was dreaming at the time—something to do with me and Hester, naked as jaybirds on a playground teeter-totter, up and down and smiling, and up and down again, and more smiling . . .

*Chirrrrr-up.*

The damn phone. It was one of those stylish push-button

things, a Christmas gift from a former acquaintance whose absentee husband owned an electronics store. An insistent little red light on the console enabled my hand to find the receiver in the pitch black of the bedroom.

"Whaa . . . ?"

"Hackshaw?"

"Uh-hum." I fought off a catarrh. "Um—Hester?"

"I didn't know who else . . . I tried to reach . . . shit, I don't know what I'm doing," she wailed.

"Slow down a sec, sweetheart." Fuzzy head and all, I'd never heard a woman jabber so.

"Oh, God, Hackshaw—just come quick!"

Something else I'd never heard from a woman.

"For chrissake, Hester, do you have any idea what time it is?" I certainly didn't.

"*Please*, Hackshaw! I don't . . . she looks . . . somebody's *killed* her!"

That thud you heard was my natural high crashing to earth.

"What d'you mean, you haven't called the police?"

"I forgot! I just panicked—"

"You find a dead girl lying on the porch and you *forget* to call the cops?"

"Don't bully me! I went into shock, okay? I mean, I came home and there she was and she was *dead* and there wasn't anything I could do for her and I didn't know *what* to do—and I just never thought to call the *goddamn police!*"

"Well. Somebody did."

The sirens were just then cutting the predawn stillness, moving swiftly closer. Hester and I were standing on the sidewalk in front of the stairs leading up onto the small back porch of the Mott house. Lying on the porch floor slightly below our eye level, illuminated by the dim yellow glow of the porch light, was the dead girl. Her arms flung wide, her neck rimmed with an ugly raw contusion, and her horribly contorted face turned toward us in hopeless supplication.

Sue Krevin.

Strangled, by the looks of it.

A young life snuffed out—no, two young lives, I realized sadly, taking in the voluminous maternity top. And worse, somehow, so casually discarded. Left on the back stoop like yesterday's empty milk bottle.

I thrust my hands in my pockets and looked heavenward, trying to forget that face, those bulging, bloodshot eyes—but knowing I never would. And then, as the screaming sirens were racing up the driveway, a shameful sense of self-preservation crept in and another thought occurred to me: there we were, standing over a body neither of us had gotten around to reporting.

"Jesus," I said. "This isn't going to look too good."

Birdy Wade was of the same mind.

He was in the lead car, his personal vehicle, a Ford Crown Victoria with a whirring red cherry ball attached to the roof. Immediately behind him came a Port Erie PD cruiser, red and blue bar lights blazing, siren mercifully winding down. Two uniformed patrolmen jumped out, one of them Ricky Reimer, the ex–high school jock I'd seen in Birdy's office a few days previous. He had a revolver in his hand, pointed straight up into the air. His partner—a skinny middle-aged cop I didn't know offhand—was waving a flashlight.

Reimer, I noticed, wasn't wearing any socks and the other guy's shirt tail was hanging out. As for Birdy, he had eschewed his official tan double knits in favor of baggy slacks and a Buffalo Bills sweatshirt. It was well past one in the morning, which meant that the Port Erie Police Department was unmanned, which further meant that any emergency calls that came in were electronically rerouted to the chief's home phone. It was then up to Birdy whether to rouse his own troops or to pass it on to the sheriff's patrol. Obviously, he had decided that anything relating to the Mott house was deserving of his personal attention.

I automatically went into suck-up mode.

"Thank God, Birdy. We were just about to—"

"Shut up, Hackshaw." The police chief hurried past Hester and me and up the porch stairs. Kneeling beside the body, he studied the scene for several moments, then lightly rested his fingertips on the girl's bare wrist. Then he abruptly stood and began barking orders.

"Roger, get on the radio to Sally and have her call Dr. Ramathan. Tell her to send out Morton and McGann, too. Ricky"—the younger officer was staring at the body slack jawed, like he was about to lose his lunch—"holster the iron and give the lady here a seat in the back of your cruiser. And lock it. Then get the camera out of my glove compartment." Birdy turned to me. "Hackshaw, go sit in my car. Don't touch anything and don't move a muscle until I tell you."

"Listen, Chief—"

"In the car, Hackshaw. *Now.*"

It was light out by the time Hester and I were allowed in the same room together, that room being the living room of the Mott house. Some two hours had passed—two hours of alternate grilling from Birdy. First me, then Hester, then me, et cetera. It was exhausting, but the stocky police chief seemed to thrive on it. He was standing near the doorway leading to the foyer, hands clasped behind him, stomach straining the limits of his Bills sweatshirt.

"All right," he said. "We talked with your sister, Hackshaw. She's got you alibied up until midnight, which, according to the doc here"—he nodded toward Dr. Ramathan, a Port Erie GP and the town's ex officio coroner—"probably takes you out of the picture. Same with you for the time being, ma'am," he said to Hester, who was sitting pale and still as a lily beside me on the worn sofa. "Your Rochester friend verified that you didn't leave the city until sometime after one."

I crooked an eye at Hester—this was the first I'd heard of any Rochester friend—but her gaze stayed on Birdy, who was still talking.

"Now, I'm not giving either of you a clean bill of health, understand. Just because the doc's prelim estimates the girl died earlier in the evening—"

"Oh, yes." This from Ramathan, whose round, nut-brown face seemed to bob in time with the sing-song rhythms of his voice. "The victim's body temperature and the rigor present suggests death occurred sometime before ten o'clock last night—"

"If you don't mind, Doctor—"

"Oh, yes." More head bobs. "I only meant to say, we will know with more precision after the postmortem, but in my professional opinion—"

"Okay, Doc. Fine. We get the picture." The chief homed in on the room's only other occupant, Jennifer Hadley. She was seated in a club chair near the fireplace, her left hand resting atop her ponderous belly, her right holding a crumpled tissue under her red nose. "As for you, miss, I hope you're feeling up to a few more questions. I don't mean to push, but we've got a homicide investigation here."

In the frenzy of the early morning, everyone had forgotten about Jennifer, until Birdy Wade thought to ask Hester if anyone else was living on the premises. She'd let out an "Oh, my God!" and then demanded that the cops search the house for her remaining boarder, fearing the worst. But one of the patrolmen had found Jennifer in her bed, fast asleep, adenoids thrumming, oblivious to the murder, the sirens, everything.

"I already told you," she said now. "I was so worn out, I had a hot milk and went to bed before nine. Sue wasn't home and neither was Hester. That's all I know."

The whole thing came out in a pitiful whine, not that I couldn't sympathize. She was haggard and bloated and big as a house—in her eighth month, Hester had said. The least likely candidate I could think of to be out strangling people. To his credit, Birdy apparently agreed.

"Now, nobody's accusing *you* of anything, dear," he said, turning on the fatherly charm. "A young lady in your condition—"

"Very true." Dr. Ramathan couldn't contain himself. "Statistically speaking, you know, it is highly unusual for a woman to employ strangulation, even against another woman. And given this woman's advanced—"

"Listen, Doc," Birdy said with borderline patience. "Maybe you should run along and make sure the medivan boys get the body over to your place in good order."

"Ah, of course." He grinned for some reason I couldn't fathom. "I'm being dismissed. Very good."

The doctor nodded smartly and strode out into the foyer, passing along the way Officer Reimer, who was just coming in. Reimer moved alongside his mentor and mumbled something in his ear.

"Okay. Bag it and bring it to me," Birdy said. Then, studying the kid's face, he added, "You doing all right?"

"Absolutely, Chief."

"Okay, Ricky. You better get back to the search—and make sure Morton and McGann are keeping the rubberneckers away from the crime scene."

When Reimer was gone, the chief turned back to the rest of us and, again with the fatherly tones, said, "His first fatal. And he knew the girl, too—went to high school together. Rough way to break in."

We all agreed it was.

"So, uh, Jennifer," Birdy said. "You were here all by yourself last night?"

"Uh-huh. I think so, anyway."

"You think so?"

"Well, the handyman was working around back earlier," she said innocently. "But I'm pretty sure Sue chased him off before she left herself. That was like around seven."

"Wait a second, the handyman?"

Hester spoke up hoarsely. "Step Garris. He handles odd jobs around the house for me."

Birdy was concentrating on the girl. "What d'you mean about Sue chasing him off?"

"Well, they were fighting again, is all. Out in the backyard. They didn't get along." She sniffed at the tissue. "The old guy was always talkin' religious stuff, like he disapproved of us—mostly Sue, I think. I didn't pay that much attention to him myself. I figured he was pretty harmless."

"They bickered all the time, Step and Sue," Hester offered. "It didn't amount to anything."

But Birdy stayed with Jennifer. "So the last time you saw either one of them, they were arguing?"

"Not arguing. I mean, Sue was, like, dissin' him, telling him to go home. She didn't like him hanging around the place when Hester wasn't here. She thought he was like a drunken pervert or somethin'." Jennifer ended with a shrug.

"Can you remember anything specific she said?"

She thought about it. " 'Bite me.' "

Birdy's left eyebrow arched.

"That's one thing I heard her say. 'Bite me.' And I think she told him to mind his own business. That was about it. Pretty typical for them." The girl sighed. "Anyway, I was too beat to care. Sue took off right after and I went up to my room with my milk awhile later. The place was real quiet after that."

"Hmm." He looked at Hester. "So you've had Garris around quite a bit? Doing odd jobs, you said?"

"Yes. There're lots of small jobs I need—"

"What specifically was he doing here yesterday?"

"Well, I gave him a list. Replace some broken window glass. Run a new clothesline off the side of the garage. Cut back the privet hedge along the side yard. Let's see, what else?"

"That's enough," Birdy told her. As if on cue, Reimer had returned, clutching a plastic sandwich bag, which he handed to Birdy. Even with the clear plastic I couldn't make out the contents. Until Birdy held the bag up for all to see.

"My men found this in the shrub beside the porch," he said with grim satisfaction.

Coiled in the bag was a short length of rope. The kind used for clotheslines.

"Better back my car around to the street, Ricky," the chief said. "And grab the shotgun out of your unit."

"Where we headed, Chief?"

"We're gonna take a run out to Muletown, see if we can round up Step Garris."

# 11

Well, I for one thought that was a good idea, arresting Step Garris.

For one thing, if means, motive, and opportunity count for anything, it seemed obvious that he *did* kill the poor girl and thus deserved whatever the wheels of justice had in store for him. For another thing, I was relieved just to be out of the picture myself. Call me a coward if you will, but I'd been an unofficial murder suspect before and I had absolutely no desire to find myself in the crosshairs again. Ever.

And then there was Hester. Thank God, Jennifer Hadley's recounting of events leading up to the murder had taken the spotlight off Hester as well. Our romance had barely blossomed, a romance that would never fully flower if she had to hold up her end on visiting days through the bars of the Monroe County Jail.

Not that I ever thought she could've done it. Not for more than a fleeting nanosecond, anyway. I'll admit, there may've been a moment of doubt—when we were standing there staring at the horrible scene on the porch floor, when her strongest emotion seemed to be confusion rather than revulsion or pity, when she seemed distracted and cold and somehow reluctant to call in the police. And all of that bundled with the odd set of events that had plagued the neighborhood in recent days. It was enough to make a blind man blink once or twice.

But the revelations about Garris had wiped all that away. Occam's razor, the intellectual whizbangs call it: the simplest of two or more competing theories is preferable. In other words, don't sweat the niggling details. Like most murders, this one, boiled down to its essence, would undoubtedly prove to be a numbingly mundane, impetuous act of rage—a hapless, middle-aged handyman striking out at a young, mean-spirited tormentor in the only way his whiskey-soaked brain could fathom: with sudden violence.

Don't misread my sympathies. I mean, Sue Krevin may've been a snippy little tart—I'd seen evidence of that myself—and according to Jennifer's account, the girl had gone out of her way to belittle and provoke Garris. But you don't kill someone for being venal or thoughtless.

"It's a crying shame," I said to Hester after the police chief and his men had taken off.

"What? Oh. My God, poor Sue," she responded, her eyes unfocused. "It's just—unbelievable."

"Unbelievable," I echoed uselessly.

It was still early, approaching eight o'clock. Birdy had left behind strict instructions for each of us—Hester, Jennifer, and myself—to appear at his office before the end of the day so that his duty officer could record our official statements. Not that any revelations were expected. Of the three only Hester's promised any narrative drama—how she had arrived home at around two in the morning, bone weary from a long day, half asleep as she plodded up the back steps in the dark and literally stumbled over the body on the porch. And how she had gagged back a scream and merely gaped for a while, dumbstruck and sickened, until it finally sank in that she'd better do *something*. So she'd hurried around to the front porch and let herself into the house and called yours truly. For emotional support, she said, adding a half dozen other New Age psychobabble catchphrases I won't bother repeating.

The chief had been understandably suspicious about Hester's failure to call the cops—a nosy neighbor, Mrs. Mobley, had done that sometime later, spying the girl's body after Hester had switched on the back porch light in anticipation of my arrival. And speaking of my part in all this, Birdy was none too happy with me, either, for failing to mention during our Monday interview that I was personally involved with Hester. He'd made that very clear during his frequent commutes to and from my spot in the backseat of his Ford, berating me as a double-dealer and a sneak, along with a half dozen old-fashioned profanities that also don't bear repeating.

But all of Birdy's implicit accusations—about me and Hester, and about the local Satan scare, and whether she or I or the both of us had anything to do with it—were pretty much forgotten the minute he lasered in on Step Garris as the prime murder suspect.

"You really think he did it?" Hester asked now. We were standing in the foyer, both still a little disoriented from lack of sleep and the pace of events.

"Well . . . sure," I said. "Don't you?"

"I guess." She sighed, then slowly stretched her neck and shoulders. "Wow. I feel like my chakras are all, like, shutting down on me."

I mumbled sympathetically, even though I had no idea what she was talking about.

"What you need, dearheart, is a hot bath and a little rest," I said. "I could fix some coffee—"

"That sounds dreamy, Hackshaw, but I just can't. I'm not even dressed for work yet, and I'll have to stop at the police station on my way into the city." She grimaced. "I'll have to call poor Sue's family at some point, too, to give my condolences. I think I should wait a bit on that, though, until the police have had time to notify them officially, don't you think?"

But I was distracted by her first comment. "You're not planning to go to work today, after all this?"

"I don't have any choice. We're in the middle of our FY inventory and we're already shorthanded and I've just been named assistant manager. Anyway"—she did this Vivien Leigh thing with her eyes—"life goes on, right?"

"For some." Not the kindest observation, but I was a little nonplussed. Where I come from you make some small effort to mourn the dearly departed, even if you don't consider them all that dear. "Look, I thought we might sit down together and talk about . . . things."

"I really think it's better to carry on, Hackshaw. Besides, you'll be busy, too. Wasn't that carpenter friend of yours supposed to come by later to work on my doors?"

"That's right. I forgot all about him. But, under the circumstances, I can have him delay another day—"

"No." Her head shook adamantly. "I want you to keep the renovation plans moving. Just see to it no one uses the back entry and disturbs the, um, crime scene. Chief Wade was very explicit about that." She checked herself in a horsecollar mirror hanging on the wall. "God, look at me. My hair looks like a rat's nest, my makeup is flaking off—I've got to get a move on."

And that was that. Hester hurried upstairs to put herself together, leaving me standing there in the foyer with my face hanging. After a minute or so of inner conflict—first thinking, *No matter that she's gorgeous and willing, I should give her a piece of my mind.* Then thinking, *Beauty has its price, and anyway, Hackshaw, you've already deposited her check*—I concluded that my best option was to wander out to the kitchen, make a pot of coffee and a few phone calls, and get on with the job I'd been hired to do.

Jackie Plummer was right, of course. Beautiful women make me stupid.

I was out in the garage, stripping the hardware off a pair of old doors and sweating with the midday heat, when Jennifer found me. The doors were the spares we'd hauled down, Step Garris and I, from the garage loft the previous Sunday. Unlike most of the interior doors in the Mott house, these had only two panels rather than four; probably had been removed from the former butler's pantry during a 1950s kitchen remodeling. But the important thing was they were an inch and a half thick and made of chestnut, just like most of the butchered doors. George Andruchek, the stair mechanic I'd brought in, thought they'd provide all of the material he'd need for his repairs.

I tossed a mortised lock set into a plastic bucket at my feet and said easily, "Starting to feel a little like your old self again?"

She grunted and rubbed her big belly. "I don't think I'll ever be like my old self again, but I felt that way even before Sue went and got killed."

"I guess nine months can seem like a long time."

"Hmmph." She leaned back against the side wall, her legs splayed to support the added weight, and stared wordlessly for a couple of minutes while I removed the hinge plates and pitched them into the bucket. Something had drawn her out there, and it wasn't the fascinating world of architectural salvage or the dashing figure I cut in my dusty chinos, but I figured she'd get around to it when she was ready.

"What happened to the other guy?" she asked eventually.

"George? He took his measurements and made up a materials list and then did what every blessed subcontractor on the planet does: he went to lunch." I flicked a drop of perspiration off the tip of my nose. "With any luck he'll be back later this afternoon, but don't bet the rent."

More silence while I hefted the one door off the sawhorses and replaced it with the other. Then: "I can't understand why Garris let her get to him that bad. I mean, why would an old guy like that care if some girl teased him about his drinkin' and stuff?"

"I suppose some men just can't stand to be put down by anyone, particularly an attractive young woman. Anyway, he isn't that old—around fifty. The gray hair and beard make him look older."

I could see by her expression that she wasn't buying it; fifty was ancient, period.

After another pause, she said, "They searched her room—two of the cops."

"And did they find anything of interest?"

Her left shoulder rose and fell laconically. "I dunno. I don't think they knew what they were lookin' for, or why, even. It's like they were—actin' something out, y'know? Like on one of those real-life cop shows on TV."

I smiled. "You're probably right, Jennifer."

I'd noticed it myself, the way Birdy's men seemed lost half the time. They don't catch many homicides in Port Erie, and when they do, it's usually a no-brainer, like a bad domestic scene—husband and wife, or feuding neighbors—with the guilty party standing paralyzed in the yard, crying and confessing before the medivan guys have even rolled out the gurney.

And even then, normal procedure is to call in the sheriff's department to do the heavy lifting. Of course, that was before—before the Port Erie PD had come under attack from some of the local bean counters. Now, like a cat with a field mouse, Birdy had an honest-to-God murder and an honest-to-God murderer he could show off, and he wasn't about to let loose easily.

"I didn't say anything, but . . ." She looked away, then came back to me. "I didn't know if it mattered or anything. I still don't, but . . . Sue had some stuff she didn't keep in her room."

I straightened over the door. " 'Stuff'?"

"She didn't know, but I saw her stashing it once, down in the basement, near where we do the laundry." She exhaled a gale. "I don't know if it's important now. I mean, whatever she was up to. I've got my own problems, y'know? I figured I should maybe, like, forget the whole thing. But . . . I don't know."

I put down my screwdriver. "Why don't you show me what you found."

A can of Krylon spray paint. Candy apple red, if you couldn't guess. Wrapped in a black ski mask.

The tidy bundle was stuck up in a cavity in the house framing, just above the foundation's sill. High enough so that a girl of Sue Krevin's height could reach it only by standing on one of the storage boxes that littered that corner of the basement. And high enough that a girl in Jennifer Hadley's condition would've been hard-pressed to reach it at all. But I had to ask.

"You're sure it was Sue who put this stuff up there?"

"Positively. I had a load of laundry in the other night and I was resting over there"—she indicated a beat-up vinyl recliner that sat in the shadows over beyond the washing machine—"and Sue came down with the paint can. I saw her wrap it in something dark, then climb up and hide it in there. I almost said something, but then—I just didn't." She frowned. "I don't mean this to sound bad, now that she's gone, but we didn't hit it off that great. She was kind of a bitch."

I stared at the can, then at the girl. "You realize what she was up to with this?"

She shrugged. "I heard Hester say there was some stuff goin' on around the neighborhood. Graffiti. I guess I just figured Sue was getting back at some of the neighbors who've been goin' around with their noses in the air." I started another question, but she cut me off. "Lookit, that's really all I know, okay? And I've got to go now—Bobby's mom is picking me up."

"One more thing, Jennifer. Was Sue into rock music? Like heavy metal?"

"Sure. I mean, who isn't? But she was really into it, like a real head banger. You should see all the tapes she's got up in her room."

"Yeah," I said. "Maybe I should."

12

It was almost four o'clock by the time I managed to get away from the Mott house. George, the door man, did come back after all, and he seemed eager to get started now that there was so little left of the day. I helped him carry a few of the butchered doors out to the garage, watched him set up his portable table saw, and then left him to it.

I was tired and grungy and hungry, wanting no more than to go home and scarf down a sandwich, then grab a hot shower and a cool pillow. Had I known what I was about to encounter at the Port Erie Police Department, I probably would have done just that. But duty called and, for once, I figured I'd better answer.

The aggravation began with Mel Stoneman.

"Hackshaw. Jesus, I knew I'd find your sorry butt tied up in this somehow."

We bumped into each other on the walkway outside the new town hall annex, him leaving and me going in. He was a large, square man with a small, square point of view—obvious, predictable, and hard-edged. But he was also the county sheriff's chief criminal investigator for our sector, which made him difficult to ignore. Heaven knows I've tried often enough.

"Nice to see you, too, Stoneman."

He aimed a blunt index finger at my face. "Don't start with me. I've taken about all the crap I need for one day."

"Let me guess. Birdy won't hand over jurisdiction on the Krevin homicide."

"All of a sudden he thinks he's Sherlock fucking Holmes. Why, his people don't know the first thing about criminal investigation technique. If he didn't luck onto this Garris clown—" He stopped abruptly, his face glowing like Chernobyl. I thought he might pop an aneurysm right then and there, but it proved to be wishful thinking. Almost immediately his primitive political survival instincts kicked in.

"That was strictly off the record, understand? Officially my department will cooperate with the Port Erie PD in any way Chief Wade sees fit." He did the finger thing again. "And if I read anything in the *Trite* that suggests otherwise, I'll be all over your butt like flies on a road apple."

"You seem to be fixated on my butt today, Stoneman."

"What the hell's that supposed to mean?"

"Well, I'm no psychiatrist, but I think the Freudians would say you were compensating for deeply suppressed homoerotic fantasies—"

"Homo . . . ?" The raised hand curled into a fist, which, on reflection, he decided to plunge into the pocket of his omnipresent raincoat. "That's a low thing to say about a man, even coming from you, Hackshaw. Christ." He stomped off across the parking lot, muttering and shaking his head as he went.

Folks weren't any friendlier inside the annex.

First, walking along the corridor, I was stared down in passing by a pair of Birdy's officers. If looks could kill, et cetera. Next it was the dispatcher working behind the counter, a hefty woman whose left breast was named P. SMITH.

"Hi. I'm Hackshaw. Here to give a statement on—"

"*You.*" She looked ready to spit, presumably in my eye.

"Me?"

"You've got your nerve strolling in here like you owned the place, that's all I can say." Unfortunately, that wasn't all she *did* say. "Call yourself a professional. I don't know how you people live with yourself, I really don't."

I was slowly shaking my head by then. "I think I must've missed something. I don't even know you, do I?"

But she was through with me. "Sit down. The chief'll see you when he's good and ready."

He was good and ready about five minutes later.

"My office, Hackshaw."

He blew past my chair almost before I saw him coming, Officer Reimer in lockstep behind him. I joined the parade and we force marched twenty feet to Birdy's half-glassed cubicle.

He settled behind his desk and said, "Close the door on your way out, Ricky."

"Aw, Chief—"

"I'll handle this myself."

The boy cop left. I sat. Birdy glared.

I took it for about three seconds.

"Look, what's with everybody around here, Birdy? Christ, you'd think *I* killed that poor girl."

"Oh, no, not you, Hackshaw. Wrong MO. You'd have cut her heart out with a fountain pen."

Maybe it was just fatigue, but I still didn't get it. Until Birdy, with a vicious gleam in his eye, reached under that damn blotter of his and whipped out a copy of the *Advertiser*. That very week's edition, delivered that very day. And carry-

102

ing below the fold a very pro-Hester bit of agitprop I'd managed to forget all about.

"Oh. That."

"It's bad enough you buried my crime briefing on the page-two police blotter, Hackshaw. And that you failed to tell me, while I was briefing you, that you were literally in bed with a woman my department was investigating—"

"I wasn't in bed with her." Yet.

"But then to turn around and write this one-sided pseudo-news story about how this champion of social responsibility, this Mother Teresa in love beads, is being harassed at every turn by, by"—he fumbled a pair of reading glasses from his desk drawer and scanned my article—"by 'a small but vocal group of nearby residents, some of whom have successfully pressured local law enforcement officials into joining in the witch hunt.' " He whipped off the spectacles. "If you'd slanted this thing any more, the print would've fallen right off the page."

"Look, Chief, anything can sound bad taken out of context like that. Anyway, all I was doing was reporting what I was hearing from people—"

"That's another thing. This unnamed and so-called reliable source you keep quoting. Who the hell is it—and don't try to tell me somebody in my department's feeding you this claptrap."

My chair seemed to be moving, or maybe it was just me squirming. "You can't expect me to reveal my sources, Birdy, that wouldn't be ethical." It also wouldn't be prudent, since the source I was quoting was me.

I know, I know. That's not quite the methodology they teach in journalism schools, but I'm a self-made man—I didn't go to journalism school. And besides, *I* knew as much about the Virginia Street situation as anybody I possibly could've dug up. And besides that, I was up against a deadline. Who has time for a lot of iffy phone calls?

True, I could've written the thing as an editorial, which would've made it perfectly okay to inject my personal point of view. The problem with that is, too many of our readers automatically discount anything I say in my editorials under the assumption that my opinions are irredeemably biased and self-serving—the *Wall Street Journal* factor, I call it. The bottom line is, I wanted people to give Hester and her halfway house a fair hearing, and a front-page headline was my best bet.

Of course, had I known she was going to end up with one of her girls dead on the doorstep, I might not have written the article at all. At the very least, I would've trod lighter on the David-versus-the-Philistines angle.

But it wouldn't have done any good to explain all of that to Chief Wade, who was teetering forward and back in his swivel chair, considering me with those doleful eyes.

"I'm disappointed more than anything, Hackshaw. Haven't I always played fair with you?"

"Yes, you have, Chief." Except for that time he privately told me he was against moving his department out to the new annex, then publicly denounced me when I argued the same position in one of my editorials.

"And yet you go and make me look bad like this." He stopped rocking so he could shake his head. "Imagine how you'd like it if I used *my* position to put the screws to you."

Something in the delivery convinced me this wasn't just a hypothetical he was posing. "Let's not do something we'll both regret later, Birdy," I said. "I come with a peace offering. Just to show my continuing support for your department." Then I took a prerecorded cassette from my jacket and placed it on his desk.

"What's that?"

"A new release from a heavy metal band called Death Squad. I found it in Sue Krevin's room."

"Who the hell said you could poke around in the murder victim's bedroom, Hackshaw?"

I shrugged. "Nobody said I couldn't, and your boys didn't seal the room." He started to object again, but I cut in. "Take a look at the cover art, Chief."

He hesitated long enough to establish that he had a mind of his own, then reached out and grabbed the tape. "Huh," he said after slipping the glasses back on. "Now, that's interesting."

"Thought you'd like it." The group's logo was a circle, in the middle of which was a red, slobbering winged goat, just as Krista Plummer had described it. Across the top of the cover was a band of strange symbols, bracketed on either end with pentagrams.

"Very interesting," Birdy muttered. "But circumstantial. Half the kids in town probably listen to this junk. We'll have to investigate a little more, see if we can come up with anything else—"

"I already have." I told him about the can of spray paint and the black ski mask, and how Jennifer Hadley had led me to them. "I handled the can, unfortunately, so you'll have to discount my fingerprints, but assuming a second set belongs to the dead girl—"

"Yeah, right. So where's the mask and paint can?"

"I put it back in its hidey-hole. I wasn't sure what the rules of evidence say about a situation like that, and, anyway, I thought it might read better—in your official report, I mean—if you guys discovered it for yourselves."

I sat back, smug as Sherlock fucking Holmes. Birdy was pleased, too.

"You did the right thing, Hackshaw, evidencewise. You happen to know if the girl's out at the house now?"

"She was twenty minutes ago."

He grabbed his phone and punched in the intercom button. "Smitty? Who's available in the squad room right now? Okay. Tell him to bring a car around front. Ten minutes." He replaced the handset and popped off his glasses. "You know what this means, Hackshaw. That my instincts about this Satan business were right all along."

"Half right, anyway."

The chief frowned. "How d'you figure?"

To tell you the truth, there'd been a moment, back in the basement, when I thought about not reporting any of this. I knew Birdy and the rest of Hester's detractors would sieze on it as proof positive that she was a bad influence on the neighborhood. And I knew that with Sue gone, the problem would likely disappear. But I also knew I couldn't keep quiet about it and still sleep nights. So the whole thing came down to applying the proper spin—and for that I have to thank Jennifer Hadley.

I said, "You were apparently right that the satanic graffiti—and maybe some of the other vandalism—was originating out of the Mott house. But you were wrong about it being some devilish cult conspiracy hatched by Hester DelGado. It comes down to a petulant, headstrong girl—Sue Krevin—poking her thumb in the eye of all those nosy, pious neighbors for giving Hester such a hard time."

"Well—maybe."

"There's no hidden agenda, Birdy," I said. "Just one pregnant twenty-year-old kid lashing out at the status quo."

He was ready to believe me, in part because it made sense, in part because it suited his purpose. He no longer needed a halfhearted Satan scare to firm up public support for his department; he had a titillating murder case to wave before the town council.

"But you know, Hackshaw," he said, his tone almost

collegial now. "This might just cast a new light on why Garris strangled the girl. I assumed he was just getting back at her for ridiculing him, but maybe there was more to it. Like, if he found out what she was up to and decided, out of some screwy sense of loyalty, to protect his new employer by getting rid of a troublemaker."

"You think he was afraid Sue's mischief would rebound to Hester and maybe force her out? And cost him his job?"

"Well, you have to figure he knew Ms. DelGado was under some pressure—he was over there working the last time one of my men stopped by to question her about the graffiti." He shrugged. "It's a theory, anyway, an avenue I can explore to try and get a confession out of him."

"You have any trouble bringing him in?"

"Nah. We rounded him up at that shack of his out at Muletown, stoked to the gills. Just about had to pour him into the car." He tilted his head. "Got him back in one of our new lockups. All he does is mumble and say he didn't kill anybody. Typical. Anyway, we lined up a public defender for him, and Tom Glomer will be handling the arraignment tomorrow morning."

"Glomer?" The Port Erie justice of the peace. "You're handling this through the town court?"

"Just the arraignment, then we'll turn him over to the county DA. Might ask to keep him in our lockup until the trial, though—it'd make visitation easier on his family."

"Uh-huh." And keep public attention focused on Birdy and his department.

"By the way, Hackshaw, shouldn't you be writing some of this down? For the paper?"

"We just published today, Birdy. Won't have another edition out for a week. Every media outlet in the area will have covered the story by then."

"Yeah, that's true. A couple of TV crews have already

called about coming out for a shoot." Just the thought of all that publicity brought a tiny grin to the corners of his mouth. He pushed his chair back. "Well, I got to run out to the Mott house and follow up on this lead. Meanwhile, you can give your statement to Smitty—" His phone rang. "Chief Wade. Yeah? Good. Just a sec." He cupped his hand over the mouthpiece. "Why don't you go get the ball rolling on that statement, Hackshaw."

I left him to his call and went out to the squad room. The dispatcher with the P. SMITH name tag still wasn't happy to see me, but she rolled a report form into her typewriter and got cracking, starting with her knuckles.

"First name," she barked, index fingers at the ready.

"Elias." When she snickered I added, "And may I call you P?"

After about two minutes, in which time she managed to mistype my name and address twice, I convinced her that things would go a lot faster if we changed places. I was still behind the typewriter a few minutes later, hammering out the last of my statement, when Birdy came out of his office. He started toward the exit door, then changed his mind and leaned over the counter above us.

"I just got off the horn with Dr. Ramathan, Hackshaw," he said. "Could be your lady friend still has a few things to answer for."

"Like what?"

"Like what's she really up to with that so-called boarding house setup of hers."

I didn't like the twinkle I saw behind those sad brown eyes. "I don't get it, Birdy."

"The Krevin girl? Doc says she wasn't pregnant. How about that?"

# 13

How about that indeed.

I was ruminating on Birdy's bombshell as I left the annex and headed across the nearly empty parking lot toward my wheels. Looking downward and lost in thought, which is why I didn't notice Reimer until I was almost on top of him. He was leaning against the fender of my Jeep, in full uniform, including those mirrored sunglasses they all seem to enjoy.

I said lightly, "I'm not sure, Ricky, but I think loitering's a misdemeanor in this town."

He stepped away from the Jeep, revealing a ticket tucked under the windshield wiper. "So's running on bald tires—and that's *Officer* Reimer to you."

I sighed and ran a hand across the stubble of my unshaved chin. "Look, *Officer* Reimer, maybe you should check with your boss. I think he's decided to call off the vendetta."

"I don't know what you're talking about—sir. I'm just doing my job."

"Yeah, well, fine." I was too exhausted to care by then.

I brought my arm up, intending to pluck the summons off my windshield. As I did, Reimer's hand shot out and clamped onto my wrist like a hawk picking off a sparrow in midflight.

"Hey—ow!" He was slowly twisting my hand back while simultaneously digging his fingertips into the underside of my wrist. "Okay, okay—I give!"

He let loose and smiled the predatory smile of a schoolyard bully. "You shouldn't make threatening gestures. We're trained to react instinctively. Sir."

"Threatening? I was reaching for the goddamn ticket, you—" I left off before calling him a fascist moron. One of us needed to behave maturely and it seemed only right it should be the one who wasn't packing a .38, a badge, and a twenty-pound muscle advantage.

"Sorry about that," he said with the sincerity of a French waiter. "Wouldn't want to damage your writing hand, now, would I?"

"Look, I already told you I've squared things with Birdy," I said, flexing the wrist. "That should be good enough—unless my article isn't all that's bugging you."

"Meaning what?"

"Meaning you seem to be taking all of this very personally. Is it just loyalty to the chief? Or is it you're upset with the world in general right now, because of the girl?"

"The girl?"

"Birdy said Sue Krevin was a friend of yours."

He briefly looked away. "She wasn't a friend, not really. I knew her from high school is all."

"Still, it had to be unnerving, your first homicide call, seeing someone you grew up with—end up like that."

"It wasn't just me. All the guys were a little shook."

"Understandably." I swear, I wasn't trying to provoke the kid. Just the opposite. I was hoping to defuse the situation a bit. And it seemed to be working, too. Until my old nemesis—curiosity—got the better of me. "A young woman like her. And pregnant, too—or so we all thought." When that last bit didn't register a noticeable response, I said, "You've heard? About her not really being pregnant after all?"

"Yeah, I heard about it. So how'd you find out?" The boy cop showed all the emotional range of Jack Webb, but then he'd probably grown up on "Dragnet" reruns. Even so, his sudden stoicism rang false.

"From your boss, who got it from Dr. Ramathan." My mouth sometimes gets ahead of my brain—you may have noticed—and this was one of those times. "They only got off the phone a few minutes ago. I guess news travels fast, unless . . ."

"Unless what?"

"Well, unless . . . maybe you already knew Sue wasn't pregnant?"

He moved a step closer. "I don't know what kinda shit you think you're peddling"—and another step, close enough now I could smell the spearmint on his breath and see my own mortality reflected in his sunglasses—"but whatever it is, we damn sure don't need it in Port Erie."

"Hold it a second, Officer." I'd played enough poker to know a bluff when I saw one. He was big and young and probably stupid, but not stupid enough to squash me right there in broad daylight in front of the police department. At least I hoped he wasn't. So I told him, "Don't move a muscle." Then I pulled a comb from my hip pocket and began combing my hair in his mirrors.

Reimer's jaw went rigid, and for a second there I thought I'd made a potentially painful misjudgment. But no. After a moment's indecision, he backed off and manufactured a look of professional indifference.

"You'd be better off keeping an eye on your rearview mirror, Hackshaw. 'Cause I plan on keeping an eye on you and this heap of yours." He began to walk off, then turned back. "Oh—and have a nice day. Sir."

The late Sue Krevin shared the ride with me all the way to my place in Kirkville. As if she were sitting in the passenger seat, silently mocking me with her lazy grin, refusing to answer or even acknowledge the questions that kept bubbling to the surface of my weary brain.

Like: Why was the girl masquerading as an unwed mother-to-be? What was she up to when I caught her rifling through Hester's desk? Why was Ricky Reimer so determined to give me a hard time? And why did I have this nagging perception that he knew more about Sue Krevin and her condition—or lack of one—than he had let on?

The only question I was able to answer, as I pulled into the driveway of my carriage house, was the one that went: why should I worry about any of this in the first place? And the answer I gave myself was: I shouldn't.

Understand, I don't like mysteries. They make my head hurt, all that deductive reasoning. And frankly, I'm not very good at it. I mean, show me a red herring and my inevitable response is likely to be *ah-ha!* Face it, if I had any aptitude for intrigue I'd be an intrepid investigative reporter for an aggressive daily paper somewhere instead of chief wordsmith for a piddling weekly shopper. That's not to say I didn't care. I did—about seeing poor Sue's murderer come to justice, and about seeing Hester DelGado get clear of this mess with her plans and her peace of mind intact. I just didn't see how I could be of any help, outside of boosting her cause with that little news item I'd fabricated. And given my standing with many of the sticks-in-the-mud in our area, even that small gesture was apt to alienate more people than it won over.

Better if I just stayed on the sidelines, I decided. Offer Hester moral support and counsel, certainly. And a sympathetic shoulder—or whatever—to cry on. But leave the rest to the police. After all, they already had Step Garris nailed for the crime; the worst was over, wasn't it?

I pulled to a stop in front of the center bay of the carriage house and dragged myself from behind the wheel. As an afterthought I took a penny from my pocket and ran the Lincoln's head check on the Jeep's tires. According to the rule of thumb, you hold the coin in the tread and if it isn't deep enough to cover the hairline on the top of the great man's likeness, the tire isn't legal. Three of mine were, if barely; number four, the right rear tire, was a blowout waiting to happen. So score one for jock-cum-cop Ricky Reimer.

I trudged up the stairs to my little apartment and shed some clothes, dumped a can of chicken noodle soup into a pan, and placed it on one of the twenty-inch stove's small burners. Then, like a grateful pilgrim cresting the hills outside Mecca, I stumbled onward to the bathroom shower.

Soon thereafter I was seated in my platform rocker, dressed only in an old robe, my feet up on the wicker coffee table. Having finished a bowl of soup and started on a bowl of pipe tobacco, I was savoring the solitude and trying to work up enough energy to move on to bed.

Of course, that's when the phone rang.

Reflex. "Yeah?"

"There you are." Jackie Plummer. "I've been trying to reach you half the day, Hackshaw. I called your office, the Nook—where've you been?"

"Working."

"That's what I love about you, always willing to try something new—"

I hung up on her.

It rang again. Repeatedly. I thought about reaching down and unplugging the thing, but it somehow seemed less taxing to simply answer it. Dumb.

"It was just a joke, for pity's sake."

"I laughed so hard I dropped the phone."

She exhaled. "Either you're still mad at me about the other night at my place or you've heard about the trouble at the Mott house."

"Both," I said without thinking.

"It was on the news earlier. My God, that poor girl murdered, her body dumped on her doorstep—I can't imagine. It must've been a terrible thing to see."

"It was." *Damn.*

"You were there?"

"Well . . . yeah. I happened to show up right around the time the cops came, give or take."

I could hear the tumblers in her head clicking. "The radio report said *Miss* DelGado found the body early this morning."

"I guess so—"

"What were you doing over there at that hour?"

"It wasn't all that early." When you lie to protect the other person's feelings, it shouldn't count. "I'm working on the house, remember? I had to meet a stair mechanic to go over a job. Look, Jackie, it's been a long, hard day and I'd just as soon not relive it, okay?"

"All right, already." I waited while she thought out a new offensive strategy. It took her about five seconds. "I understand they've arrested somebody."

I sighed, resigned. "Step Garris. He's like the town"—I hesitated, mindful of Jackie's fondness for political correctness—"chemical dependent. Hester hired him as a handyman."

"Well, I have to give her credit for her social consciousness, anyway. Taking in troubled young women, giving a break to a man down on his luck. What a tragedy that it turned out the way it did."

"Yeah." I stifled a yawn.

"They didn't say on the news report—I mean, she wasn't molested or anything?"

"It didn't look like it; her clothes weren't disturbed. According to Chief Wade."

"Well, that's something, anyway. Not that being strangled isn't horrible enough, but at least the poor girl didn't—oh, you know what I mean."

"Mmm."

"A shame," she muttered. Then, "But that wasn't why I've been trying to reach you."

"It wasn't?" Women, like wonders, never cease.

"Not directly, although part of the reason had to do with this Hester DelGado of yours. I saw your article, by the way. I don't care what Ruth or anyone else thinks, Hackshaw, I thought it was courageous of you to go out on a limb for this Mott house project of hers. Not that it'll do much good at this point, I suppose—"

"Wait a minute, what d'ya mean 'what Ruth thinks'?"

"Oh, well, when I called the *Advertiser*, she and I got to talking about the murder and your article naturally came up. Your sister was annoyed, is all. She'd had several irate calls from people in Port Erie, I guess, and she had no idea where *you* were—"

"Thursday's our slowest day," I said defensively. "There's lots of times I don't go into the office on Thursday." At least, every other Thursday, now that Ruth had switched us to a two-week pay cycle. Also, it's the day the paper goes out and the angry calls come in, but that was coincidental.

"I'm only relaying what Ruth said. At any rate, what I meant to tell you is that I remembered something about your new friend." That last part was very frosty.

"You mean Hester?" I said innocently.

"Remember I told you how familiar she seemed, that day

115

I drove past the Mott house on my way to see my mother?"

"Uh-huh."

"Well, it kept nagging at me. But then I remembered where I knew her from. The Downtown Craft Fair. You know how I share a stall with the MacDennys every year?"

"Yeah." She'd dragged me along to the thing once, a monstrous artsy affair held at the Rochester Convention Center. The MacDennys were a couple of "ceramists"—pot throwers, like Jackie—both of them transplants from merry olde England. A double dose of eccentricity, in other words.

"I realized that's where I knew her from. Nigel and Honoria introduced me to her last spring. As their channeler, of all things."

"What's a channeler?"

She tittered. "A sort of a spirit guide. Someone who can connect us mortals to those who've already passed on to the other side. I called the MacDennys—just to see if my recollection was accurate," she added hastily.

"Very thorough of you."

"Honoria told me Hester DelGado wasn't doing that sort of thing anymore. The last they'd heard, she was dabbling in crystal healing these days. Honoria also said there may've been a legal problem involving Hester's channeling—a disgruntled client or something. The MacDennys were both deliberately vague; they still believe in such craziness, although they don't take it that seriously. Anyway, Hackshaw, I thought you should know the sort of person you're dealing with. Frankly, she sounds like a complete flake."

"Thanks for your concern, Jackie," I said as sincerely as I could manage. "But all I'm doing for the woman is handling a few renovation problems—"

"I've *seen* her, Hackshaw."

There was no good way I could respond to that, so I didn't. "Was there anything else you wanted, dearheart?"

"Well, no. Nothing in particular, except—" She paused, and when she continued, the tenor of her voice had changed from sulky to sultry. "I thought you might like to come over. Krista has an overnighter at her girlfriend's house. I thought you and I might make up for lost opportunities."

"Tonight? Gee, normally I'd love to, but I'm just so doggone beat—"

"Yes," she said, suddenly glacial. "And we both know why, don't we?"

This time she hung up on me.

I almost felt guilty, until I remembered the toothy real estate agent Jackie had been seeing semiregularly behind my back. The guy was a real dweeb, according to Krista. Not that I cared. If Jackie wanted to waste her time listening to a three-piece suit wax philosophical about adjustable rate mortgages, it was her business.

As for Hester being a flake, I'd already determined that on my own and concluded that a scrambled egg is just as tasty as any other. Still, this channeling stuff reminded me just how little I actually knew about her. Which is why, despite my weariness, and in complete disregard for my earlier vow to stay on the sidelines, I found myself digging through the pocket of my corduroy sportcoat, looking for the small spiral notepad I always carry with me.

The name and number were right where I'd scribbled them Tuesday night, after I'd found Sue Krevin going through Hester's desk. I stared at the page for a moment, ready to forget the whole thing but not quite able to do so. Fixated on the curious notation Hester had made on the back of that invoice, an estimate for a security system.

"Check with Janus."

Against my better judgment, I picked up the phone and dialed. It rang four times before an impatient male voice picked up.

"Yes?"

"Um . . . can I speak to Janus?"

A weary exhalation. "Speaking. And it's *Janus*."

"Isn't that what I just said?"

"No, you didn't," he snapped. "You pronounced it *Janis*, like a woman's name. It's *Jay*-nus."

"Ah." Prickly bastard. "Rhymes with anus, then?"

He muttered, "Asshole."

"If you prefer."

"For Christ's—who the hell is this? And how'd you get this number?" Judging by the way he mangled the language, he was from the big city originally—a New Yawker.

"Sorry about the hour. I'm doing a credit check for a home improvement loan and the applicant gave your name as a reference." Okay, so some of us prefer reruns of "The Rockford Files"—but it always worked, didn't it?

Alas, not this time it didn't.

"Credit reference? For whom?"

"A, uh, woman named Hester DelGado."

There may've been a sudden intake of breath, definitely a longish pause, before he said, "All right, who is this? And what's this really about?"

I remember thinking, as I softly hung up the phone, *I wish I knew.*

118

14

Mrs. Hobarth, our fire-and-brimstone receptionist, was actually smiling when I arrived at the office the next morning. Stranger still, she seemed to be smiling at our young intern, Alan Harvey, who was grinning back.

I couldn't understand it—until the dog rushed out from under the desk and began gnawing at my shoelaces like a curly haired termite.

"What the hell—"

Mrs. H. reapplied her standard frown. "Watch your mouth, Hackshaw. And your feet."

Alan, beaming, said, "It's a toy poodle."

"How many batteries does it take?"

"Ha-ha." He flapped his hand dismissively. "I bought her for my mother—we had to put poor old Muffins to sleep last week."

"Muffins?"

"Mother's last poodle. He was arthritic." He slipped me a wink to tip me that the next bit was aimed at Mrs. H. At least

I hoped that was his intention. "I brought her in to get a few ideas for names."

"Ah, I see." Like any crocodile, Mrs. Hobarth had a soft underbelly. Little dogs, in her case. She had a couple of terriers, last I knew—Samson and Delilah, naturally. Alan, clever boy, was presenting the old bat with a peace offering she couldn't refuse.

The puppy was now gumming my ankle. "Uh, has it had its shots yet?"

"She's a she, not an it." Leave it to Mrs. Hobarth to know a bitch when she saw one. She leaned out over her desk for a better view. "Anyway, it's the dog we should be worried about. Best get her away from there, Alan, before she contaminates herself."

He scooped the pup off the floor and cradled it in the crook of his arm. "We've been wracking our brains for a good name, Hackshaw," he said, absently stroking its squirming head. "Any suggestions?"

"How about Fay?"

"Fay. I think I like it." He said to Mrs. H., "What do you think, dear?"

She hated it, if only because it was my idea. While they busied themselves kicking it around—the name, not the dog—I slipped away to the newsroom.

The first words out of Ruth's mouth were promising.

"I'm not talking to you, Elias."

"Thanks, Sis. I've got a lot on my mind, and—"

"I never should've let you slide that Mott house piece past me." While she paced the aisle, arms firmly folded, I settled in at my littered desk and began picking through my phone messages. "I *knew* it was trouble the minute I saw it, and now, to make matters even worse, that young girl's been killed over there—are you listening to me, Elias?"

I glanced up. "I thought you weren't talking to me."

"I'm not. I just thought you should know why."

There's no sense arguing with logic like that.

"I can't fault you for your lousy timing, since you couldn't know a murder would come along—"

"Of course not."

"—even though you *do* seem to have developed a knack lately for getting mixed up with dead bodies."

Unfortunately, I couldn't argue with her there, either.

"But your lousy judgment is another thing. That article was an embarrassment to this newspaper, Elias."

"What was so wrong with it?"

"It was unprofessional. Completely biased. Self-serving and cynical and unethical."

"Oh." I shuffled the pink phone memos into two stacks. "I guess it's not unprofessional when you publish verbatim press releases from the Kirkville Players and let our readers think they're legitimate reviews." The local amateur theater group was one of Ruth's passions; she had played Witch Number Three in their most recent stab at Shakespeare.

"That's different." She exchanged folded arms for hands on hips. "We're getting off the point. The article was bad enough, Elias, but you could've at least had the decency to show up here yesterday and take some of the heat. That's the real reason I'm not speaking to you. Liz and Alan and I were stuck fielding one angry call after another while you were out gallivanting, doing who knows what."

I pushed back in my chair and sighed. We'd been bickering like this since we were kids and it always blew over sooner or later, but there were ground rules to be honored. "Look, Sis, I'm sorry. You're mostly right and I'm mostly wrong, as usual, okay? But"—I indicated one of the short piles of phone messages—"let's examine the evidence. These calls came from your irate readers, pretty much the same calcified bunch who always call to cancel their subscriptions whenever I write anything they don't agree with. Funny how people who've supposedly dropped their subscriptions somehow manage to pick up on my next controversial piece the minute the paper hits the street."

"Well, just because they continue to read it doesn't mean they like it."

"But they *do* continue to read it—because some folks aren't happy unless they have something to be unhappy about. As for my 'gallivanting,' flitting around our circulation area is how I put together my Ramblings column, which, you have to admit, is the most popular feature in the paper." I began reading off select phone messages. "Here's one from Harv Stedman, one of our best advertisers: 'Thanks much for the yogurt machine plug.' And another, from Corrine Brooks, thanking me for saluting her husband on his impending fortieth." I omitted her additional comment, a complaint about the Mott house piece. "Here's a kudo from the president of the Chil-Kirk PTA for including a nice item on their latest fund-raiser. And one from the D'Angelos for writing up their family reunion. And so on."

Ruthie was ready to give up, if not give in. "Since we're back on the subject of *legitimate* news gathering," she said stiffly, "the Chilton College provost would like you to swing by the campus around noon to cover the luncheon speaker for their summer lecture series." She tossed a press release onto my desk. "And I'm *still* not talking to you."

I watched her reverse her field and stride purposefully down the corridor that connects our newsroom with hubby Ron's printing shop. That left me all on my lonely in the office, wondering where Liz Fleegle was and why nobody seemed to mind *her* spotty attendance record.

For the next half hour I busied myself answering the phone—a couple of routine pleas for coverage of this or that event—and alternately flipping through my notepad, culling out the best anecdotes and tidbits for inclusion in next week's Ramblings column. I was typing up a paragraph on the Beck Farm's you-pick-em strawberry harvest when Alan Harvey sashayed in from the reception area, sans pooch.

"All through finessing Mrs. Hobarth?" I asked, still pecking at my Royal manual.

"Mmm-hmm. I helped her redo the classified ad rate schedule, now she's minding the pup for me."

"Glad you're free. I have a nice little assignment for you, but not so little you won't pick up a byline for your clips file." I handed him the press release on the college lecture series and explained the assignment to him the way Ruth had explained it to me. "And you get a free lunch out of it to boot. Think you can handle it okay?"

"Sure, no problem. But I can't say I'm entirely looking forward to it." He rolled his eyes. "Professor Mortensen, the program director? He positively hates me."

"Better get used to scorn if you're planning a career in journalism." Just then the phone chirped. "Better take the Minolta with you, too," I told Alan as I picked up.

"Hackshaw? Am I disturbing you?" Hester. I sent Alan on his way with a little wave.

"The sound of your voice always disturbs me, dear," I said. "But in pleasant ways."

She cooed. "Glad to hear it. I was beginning to wonder. I thought I might hear from you last night, after everything that went on. In fact, I tried calling your place, but your phone was out of order or something."

"I unplugged it and went to bed early. Sorry I didn't call, but did you find my note?" I'd left her a summary of what George Andruchek had in mind for the doors and a list of which tradesmen were scheduled to come by that day.

"I found the note. George is here now, working on the doors. And the chimney guy came by this morning for a look—I was out, but Jennifer handled it. The plasterer called to say he'd be here sometime after twelve, and I'm expecting a man from the security company to show up, but I've got a problem. I'm off work today, but I have to run into the city for a few hours and Jennifer wants to go out, too." She paused to catch her breath. "Anyway, I was hoping you were planning to come by—"

"I am, only later. I have some newspaper errands I need to take care of first and some copy to file." Not to mention a beer at the Nook with my name on it. "I was thinking I'd be over around three—"

"Couldn't you maybe bring some of your work over here? I mean, you can use my phone if you need to call around. I know it's a lot to ask, but I've had to juggle my own schedule and there's so much to be done over here and I don't want to see the renovation project fall behind."

And she *was* paying me to oversee the project. That was the implication. Women automatically think everybody should have to work as hard as they do.

I surrendered a sigh. "Tell you what, ask Jennifer to stick around till I get there, probably about an hour."

"Oh, that's great, Hackshaw. You're a doll. I hate to push you like that, but I need someone here and I can't very well ask Step to do it."

"Of course not," I said, chuckling, "seeing as how he's locked up in Birdy Wade's holding cell."

"But he isn't. Didn't I mention the arraignment this morning?"

"No. Why? They didn't drop the charges—?"

"No, he's to stand trial for murdering poor Sue. But I got him out on bail—"

"*You what?*"

"And now he's in the yard, clipping the hedges and refusing to leave because he thinks he owes me—"

124

"Why in hell would you bail Garris out?"

Her turn to sigh. "It involves a lot of complicated emotions on my part, Hackshaw. I'll explain when I see you. Plan on staying for dinner and—whatever. Gotta run."

15

Jennifer Hadley was sitting on the front porch steps when I pulled up to the house, her knees splayed wide to accommodate her distended abdomen, a small suitcase resting beside her. The poor kid's face was puffy and pale, her expression woebegone, any initial excitement she may've felt at the notion of becoming a mother seemingly wrung out of her by the realities of her condition and her situation.

Frankly, just seeing her made me feel guilty about being a man.

"Hi," I said as I came up the walk. "Taking a trip?"

"Bobby's mom is driving me to birthing class, then she wants me to stay over at her place for the night." A glimmer of hope animated her eyes. "Bobby got a better job, at Kelso's Garage, so it's kind of a celebration. Like maybe he's starting to think about, you know, his future."

"Well, that's great," I said, trying for optimism. "I hope I haven't held you up. I got here as soon as I could."

"That's okay. The class isn't till one." She wiped the

sheen of perspiration from her forehead; it was humid for June. "I, uh, didn't tell Hester I probably wouldn't be home tonight. Maybe you could let her know."

"Sure. You think she'd have a problem with that?"

"Not really. She might rag on me about Bobby is all." She shrugged. "I know she'd probably want me to be here, because of the new girl, but that's the way it goes."

I frowned. "The new girl? You mean someone else has moved in already?"

"Supposed to later today. Some juvie runaway that social services dug up. That's why Hester had to go into the city, to pick her up." She looked at me. "This girl isn't pregnant. I guess her mother just couldn't handle her or something."

I shouldn't have been surprised; Hester had never made a secret of her plans for the Mott house. Still, it struck me as ill-timed at best, adding another problem child to the equation so soon after the revelations about Sue Krevin.

"Does Hester know about what we found in the basement?"

"Yeah. I told her, and Chief Wade came by to ask some questions. She was, like, shocked that Sue was doin' that stuff. But you know Hester. She bounces back in a hurry—only you never know where she'll come down when the bouncing stops, you know?"

I said I knew just what she meant.

"Like with that crazy old man," she continued. "Why she'd wanna pay his way out of jail, I don't know. I go, 'Don't you think he did it?'—meaning strangle Sue—and Hester goes, 'Probably he did, but he wouldn't have if I didn't hire him in the first place.' Like just because she gave him a job, he's her responsibility or something." She shivered her shoulders. "He's out back right now, hangin' around. That's another reason I'd just as soon spend the night at Bobby's mom's."

"Understandable." I was about to continue on into the house, but instead I took a seat beside her.

"You know what I find really weird?" I said. "That Sue was pretending to be pregnant. You hear about that?"

She nodded. "Chief Wade told us."

"Why would she do that, I wonder?"

"I dunno. Maybe just to get a cheap place to live for a while." She read my skepticism and went on, "I ran into her about a month ago, outside the drug store in the village. We knew each other from high school, but not like we were friends or anything—she was a year ahead of me and she ran with a different crowd. Anyway, we were just, like, talking— what've you been doin', where're you livin', like that." She rubbed her belly and grinned ruefully. "Well, it was pretty obvious what I'd been doing. So I tell her about my family givin' me a hard time and how I was livin' at Hester's place and how it was a pretty good deal. So Sue says she was worried herself, that she was real late with her period, and maybe she'd be needing a place. A couple weeks after that, she showed up and moved in."

"You really think Sue faked the pregnancy because she was after cheap room and board?"

"Yeah, maybe. Someplace clean and safe, too. But I guess it wasn't so safe after all."

While we dwelt silently on that irony, a Dodge minivan pulled alongside the curb, followed almost immediately by a dusty pickup truck with DAN THE CEILING MAN painted on the door panel. Bobby's mom and my plaster contractor, respectively. I carried Jennifer's bag out to the minivan, exchanged introductions with the cheery woman behind the wheel, and waved the two of them down the block. Then I walked Dan inside the house to show him the ceilings.

\* \* \*

"Who was the suit?"

"Some salesman with"—I glanced at the business card he'd foisted on me—"Greenbriar Security Systems. Oh, excuse me, not a salesman. Says here he's an electronic security consultant."

George Andruchek snorted. "Yeah, he looked like he was electronic. Sounded like it, too."

I couldn't disagree. The salesman who wasn't a salesman had stopped by to see if "the lady of the house" was prepared to "sign off" on a proposal for a home security system that he'd "specked" for her. "If it's a go," he said, he could "task out" the order within a week. I took that to mean the grunt work would be handled by somebody else, presumably an electronic installation consultant. I'd told him the lady of the house hadn't made up her mind yet as far as I knew, but that she'd call him as soon as she finished doing a cost-benefit analysis on his proposal. When he asked who I was, I told him I was Ms. DelGado's nuisance avoidance consultant. He was still chewing that over when I saw him to the door.

"How's the job going, in general?" I asked George.

"So-so. No big surprises. Tell ya, though, when I'm done with the doors, the little lady might want me to take a look-see at that stair bannister. Squeaky as hell."

We were standing in the foyer, directly in front of the stairs. While I'd taken time to deal with Dan the Ceiling Man and the security guy, George had been tinkering with the dining room's pocket doors. He'd already glued and nailed new strips of oak along the bottom of each and had sanded out the joins. I had helped him hoist one of the heavy doors back onto the overhead track, but we'd had to take it on and off again twice so he could adjust the track for smooth operation.

I said to him, "Once a stair mechanic, always a stair

mechanic, huh, George? I'll mention it to Hester, but first things first. You about done fiddling with that track?"

"Smooth as butter now." To demonstrate, he used one finger to effortlessly slide the left-hand door into its wall cavity. Then he winked. "Just in time for me to drive over to the Donut Hole for my afternoon coffee break."

I shook my head minutely—he'd only been back from lunch for little more than an hour—but I didn't say anything. When you deal with enough independent contractors, you soon learn that the accent is on *independent*. I suppose the same could be said for certain small town newsies.

"You want me to do anything in particular while you're gone?" I asked, thinking I might carry a few of the second-floor doors out to his table saw in the garage.

"You wanna do something for me, you can get rid of Garris. The bastard's mooning around out back like a freakin' zombie." He wiped a red bandana across the back of his neck. "Truth is, it makes me sick just to look at him."

Judging by the bare loathing I saw on Andruchek's face, I wondered if Garris might not be better off in jail. New York State doesn't have the death penalty, but it would have it if it were up to most of the local folks.

"Well, I'll see if he's still there," I said. "Maybe I can convince him to go home."

"You do that. I can't work back there with him around." He stuffed the bandana into the pocket of his bib overalls. He was a short, heavyset man with thinning blond hair and earnest blue eyes. "It's not just me. Hell, if my wife knew I was over here workin' with a murderer hangin' around, she'd throw a shit-fit you wouldn't believe."

"I'll see what I can do," I said. "But get the coffee and donut to go, okay? I'd like to see this job finished up by tomorrow."

He wasn't happy about it, but he conceded a nod and

went on his way. I walked through to the back of the house and out the kitchen door, stepping onto the small entry porch. Step Garris was there in the yard, holding on to a lawn rake and staring back at me. With his wild gray hair and bushy beard and holding that rake like it was a staff, he looked for all the world like an Old Testament prophet, ready and willing to bring down the wrath of God on all of us blasphemers.

I shook off a sudden chill and proceeded down the steps. It was then that I realized it wasn't me he was staring at, but the porch itself—the place where Sue Krevin's body had been found. I thought, *Thank goodness she didn't end up on the front porch; at least the neighbors can't see him back here.* Then I glanced to my left, at the house belonging to one of the chief busybodies, Mrs. Mobley. I couldn't say for sure, but I thought I saw a curtain moving in one of the first-floor windows.

"Uh, afternoon, Step."

I was standing right next to him by then, but he didn't react. Just kept his eyes riveted on the porch.

"Step? It's me, Hackshaw."

I brought my hand up cautiously, about to tap him on the arm, but changed my mind, fearing it might be like stepping on a land mine. I cleared my throat instead.

"Step, can you hear me—?"

"That girl was evil, Hack." His head suddenly swiveled ninety degrees and those distant, dark eyes were on me. "I was only tryin' to put her on the right path, I swear. I seen how she was and I told her, but she wasn't havin' none of that from the likes of me. 'Mr. Gar-ass,' she called me. And 'Step-in-shit.' "

I shifted nervously. "Pretty cold. But you know, you have to roll with the punches sometimes, Step. I mean—"

"Stephen."

"Excuse me?"

"My name. Stephen." His eyes swung back to the porch.

131

"Ma named me after one of the saints; one of the first Christian martyrs, she used to tell me." The head came around again. "Was the kids in school started callin' me Step. Step-Hen at first, then just Step. They liked to tease me, too, till I showed I could take care of myself."

"Well, listen, uh, Stephen—"

"That's okay, you can call me Step. I don't mind it."

"I was going to say, you've had a rough couple of days. Maybe it'd be better if you went home, got some rest."

His eyes seemed to focus then, as if he were really seeing me for the first time. "Lord Almighty, Hackshaw, I'm in some kinda trouble this time, ain't I?"

"Yeah. I'm afraid so."

"You think I killed that little tease? Tell me true."

I didn't want to tell him true—not while he was standing an arm's length away. So I fell back on Socrates and asked, "Are you saying you *didn't* kill her?"

He frowned at the rake in his hand. Shaking his shaggy head, he shambled over to the side of the garage and leaned the rake against the wall. "I don't think I done it," he said.

"You don't *think* . . . ?"

"Truth is, I get these spells sometimes—when I been drinkin' hard." His head drooped. "I forget things. My old lady can tell ya."

I didn't have anything to say to that, either. But I remember thinking what a cakewalk Birdy Wade and the DA had ahead of them.

Garris's head came up. "I been standin' out here, tryin' to remember. Tryin' to see myself doin' harm to that girl. Hard as I might, I can't remember nothin'. Sure, I mighta hated the little bitch, but I didn't kill nobody— I'd almost swear to that."

"Well, you'll get your chance to do that, Step, at your trial." If his defense attorney was stupid enough to let him take the stand. "In the meantime, I think it'd be best if you went on home."

"Yeah. Yeah, I guess so. Only"—a bit of his normal demeanor surfaced, a blend of savvy and subservience—"that's a long walk out to Muletown, Hack, and besides, I don't think people'd be real happy to see me traipsin' through town right now. You gimme a lift?"

That was all I needed, for people to see me chauffeuring Step Garris. "The thing is, I can't leave right now, Step. George went to run an errand and I can't leave the place unattended—"

"We can wait'll he comes back. I don't mind." He squinted at me. "It ain't just the ride, Hackshaw. I got things to tell ya 'bout that girl."

Something else to look forward to. Like root canal surgery.

# 16

To paraphrase General Sherman, if I owned both hell and Muletown, I'd live in hell and rent out Muletown.

To begin with, it wasn't a town at all, but essentially a community of squatters living in sorry little frame houses perched on cinderblock piers. The land the houses occupied sat hard and fast alongside the Erie Canal and was owned by the state. That the land had, over more than a century and a half, evolved into an unofficial hamlet can be traced back to one key fact: the site included the only canal lock between Rochester and Lockport, some forty miles west.

A little history. Back in the 1820s, when the Erie Canal first opened for business and overnight became proof positive of America's manifest destiny, western New York was still a sparsely settled frontier. Where there were any roads at all, they were horrible roads, which is why waterways were the preferred route of travel and why the canal itself was built—a man-made waterway that moved people in the direction they wanted to go: west, young man. And just as folks since time immemorial had always formed communities along navigable rivers, so did new towns, like Port Erie, spring up along the latest eighth wonder of the world.

So what's that have to do with Muletown and canal locks? I'm getting to that.

In what is now the town of Port Erie, there were two locations that attracted early settlers. One was next to a low bridge that had been built over the canal to connect an old farm road; that's where the village proper of Port Erie sits today. The other was about three miles west, beside the canal lock, which had its own attractions for a certain element of the frontier population.

You see, it took time to move packet boats and barges through a lock, and it also took a lock tender—someone who knew how to operate the thing. The lock tender needed a place to live with his family, so a modest house would be built near the lock. And since many of the passengers would get off the packet boats to stretch their legs while the lock was being filled, often the lock tender's wife would take advantage of the situation to sell food and drink and homemade curatives to the weary travelers. Before long, other industrious types—drummers, patent medicine hawkers, itinerant gamblers, and so on—got wise to the benefits of a captive audience and began showing up at lock locations all along the Erie Canal.

In the case of Muletown, there was a second factor at work, and it was this factor that gave the place its name. In addition to the lock tender's house, the site from its earliest days also had included a stable for the mules that trudged the towpath, pulling the boats along, as well as a kind of barracks for the mule skinners who tended them. And the mule skinners were a hardworking, hard-drinking, and hard-playing bunch.

Add up the various elements—mule skinners, drummers, travelers, gamblers, whiskey salesmen, working girls—

135

and you can imagine the sort of loose, boom-and-bust shanty-town that evolved. And why the more respectable pioneers who settled in the area avoided Muletown and instead gravitated toward the other end of town, the tiny village sprouting up around the bridge. And why, to this day, the proper citizens of Port Erie thought of the denizens of Muletown with disdain, when they bothered to think of them at all.

The fact is, most Port Eriens would just as soon see Muletown disappear entirely, and eventually they'd get their wish. Since the canal was first modernized early in this century—rendering the original Muletown lock obsolete, by the way—state officials had made several half-hearted attempts to remove the residents of Muletown from what had always been a public right-of-way. The Muletowners fought back in court, naturally, and in the end the state agreed to let them stay in their homes until the last surviving family members either died or moved away, at which time all property rights would revert to the state and the abandoned house would be torn down. Since the agreement, a dozen or so homes had come down, but a dozen others had persisted, including the one that had sheltered several generations of Garrises.

"It's the green one there, Hack. Pull in by that heating oil tank."

I followed his directions and parked the Jeep on a patch of gravel fronting a low, tired single-story house covered in the same type of asphalt shingles that had formerly uglified the Mott place. It was the only thing the stylish Mott house had in common with the Garris abode, or with any of the other houses that made up Muletown.

They were hardly houses at all, really; more like fishing shacks or summer cottages that over time had undergone modest upgrades, like indoor plumbing and electricity and homely shed-roof add-ons. Some had acquired insulation and storm windows, too, but despite that, the scattering of houses

136

reflected the impermanency of their occupants' situation. None had seen a fresh coat of paint in years. Broken windows were boarded over with plywood. Yards were muddy catch-alls for scavenged cars and abandoned kitchen appliances and lean, nervous dogs straining at their chains. It was the modern mantra of low maintenance reduced to its base element—no maintenance. But what could you expect? The Muletowners were regarded as transients, even if their ancestors had occupied the same spot of land since before the Civil War.

"You better come in, I guess."

He led me through a screened front porch crammed with bundles of yellowing newspapers and scatterings of rusty engine parts and into a small, overfurnished living room. The interior of the house gave off a potent mixture of conflicting odors—menthol, boiled cabbage, mildew, tobacco and cat—and the gloomy room trapped all of the outside air's humidity without its leavening breezes.

"You wanna wet your whistle, Hack?" Garris asked, after directing me onto the lumpy sofa.

"No, thanks." My lips weren't about to touch anything in that place.

"Well, I do." He disappeared through a door leading into the kitchen. I heard the refrigerator open and close, followed by the distinctive pop of a can opening. Thirty seconds later there was another pop, and Garris returned to the living room holding a fresh can of Genesee beer, presumably his second.

He sat in an old brown vinyl recliner patched with gray duct tape and took a long pull at the brew.

"A man gets a terrible thirst sittin' around old Birdy Wade's jail."

He should know, having spent his share of time in the town lockup on various public nuisance charges.

"You had something you wanted to tell me, Step?" Not

137

that I was eager to hear it, but it was the only way I was going to get out of there.

"That girl wasn't right, Hackshaw."

"How do you mean?"

He leaned forward. "I mean she was up to no good from the start, is what I mean. I seen the way she cut folks up—not just me, but the other one, Jennifer? And Miz Hester, too. That Krevin girl didn't respect none of us. It's like her bein' there was a joke or somethin'."

"Well, she was a calculating little snip, I'll give you that—"

"She was out to start trouble from the get-go. I seen her more than once, sneakin' out of the house after dark—"

"Wait a minute. What were *you* doing over at the Mott house after dark, that you could see anything?"

He wiped his sleeve across his hairy mouth and hung his head. "Sometimes I was late finishin' up a job, is all, like puttyin' them storm windows. Then again, sometimes, after I got paid"—he glanced up, a kid caught with his hand in the cookie jar—"I'd get me a bottle over to Cap's Liquor Store and head on back to this little spot I made for myself in Miz Hester's garage, so's I could get a little peace. My old lady, she gives me hellfire sometimes."

"Uh-huh." Which had me wondering where his wife was at the moment; aside from Garris's raspy breathing, the house was quiet as a tomb.

"What I'm tellin' ya is, I seen her sneakin' off at night, up to no good."

"I already know about that, Step. And so does Birdy." I filled him in on the spray paint and ski mask and the Death Squad tape, and the connection they all had with the satanic graffiti plaguing the neighborhood.

He nodded, accepting it as testimony in a judgment already rendered. "I knew that godless little bitch—"

138

The porch's screen door slammed shut, and we both turned expectantly. The inner door opened and a slim young man entered, puffing on a cigarette. The smock he was wearing bore the unmistakable colors of the local fast-food hamburger franchise, and the paper hat clutched in his hand sealed the deal. His face was narrow and pale and stoic, his longish hair matted down and greasy as his employer's french fries. If memory served, this had to be Chucky, the younger of the Garris's two sons.

He showed every intention of passing through to the back of the house without a word until his father spoke up.

"You got nothin' to say to your old man, sonny?"

The kid—if midtwenties still qualified him as such— paused at the kitchen door and blew a plume of smoke out of the side of his mouth.

"Hi, Pa. They let you go, huh?" Not *Good to see ya, Pa,* or even *Did you do it, Pa.*

"Temporary, anyhow. Where's your ma at?"

Chucky shuffled his feet. "Over to Aunt Marla's, I think. She was pissed big time when she heard what you got picked up for."

"She was, huh?" Garris turned back to me. "I guess that figures. She'll come back sooner or later. Question is, will I still be here when she does?"

I couldn't answer that one for him. Chucky didn't seem to care either way. He slipped away to the kitchen. It appeared that Step was used to his family's indifference.

"Well, leastways the Lord loves a sinner," he intoned, then punctuated it with another long hit on the beer can.

"Look, Step, I really have to be going—"

"Stay a minute, Hackshaw. Please."

It was a word he didn't say often, and I could see it didn't come easy. Still, to be honest, it was the wild desperation in

139

his eyes and the unpredictability of the man, not sympathy, that kept me in my seat.

"I seen the girl out around town a couple other times. One time at night, usin' the pay phone down there on Main near the Rexall Drugs. Chewin' somebody's ear off, it looked like."

I pointed out that that was hardly unusual behavior for a young woman, gabbing on a telephone.

"Yeah," he came back, "but they got a phone at the Mott house. Why'd she have to walk four blocks to gab, huh?"

"Maybe Hester has a time limit for phone use. Maybe Sue, like most kids, wanted some privacy."

He snorted. "Privacy. That's what I mean. What was she up to, she needed privacy? Then there's the other time." He finished the beer and plunked down the can on the side table. "Broad daylight, this was, about a week ago. I'm headin' into town, takin' the towpath like I usually do, right?"

The old Erie Canal towpath was now a public trail for hikers, runners, and bicyclists. Anyone with enough stamina could start down it at one end of the county and follow it all the way to the other end and beyond. In Step's case, physical fitness wasn't the issue; his drinking had cost him his driver's license long since.

"So I come to the part where they got that boat launch there, back in them trees off Sandpit Road?"

I nodded that I knew the spot.

"I just come down off that little foot bridge, you know? And I'm walkin' along where all that sumac and shit is so high? And I seen the Krevin girl down in the gravel lot there, where the boaters leave their cars and trailers and stuff. Only there weren't no other cars or nothin' in the lot, that bein' a week-day mornin'. There was just this one car—the one I seen the girl gettin' out of."

I could see by his expression I was supposed to be impressed, but I wasn't. Because even if this wasn't just a tall tale Garris had concocted to divert attention from himself, it didn't add up to much.

"There's nothing sinister about a young woman turning up out at the local lover's lane, even in the middle of the day. She was probably just making out with a boyfriend."

"So if there was nothin' sneaky about it, why'd he leave her out there like that, make her walk back to town?"

"He did?"

"Right after I seen her get outa the car. She give him a little wave, like, through the window, and the guy guns his engine and takes off outa there." He finished with a smirk. "Let's hear you explain that."

"Christ, I don't know. Maybe the guy's married, or maybe they had an argument, or . . ." I threw my hands up, frustrated at being trumped by the likes of Step Garris. "Maybe if you think it's so all-fired important, you should be telling this to Birdy Wade."

"Nuh-uh. Don't think I better be doin' that."

"Why not?"

"That car I saw? It was a Port Erie PD cruiser."

# 17

I started cursing Step Garris under my breath the minute I got in my Jeep and kept it up all the way back out to the main road.

Didn't I tell you? The worst thing about this news business is that people are constantly unburdening themselves on you, telling you things you didn't want to know. Here we had this nice, neat murder case—girl meets town drunk, girl mocks town drunk, town drunk strangles girl—and the town drunk, in one of the few lucid moments he's had since LBJ, has to complicate things with a disturbing tale involving said girl and the local cops.

Just what did he expect me to do about it? I mean, assuming I believed him in the first place, which I didn't.

I know what you're thinking. The poor guy's pathetic, Hackshaw. The lowest of the low, never an even break in his miserable life, and now he's quite possibly been made the convenient patsy in a diabolical plot hatched by Chief Birdy Wade's corrupt police department. In the name of all that's right and good, the man *needs* a champion.

Do me a favor and put your heart back in your chest where it belongs; you're bleeding all over everything.

Look. In the first place, Step Garris isn't some misunderstood eccentric with a heart of gold. He's got a record as long as a Bill Clinton speech for everything from public intoxication and disturbing the peace to criminal trespass, shoplifting, drunken driving, and even assault and battery, for punching out a barmaid—yes, a bar*maid*—who once tried shutting him off. This ain't Otis of Mayberry we're dealing with here.

In the second place, the man wasn't even sure in his own mind that he hadn't killed Sue Krevin. He didn't *think* so, but he couldn't remember, because he'd had a blackout. Which meant that he must've been hitting the hooch pretty heavy sometime shortly after he'd had his last shouting match with Sue in Hester's backyard. On top of that, he'd just admitted to me that his latest favorite spot to crash with a bottle was in Hester's garage, forty feet from the porch where the girl's body was found. And we already knew he had ready access to the probable murder weapon, a length of discarded clothesline.

Motive, means, and opportunity.

I hardly need mention my final point: Garris's kneejerk belief in conspiracy theories. The CIA killed Kennedy for the Bay of Pigs. The moon landings were faked on a Hollywood sound stage. The Trilateral Commission was a front organization for international communism. Microwave ovens were part of a Japanese plot to control our inquiring minds.

Give me a break.

Okay, so if Garris wasn't credible in the first place, why was I so upset about him dumping this new Sue Krevin anomaly on me?

Because, credible source or not, it added fuel to all of the other stuff that'd been bugging me. The girl's phony pregnancy and her penchant for late-night paint jobs. Her connection to the boy cop, Ricky Reimer. His blind loyalty to Birdy Wade and his clumsy attempt to intimidate me. Even Hester DelGado's odd behavior—why she bailed Garris out of jail, why she had hired him in the first place, why she needed to "check with Janus" about installing a security system . . .

Something strange was going on, and in good conscience, it was tough to ignore. But I was determined to try, to put the whole thing out of my mind and concentrate on the two things that really *did* concern me: the renovation work on Hester's house and lovely Hester herself. The rest of it was somebody else's problem, I figured.

Until I happened to glance up at my rearview mirror.

And saw the Port Erie cruiser rapidly closing on the Jeep's tailgate.

At first I thought it was going to smash right into me and I reflexively hunched my shoulders and closed my eyes. But when I opened them again, the cruiser was just there, crowding my backside like a pervert on a city bus. Close enough I could readily make out the driver's mirrored shades and tight grin.

Guess who?

No siren, no lights—just Reimer staring at me through those insectoid sunglasses.

I snuck a peek at my speedometer; I was ambling along five miles under the speed limit. *Too slow maybe. Should I pick up the pace a little, see if he falls back? Or slow down even more, let him pass if he wants to?*

I decided to speed up a little. And it seemed to do the trick. When I looked in the rearview again, he had dropped back a couple of car lengths. I let out the breath I'd been holding.

But then a pickup passed us going in the other direction, and almost immediately the cruiser snuggled up to my bumper again.

144

The thought *No witnesses* flashed through my mind.

I gulped—more of a dry heave—and studied the terrain. Big Ridge Road was lonely along this stretch, with the high berm of the canal off to my right and on the left an overgrown pasture without so much as a friendly cow in sight. Then, up ahead, I saw another vehicle approaching. But no—it was turning off onto a side road.

I checked my mirror. Reimer had seen the other car, too, and had dropped back again. But now he was closing up.

Another thought zipped by: *Safety in numbers.*

I flipped on my blinker and decelerated just enough to make the turn onto the side road. Reimer followed suit. In no time I was tailgating the other car, a plodding Chevy sedan driven by somebody with blue hair, with the Port Erie cruiser still tailgating me.

We carried on that way for a few hundred yards. Then the old gal's directional flashed and the world's slowest car chase got even slower as she made a left onto another narrow country road. Me in cold pursuit, ditto for Reimer. The former sweating bullets, the latter biding his time with malicious indifference.

The road began to curve to the south and it dawned on me that eventually we'd be right back to Big Ridge Road, a mile or so west of where we'd initially turned off. Then the Chevy's signal flashed again and the old lady swung slow as a molasses flow into the gravel driveway of a farmhouse.

If I wasn't such a numbskull, I'd have followed the old girl right up the drive and tried to sell her a subscription to the *Advertiser* or something. Anything to spoil whatever the boy cop intended for me. But by the time I thought of it, we were already past the farmhouse. So instead I downshifted and punched the gas, the surge snapping me back against the seat. But it was no use. The cruiser caught up effortlessly and we were grill to bumper again.

He was about to fire up his light bar and pull me over—I could sense his finger inching toward the toggle switch. But no sooner had I regained speed than I had to brake again, this time for the stop sign at Big Ridge Road.

There we were, idling at the intersection, my old Jeep gurgling indignantly at the unaccustomed wear and tear, the powerful engine in Reimer's big Ford throbbing impatiently, Reimer's image staring down from my rearview mirror, jaw set like concrete, tired of playing cat and mouse and ready to pounce.

So why didn't he?

Because, unlike yours truly, he'd already spotted the other car making its way toward us along Big Ridge Road. A little Toyota, coming at a good clip. Probably a commuter on his way home to Chilton or Kirkville, bypassing the minor rush-hour congestion in downtown Port Erie by taking the old bridge . . .

*The old bridge.*

Reimer no doubt expected me to turn left and head back toward Port Erie, the same direction I'd been going when he began stalking me. Right back over the same stretch of lonely highway as before. And, dumb as it sounds, that's just what I'd intended to do. But now I realized I had a better option: a right turn onto Big Ridge Road, which ran west for a half mile or so before doglegging south and crossing over the canal.

In the nanosecond it took to figure all of that out, the Toyota had closed within fifty yards of the intersection. It was do or die. Maybe both.

At the last possible moment, I gunned the engine and pulled out in front of the little import. I heard its tires scream, then the quick, angry bleat of its horn. I braced myself for the expected whiplash and the simultaneous sickening sound of metal tearing metal. But it didn't happen.

In the rearview mirror I saw the Toyota fishtailing to a stop astride the yellow divider lines even as Reimer's cruiser tore out of the side road and tried to get around it. I forced my attention back to the road ahead, accelerator flush to the floorboard, willing the battered old Jeep to match my own adrenaline rush.

Momentum pulled my body to the right as I steered through the leftward curve of the dogleg, still gaining speed. Then, maddeningly, we were slowing again, the Jeep rattling like grandma's tea kettle as it strained to climb the steep grade leading to the old bridge.

A siren screamed behind me—closer than I'd hoped— but this time I didn't look back. Just kept the pedal to the metal, struggling to the top of the grade, gaining speed again as I drove under the square arch of the bridge's girdered superstructure, fairly flying as I crossed the noisy steel deck to the south side of the canal.

And finally, easing off the gas and letting go a quaking sigh as I sped past a familiar road sign: WELCOME TO CHILTON, A TOWNSHIP OF FRIENDSHIP.

"Hey, Hacky boy. How 'bout a game of gin?"

"Not today, Dutch. I've taken a vow of poverty."

Buddy McCabe had a Twelve Horse drawn and ready before I'd even settled on the bar stool, bless his soul.

"Uh, about that tab of yours, Hack."

"Oh, yeah." I dug into my jeans and extracted a small roll—when I'd deposited Hester's advance check, I'd taken my 10 percent in cash. I counted out a good portion of it now and slid it across the bar. "Does that get me current?"

"And then some. This'll make Norb's day."

"Good thing you didn't mention that ahead of time."

Dutchie, sitting three stools down, spotted the transaction and bellowed, "Hey, numbnuts, I thought you said you were broke."

"You misunderstood, Dutch." No surprise there. "What I meant was, I don't feel like making you broke today."

"Hah!" He shook his cannonball head. "You better worry about yourself, man. I'm on a lucky streak these days. Me and Dwight Philby took second at the Legion Hall euchre tourney last Sunday and I won another hunnert bucks playin' Instant Lotto." Then he smirked. "Even got my ashes hauled last night."

Buddy chuckled. "Yeah, but you were alone at the time, so it doesn't count."

"Hey, McCabe? Fuck you. And gimme another Gennie."

While Buddy went off to cater to the clientele, I nursed the head off the glass of ale and hoped nobody would notice the slight tremble in my hands.

If he'd wanted me bad enough, Reimer could've followed me right across the town line, jurisdiction or no. But then he might've had some explaining to do to Birdy Wade, like why he'd risked a high-speed chase just to lay another Mickey Mouse summons on me. Assuming that a traffic violation was all he was planning to hit me with.

That he had it in for me was obvious. But was he merely harassing me as payback for my article on Hester's halfway house and the insinuation that the Port Erie PD was taking sides with the local xenophobes? Or did it have to do with the girl, Sue Krevin? Some connection he thought I'd made? Like maybe the girl's satanic graffiti campaign wasn't just random mischief, but a scheme the two of them had hatched? A scheme designed to provide a phony crime scare for Birdy Wade's besieged department, so that it could justify its existence to the naysayers?

If I was right, it was bad enough. But there was something

else. The girl had been murdered. By Step Garris, we all assumed. But *if* Reimer and Sue were in cahoots, and *if* there'd been some sort of falling out among thieves, so to speak . . . *damn.*

I felt a major headache coming on.

"Hey, Hack. What's with the long face?"

"Huh? Oh. Nothing. Working too hard, I guess."

"So you could use a little R and R." Buddy leaned forward on one elbow and said quietly, "You hear about the game tomorrow night?"

"Which game is that?"

Still mumbling. "At Lou Edelman's place. Serious draw and stud players only, he says, if you get my drift."

I did. It meant Dutchie Prine wasn't invited. I looked to my left. Conveniently, the Dutchman just then plucked his glass off the bar and strolled out to the side room where the coin pool table was kept. It's not that we didn't like him, you understand. He was an okay enough sort, once you got past the bluster and the casual bigotry and the quixotic temper. In that respect Dutch was much like a lot of the other townies around our parts, except that he was bigger and stronger and thus harder to control—unless you were Buddy McCabe, who happened to be bigger and stronger still. Dutch was also a notoriously bad but streaky poker player who, when he got the deal, liked to call every gimmicky, wild card–filled game known to man.

"Lou's house, huh?" Edelman lived in Port Erie, of all places. "I don't know if I'll make it." Then, "Maybe I could sneak by late."

Buddy didn't question my choice of verb, probably because he was used to my having to sneak around for various reasons. People are so cynical sometimes.

"Don't make it too late," he said. "Jan says we can only

play till midnight, then it's vamoose. I think she just had the floors waxed. Or maybe it was her legs."

Jan was Lou's wife. He liked to say her name stood for Jewish-American Nag, but not when she was within earshot.

I finished my ale, then checked the Budweiser clock behind the bar. Nearing five o'clock. Reluctantly I pushed the glass away and said, "Gotta go."

"What's the rush, Hack? You just got here."

"I have to check on George Andruchek, the stair mechanic? He's handling a job for me at the Mott house. And I'm expected for dinner."

"Ah, right." Buddy did that Satchmo grin he knows I hate. "The redhead you told me about."

"I didn't tell you anything. It was Jimbo Clark."

"Whatever. And now I see some dead chick turned up in the backyard or something. What is it with you and stiffs lately, Hack? What's this make, three in the past year?"

I bristled. "This one's got nothing to do with me, okay? I'm just doing a job for the owner," I added as I backed off the stool.

"Right. And having dinner with her." He snapped his fingers. "Hey, speaking of that Mott house, I mentioned to Lou you were spending some time over there with this choice redhead. He says you lucked out again."

"Yeah, yeah—"

"No, what he meant was, you coulda got stuck with the guy who almost bought the place last winter. Some doctor, I guess. A real asshole, Lou says."

I eased back onto the stool. "How'd Lou find that out? He doesn't live anywhere near Virginia Street."

"Yeah, but he's on the town planning commission."

"That's right. I forgot about that."

"He says this doctor wanted to buy the place and make

it into a health clinic or something, so he had to make a pitch to the town for a—I forget what he called it."

"A variance."

"Right. Anyway, he didn't get it. Lou says the guy's plan wasn't half bad, but the guy was such a jerk, and then some of the neighbors bitched, so the town caved." He shrugged. "So I guess you're lucky the place was still up for sale when this new babe came along."

Funny, I didn't feel lucky. "You remember this doctor's name?"

"Lou didn't say. We were just, you know, shooting the breeze."

"Hmm." I started to leave again, then turned back. "Uh, Buddy, is your car out back?"

"Yeah. Why?"

"I was just wondering if maybe I could borrow it tonight. I'll leave you the Jeep."

"Is that piece of crap acting up again?"

"It's running tip-top, thank you." Like Buddy's prehistoric Imperial was a fine Swiss watch. "I just think it might be better if I . . . traveled incognito tonight."

He started laughing so hard he could barely get the keys out of his pants. "Man, I *knew* it. It's got something to do with this dead chick, right?"

I sighed. "Your guess is as good as mine."

18

Hester was eyeing me across the battered oak dining table as if I were the head judge at the Pillsbury Bake-Off.

"You don't like the pudding."

"Sure I do." I spooned up another glob of the stuff. "Interesting touch, adding in these chocolate chip morsels."

"Those aren't chocolate chips," she said ruefully. "I was having trouble with my electric mixer."

Bachelors can't afford to be finicky. I immediately gobbled down the spoonful and grinned like an idiot. "Well, I think it makes for a great change of pace, myself. Like chunky peanut butter."

"I warned you I'm not much good in the kitchen."

Our main course had consisted of fried haddock, french fries, and creamy coleslaw, what the local supermarket called its Friday fish fry special. Given the saturated fat content, it's a wonder pious Catholics hadn't died off long before Vatican II. But it was very tasty, even if the tartar sauce did come in those annoying little packets.

"It all tasted homemade to me," I lied. "Too bad George couldn't stay."

"Hmmph. He doesn't approve of me any more than my neighbors do. But that's okay." She reached across and patted my hand. "At least I've got you. Although I was beginning to wonder if you'd deserted me, too."

"Sorry I was gone so long. But like I said, the Jeep was giving me some trouble on the drive back from Muletown, so I had to switch vehicles with a friend."

I'd made it from the Nook to Hester's unscathed, if you don't count the humiliation of being seen in Buddy's carbon-belching Imperial. I wasn't sure which shifts the Port Erie cops worked, but my plan had been to arrive well after five on the assumption that Reimer would have gone off duty by then.

I casually pushed aside the half-full pudding dish. "Speaking of Muletown and Step—"

"Why don't we talk about that over coffee. In the living room," she added, cautioning me with her eyes before shifting same toward the dining table's third occupant.

The new boarder's name was Regina something, better known as Reggie. She was a twig of a thing, all arms and legs and snapping gum and fractured teen syntax—what Hester, in a private aside, had called "a valley girl in search of a beach."

Personally I doubted we could say anything that would grab Reggie's attention, seeing as how both of her ears were covered by the headset from her Walkman. She'd slipped the thing on halfway through the meal, effectively zoning herself off from us adults. Hester seemed to take the snub in stride, so I had, too, less amazed at the kid's behavior than by the way she was wolfing down the lumpy pudding.

"Coffee sounds fine," I said. "Unless you happen to have a cold beer in the fridge."

Hester smiled. "Now that you mention it . . ."

\* \* \*

153

But once we'd settled on the living room's swaybacked sofa, Hester still didn't want to discuss Step Garris.

"About these baseboards," she said as she brushed back a strand of wavy hair. "Have you figured out what I should do about the damaged parts?"

I sipped at my glass while I studied one of the problem areas, a foot-long section near the fireplace surround. The baseboard had been notched out years ago to accommodate a cold air return grill for a central-heating system. Hester had had the antiquated system replaced a few weeks earlier, rendering this grill and half a dozen like it obsolete. You could simply leave the grills in place, stuffing some insulation inside the cavity to cut down on drafts and heat loss, but as Hester had pointed out, the chintzy metal grills were an eyesore. In the renovation game it's called the mushroom effect: you set out to do one job and find out it leads to several other repairs you hadn't anticipated.

"Well," I said, "we'll need to do a Dutchman of sorts on each of the bad areas, that much is obvious."

"Not to me. What's a Dutchman?"

"Strictly speaking, that's where you cut out the bad section and replace it with new material. In this case I'd do a bevel cut on either side of the butchered areas and replace the whole section with a new piece of wood. Wouldn't be much of a problem if the trim was painted, but this natural oak of yours is a different story. We can't fill with a cheaper type of wood and we'll have to try and match up the grain in the old stuff as best we can."

"Man, this is starting to sound expensive."

"It would be if you had to buy brand new oak and have it milled to match the original." The baseboards were a foot high with a fancy milled cap, not something you can order off the shelf at your local home center. "But there are a couple of cheaper alternatives. The first would be to see if I can scavenge a few sections of matching baseboards someplace, like at Ediface Wrecks."

"Ediface . . . ? What's that?"

"An architectural salvage outfit in Rochester. They've got a warehouse full of old house parts."

She waved her bejeweled hands. "Now you're talking. That sounds like a great alternative. Isn't it?"

"Maybe. *If* I can find just what we need—a big if. On the other hand, there's an easier way to get what we need, if you don't mind robbing Peter to pay Paul."

"You don't mean *steal* the wood, Hackshaw. Because I've already got enough trouble—"

I laughed. "I'm suggesting you 'steal' it from yourself. You know that big walk-in storage closet you showed me up on the second floor? It's got the same oak baseboards as the rest of the house. What I'd do is remove the trim there and use it to piece in the bad areas down here. Then I'd replace the closet baseboards with whatever decent stuff I can find at Ediface Wrecks. It won't match the rest of the house, but it's a closet, right?"

"Wow. What a neat idea." Hester inched a bit closer. "I don't know what I did before you came along, Hackshaw."

I'd been wondering about that myself, if for a different reason. I set my glass on the coffee table and stretched my arm out along the ridge of the old sofa.

"Answer a question for me," I said. "You're serious about this old place, right? Fixing it up, living here, taking in young women with problems."

"Of course. I told you, it's a self-realization thing. I get to have the sort of house I've always wanted in a small town setting, and also a chance to do some good. That is, I could if the neighbors would give me half a chance."

"That's my point. Look, Hester, I'm not one to tell anybody they should kowtow to the local yahoos. But being true to yourself and who you are is one thing, shooting yourself in the foot is another."

"I don't know what you mean."

"I mean Step Garris, for starters. I can understand why you'd hire him in the first place—you're new here, you didn't know how Port Eriens view Muletowners like Garris, and you've got this commendable instinct for helping underdogs. But why in the name of Christ would you bail him out of jail after he's been charged with murdering one of your own boarders? Don't you realize how nutty that makes you look? And bringing in this new girl so soon, a runaway that social services must've been desperate to place if they'd put her in here a day after another girl has been found dead on your doorstep—you might as well stand out on your front porch and thumb your nose at people."

I really hadn't meant to come on so strong—I almost never yell at women—but I'd built up a lot of stress as a result of my game of tag with Reimer. My outburst drew a long exhale from Hester. She placed her glass on the coffee table, and when she faced me again, her eyes were glistening.

"Don't think I didn't consider what the neighbors would say. I knew I'd be criticized for putting up Step's bond, but I feel responsible. I *am* the one who brought him here—and Sue Krevin, too."

I started to interrupt, but she shushed me with a raised palm. "As for Reggie, she didn't have much choice, and I don't see that I did, either. Her mother threw her out and she got into trouble—shoplifting, minor stuff. They stuck her in juvenile hall for three days while they tried to figure out if she could be placed somewhere. While they were dithering, Reggie was sexually assaulted by two other girls. So a friend of mine at social services called me—" She impaled me with a look of abject sorrow. "She's seventeen, Hackshaw. Should I have turned her away?"

Suddenly I felt lower than the stinking baseboards. "I guess, under the circumstances . . ."

She could've left it at that—I certainly wasn't about to press her again—but she surprised me with a question of her own. It came out cautiously, like a mouse when the house goes quiet.

"You're satisfied that Step did it, right?"

"It sounds like you're not."

"I'm not saying that. It's just, I know how quick these people are to lay blame on somebody who doesn't fit their mold. Even if he did murder Sue, I can't just write him off like a bad debt or something. Besides, did you know Step suffers from blackouts when he's in an alcohol phase?"

An alcohol phase. Alcoholic haze would be closer to the mark. Better still, booze binge. I should get Hester together with Jackie Plummer; they'd probably like each other, if it weren't for me. I sighed, nostalgic for the days when drunks were drunks and things like drugs and gambling and overeating were simply bad behavior, not diseases. But then, I've been called a curmudgeon. And worse.

"Yes," I conceded. "I know about the blackouts. I also know that he 'hated the little bitch'—that's a direct quote—*and* that he suspected Sue was making trouble for you around the neighborhood, *and* that his favorite crash pad when he's got a bottle is in *your garage.*"

I thought that might impress her, but it didn't.

"The stuff about Step and my garage came out at the arraignment this morning. I guess he told Chief Wade all about it—as much as he could remember, anyway."

"Well, that clinches it. Even if Garris didn't do it, he's the one who'll pay the piper."

"Now it sounds like *you're* not sure he's guilty." Her voice had a certain gotcha quality that set off my defenses.

"Don't put words in my mouth." I launched myself off

the spongy sofa and began pacing in front of the fireplace. "Look, it's up to the cops and the courts to decide whatever he did or didn't do, okay? You're not a lawyer and I'm not a private eye, okay? And Step Garris sure as hell isn't a babe in the woods when it comes to making trouble—"

I abruptly stopped railing and pacing when the girl walked in, the lightweight headphones draped around her neck like a Japanese necklace.

She said to Hester, "Uh, I'm gonna walk downtown and, like, scope out that little video arcade you told me about."

"Okay. Be back by ten, though, right?"

She plunged her hands into the pockets of her voluminous shorts and grimaced. "Yeah, I know the rules."

We watched her go before Hester said to me, "The court put her on a curfew."

"Mmm," I said. Then, "You think it's a good idea, letting a kid like that run around by herself right now?"

"She's only going a few blocks. Anyway, this isn't a jail."

"I'm only saying—"

"Look at it this way, Hackshaw." She scissored one leg over the other, a move I would've thought painful in those form-fitting jeans. "We can stay here and argue about her leaving, or we can go upstairs and put the next few hours to good use."

"Actually," I said, "the kid does have a right to a social life, doesn't she?"

Afterward.

Too early for moon glow this time. Just past nine o'clock, the high summer sun riding the western horizon, muted amber light cleansing Hester's bedroom like a second coat of paint. And warm in there, warm and sticky as—well, never mind.

"Wow."

Predictably, Hester spoke first. And second.

"Your muladhara chakra must be like a nuclear reactor."

"Just what are these chakra things you keep talking about?" I figured it was a New Age compliment of sorts, but it never hurts to ask.

She rolled on her side, smiling like the proverbial cat, and walked her fingers down my sweating chest. "They're like these energy fields we have in our bodies. It's a Hindu thing."

"Hmmph." The last woman I knew who was into this Hindu jazz was also a flake. In fact, she'd nearly skinned the flesh off me acting out chapter six of the *Kama Sutra*.

"The muladhara chakra is the genitals," Hester purred.

On the other hand, it's best to keep an open mind.

"Well, your chakras ain't too shabby, either."

"Such a romantic."

We lapsed back into lethargy, Hester gently touching this and that while I studied the ceiling, half of me wondering if my nuclear reactor was ready to come on line again, half of me fighting troublesome, persistent thoughts about the lovely enigma who lay next to me.

There were a dozen things I might've asked her about. Her past incarnation as a channeler to Jackie's squirrely potter friends. This shadowy Janus character, and why she seemingly needed his input before deciding to install a costly security system. Where she was coming up with the money to do anything, let alone post a bond for Step Garris.

Lots of questions.

But the most troubling—the only one that seemed worth asking just then—had to do with the dead girl, and the secrets she'd taken with her.

Still staring at the cracked ceiling, I said, "Tell me about Sue Krevin."

The gentle stroking stopped. "What d'you mean?"

"What do you know about her? What do you think she

was up to with the fake pregnancy and the graffiti? Like that."

Hester exhaled. "Well, I know she just turned twenty, that she's from right here in Port Erie, that she lived with her divorced mother until coming to stay here. That much I know is true. As for other things she told me—like how she and her mother didn't get along and how her mother's boyfriends used to hit on her all the time—I don't know how much of that to believe anymore. I do know Mrs. Krevin seemed genuinely heartbroken when I spoke to her on the phone yesterday, after the police notified her about Sue."

"Did she know Sue wasn't really pregnant?"

"She didn't know she was supposed to be pregnant in the first place. Sue told her she wanted to move into her own place, is all. An 'impulsive girl,' the mother said."

"Mmm."

Hester swung her feet over the side of the bed and shrugged into an oversized T-shirt. "As for why all the deceit, Hackshaw, I don't know. Maybe it's like Jennifer figures. Sue faked the pregnancy to get cheap room and board. Then she did the graffiti to get back at the neighbors, like out of some misplaced loyalty to me."

"I didn't get the impression she even liked you very much," I said. "Or you her."

"That was just typical female rivalry. Or maybe Sue was projecting her feelings about her mother onto me."

That didn't sufficiently answer my question, but I was ready to move on to the next one.

"Did Sue ever say who was supposed to be the cause of this nonpregnancy of hers?"

"No, she never seemed particularly concerned about that. Of course, now we know why."

"She didn't mention any boyfriends at all? A guy named Ricky Reimer, for instance?"

160

Hester frowned. "Reimer? Isn't he one of the Port Erie cops? The young one with the square jaw?"

"Mmm. A former high school gridiron hero."

She stood and stared down at me, her arms crossed, the thin T-shirt material drawn tight over her breasts, her deep red hair touseled. Stern, but still fetching.

"I'm getting some very negative vibes here, Hackshaw. Are you trying to say Sue was planted here by the local police? Like she was spying on me or something?"

"No, no. I'm not saying that at all." *Thinking* it, maybe. "It's just, Reimer and Sue knew each other, and Reimer's been, uh, coming on a bit strong since my Mott house article came out—"

"You know what I think? I think you're getting just as paranoid as the rest of us. I'm not sure what's going on anymore, but like you said, you're not a private eye. And one thing I am sure of, I don't want you to do anything that might piss off Chief Wade. I'm having a hard enough time convincing him I don't have horns. I may never be able to bring him around to my point of view on my boarding house concept, but I hope I might at least get him to stay neutral. Let's face it, whatever Sue was up to, it's over and done with and we should probably just put it behind us and move on to the next battle. Which reminds me, you're planning to come over tomorrow morning?"

She was glancing at the clock radio, my cue to roll out of the bed and search for my pants.

"I should be here by tennish," I said.

"You might want to bring along a change of clothes."

I slipped on my BVDs. "I might?"

"Some of the neighbors are supposed to have a meeting at the mayor's office at one o'clock to present their petition against me. I'm going to crash it and I'd like you along for moral support. If you don't mind. I know you don't owe me anything . . ."

I tried to think of a polite way to refuse. But, I mean, there we were, half naked, staring each other down across the width of a rumpled bed still warm from our lovemaking. A bed I hoped to see more of in the future.

So I said, "I won't need a tie, will I?"

# 19

On the way back to Kirkville, I stopped off at the Nook and reswapped vehicles with Buddy McCabe. Then I went straight home to bed, intending to get a good night's sleep and an early start on Saturday. As it turned out, I slept like a baby until nearly nine o'clock, and even at that it took a series of heavy-handed raps on the carriage house's front door to rouse me. I fumbled on a pair of jeans and a T-shirt and made my way downstairs.

Mr. Johnson, one half of the kindly duo that rents out my house, was waiting on the stoop. Dangling from one hand was a small tool box, standard issue for retired science teachers. I didn't even ask.

"We were beginning to wonder about you, Hackshaw," he said, squinting against the brilliant morning sun. "Did you know your phone was out of order?"

"Out of order—?" I slapped myself in the forehead. "I unplugged it the other night."

"I thought maybe Rochester Tel cut it off again—"

"I happen to be in good standing with the phone company just now, thank you." Forget to pay a bill once or twice and you're labeled a deadbeat for life.

"Or maybe there was a wiring problem." He hoisted the tool box. "I could take a look at it, if you want."

People just don't listen anymore, have you noticed?

"Very considerate of you, Mr. J., but I think I can manage to plug it in on my own."

I hate to be sarcastic, but I was suffering from a severe caffeine deficiency, which I planned to remedy as soon as I could run back up to the apartment and switch on Mr. Coffee. Alas, my tenant wasn't through pestering me. Why they don't raise the retirement age to eighty or ninety, I'll never know.

He droned on, oblivious. "If it was anything but the wiring, I probably couldn't have fixed it anyway. They put computer chips in everything these days. Not much a screwdriver and a pair of needle-nose pliers can do for a faulty integrated circuit. Planned obsolescence is what it is."

He was holding the tool box with both hands now and calmly rocking back and forth from heels to toes, waiting me out with patience learned over forty years of drumming photosynthesis into the heads of distracted teenagers. Meanwhile, my sinuses were beginning to close up and a dull ache was building behind my right eyeball.

Finally I said, "You wanna come up for coffee?"

"Well . . ." He consulted his watch, like he had to be somewhere this month. "I guess I've got time for a cup."

While the java brewed in the galley kitchen and Mr. J. played with the phone jack in the living room, I handled my morning ablution and finished dressing. By the time I brought him a mug, he was ensconced in my platform rocker.

He took a tentative sip, made smacky sounds, and said, "How do you feel about kale, Hackshaw?"

"Who?"

164

"For the garden. Mrs. Johnson and I are putting together the chart for the second planting in July. Kale's a good fall crop for this climate." Another sip. "So what d'ya think?"

"Uh, I'm not sure I exactly know what kale is."

"A variety of loose-leaf cabbage. For salads and soup and such. Loads of calcium."

"Oh, right. Kale." I shrugged. "Anything you two decide is okay by me."

"I think kale is the way to go."

"Uh-huh." I parked on the wicker love seat and worked on my coffee while waiting for the next nonsequitur.

"Jackie Plummer called twice," he said presently.

"She called you?"

"Twice. Once last night and again first thing this morning. She assumed your phone was disconnected again, but I told her it could be the wiring."

I took a large gulp. "Did she say what she wanted?"

"Not in so many words, but I can guess." The old satyr grinned. "Pretty divorcée like that, doesn't take a rocket scientist to figure out what's on her mind. Hell, I certainly don't have to tell *you*, of all people—"

Hubba hubba. Mr. Johnson had an exaggerated notion of my love life. I'd tried to disabuse him once or twice, but it was like explaining a sleazy mall Santa to a five year old—the truth is the last thing they want to hear.

"Well, I'll call her later," I said. "But right now I have to get over to a job in Port Erie." He showed no signs of taking the hint, so I added, "Was there anything else? I mean, any other messages to pass along?"

"No. But you did have a visitor of sorts last night, around dusk. At least, I think that was his intention. Hard to say for sure, the way he was skulking around." He raised his mug and drank, leaving me suspended.

"Someone was skulking around here?"

"Mmm." The mug came down. "A guy in a black Firebird, or maybe dark blue. My night vision isn't what it used to be. In fact, I think there were two of 'em."

"Two Firebirds?"

"No, no. One Firebird—black, I think—with two people in it. The headrest blocked my view, but I'm pretty certain there was somebody short in the passenger seat." He took a final hit from the mug and placed it on the coffee table. "I was out back turning over the compost heap when I saw the car come by, going real slow when it came around the corner and drove right past the carriage house. Nothing unusual there, coming off a turn like that. But then I go back to turning the pile, and maybe a minute later, this Firebird cruises by again in the opposite direction, still slow as a tortoise. Probably trying to spot if your Jeep was there." He chuckled. "The driver looked to be a youngish fellow, best I could tell. So I figured, well, maybe Hackshaw's been sniffing around the wrong henhouse again. Like last year, with that Dwayne Shinzer? Looking to knock your block off for diddling his wife—"

"She told me they were separated!"

"Too bad she didn't tell Dwayne. Anyway, I thought you should know about the Firebird."

"Mmm."

I thanked Mr. Johnson for his concern and gradually eased him back down the stairs and out the door. Then I got myself a second mug of coffee and drank it down while staring out the living room window at the side road where Mr. J. had witnessed the alleged skulker.

As I stared, I thought about whose toes I might've stepped on recently, but the permutations were infinite. Then I wondered what make of car Ricky Reimer drove when he wasn't stalking people in a Port Erie cruiser. Then, because worrying never solved anything, I decided not to think about it at all.

Hester DelGado was a Bohemian rhapsody that Saturday—a New Age Gypsy decked out in a flaring flowery skirt, a tight white jersey, and shoes Jackie Plummer would no doubt characterize as hooker heels. And more jangling parts than a tambourine. I counted six bracelets, three necklaces, including the blue Herkimer crystal, and nearly as many rings as an old-growth oak. I figured the eye shadow alone probably had set her back twenty bucks.

Sinfully delectable, if you want to know the truth, like a Bavarian cream puff. But I doubt if the neighbors would agree.

"I hope you remembered to bring a change of clothes, Hackshaw."

She was standing, hands on hips, in the double doorway leading off from the foyer. I was at one end of the living room, helping Dan the Ceiling Man set up his gear. The scrubbed cotton work shirt I was wearing was bibbed front and back with sweat and my old jeans were ratty enough to bring top dollar in a Tokyo boutique.

I frowned. "I brought clean duds, but are you sure you want me along? Not that I mind, but we're busy here, and I've got those baseboards to get at next—"

"I need you there, Hackshaw. You keep me centered."

Dan the Ceiling Man gave me a look; first time he'd taken his eyes off Hester, actually. I said to him, "George is out back in the garage, if you need help with your scaffolding."

"Hey, no problemo, Hack. You run along, leave the man's work to the men."

His expression was neutral, but I could read the amusement in his eyes, with a touch of envy mixed in as well. I muttered a curse at him, then shuffled off to retrieve the clean clothes from my Jeep.

Ten minutes later, having washed and changed in the half bath off the kitchen, I met Hester on the front porch.

"I guess we'd better take my wheels," I said. Her tiny Geo was blocked in the drive by George Andruchek's truck.

"Why don't we walk? It's only a few blocks."

I didn't argue, even though I wasn't crazy about the idea. Not that I mind strolling arm in arm with a beautiful woman under normal circumstances. But these circumstances were anything but. I'd swear I could feel dozens of eyes staring at us as we made our way down Virginia Street toward Main, even though I realized that most of the hard-line busybodies were probably already over at the mayor's office, giving voice to their petty petition.

"Aren't you warm in that jacket?" Hester asked.

"No, it's fine." I'd changed into a lightweight cord sport-coat, along with fresh khakis and a blue oxford shirt. My newsman uniform, aka Saturday-go-to-meeting clothes. Good thing, too, I thought, glancing out the corner of my eye at Hester. At least one of us needed to come across as a potential Republican for the mayor.

She was reading my mind again. "You probably think I'm a little too avant-garde for the occasion, but I thought it out very carefully and I decided the hell with them. I'm not interested in trying to fit into someone else's mold. I'm going to take a proactive approach from now on." She squeezed my arm and smiled radiantly. " 'To thine own self be true,' right, Hackshaw?"

"My sentiments exactly," I lied. We were on Main by then, walking north into the business district and toward the canal bridge. The traffic, both vehicular and pedestrian, was heavy even for a Saturday afternoon, but then I remembered. This was the start of the three-day Port Erie Canal Days Festival. Our path for the ensuing four blocks would be littered with sidewalk stalls set up by the local merchants and the itinerant antique dealers, hobbyists, and artisans who turn up at all of the various upstate summer festivals like ants at a picnic.

Hester was impressed. "Wow, it's like Corn Hill in miniature," she said as we ogled our way past a display of handmade teddy bears. Corn Hill was part of Rochester's third ward, one of the oldest residential neighborhoods in the city. Over the past twenty-odd years, urban homesteaders had restored most of the area's classical revival and Victorian-era houses to their former glory, an accomplishment celebrated with an annual two-day arts festival that drew as many as two hundred thousand people.

"God, it makes me kinda nostalgic for my little apartment on South Plymouth," Hester said wistfully.

It was one of the few times she'd volunteered anything about her life prior to moving to Port Erie and I was eager to press her for more, but, as is often the case, fickle fate intervened.

"Uh-oh." I stopped dead in my tracks.

Hester, still hooked to my elbow, said, "What's wrong?"

What was wrong was Jackie Plummer. Thirty feet straight ahead, standing in front of a display stall crammed with the distinctive teal pottery she turned out in her studio. She was talking to a browser, smiling and bobbing her head attentively. But I'd seen that particular smile too many times before, the one tinged with permafrost; she'd already spotted us.

"Oh, nothing," I told Hester. "I stepped on a piece of chewing gum is all."

"People can be so thoughtless," she said as I made a show of scraping the sole of my shoe against the curb edge.

"Ain't it the truth." It was too late for a graceful retreat. Anyway, military types claim that the best defense is a good offense. So I reclaimed Hester's arm and hurried her through the milling crowd, yoo-hooing cheerily and waving my free hand like the smartest kid in class.

"Jackie! There you are!" I remembered to grin. "I was hoping we'd find you."

Her potential customer having moved on to the adjacent stall, Jackie switched the brittle smile to me. "I'll bet you were, Hackshaw."

"I got your message from Mr. J. this morning, but I thought I'd track you down here rather than call—"

"I didn't leave a specific message," Jackie noted peevishly, her glance slipping irresistibly to Hester before coming back to me with a vengeance.

"Well, no, but I *assumed* you'd called to remind me about the festival, and since I was going to be covering a special town hall meeting over here in Port Erie anyway, and since I was eager to introduce you two"—I nodded at Hester, who seemed to be amused by it all—"I thought, well, why not walk to the meeting and see if we don't run into Jackie along the way. And here we are."

I was sweating like a sumo wrestler, not entirely because of the cord jacket. But my tactic seemed to work; Jackie's glare now included a measure of reasonable doubt.

"Well?" she said, whereupon Hester nudged me in the ribs.

"Hmm? Oh! Sorry. Jackie Plummer, this is Hester Del-Gado, the woman I was telling you about. New owner of the Mott house, with plans to open the place up to needy young ladies." Babbling ferociously, I turned to Hester. "Besides being something of a women's activist herself, Jackie's a highly respected, uh, ceramist, over in Kirkville, as you can see by her wares here. And a, uh, good friend of mine."

*A good friend? Jesus.* I didn't even have to look at Jackie to know I'd be paying for that one for months.

They nodded to each other, the way women do, and

170

Jackie said, "We've met before, haven't we? Through Nigel and Honoria MacDenny?"

"Oh, yeah. I thought you looked familiar." Hester was still smiling broadly, but for the first time she seemed less self-assured. "Listen, it really is a pleasure to meet you—any friend of Hackshaw's and all that—but I'm afraid we're running late for an important meeting." She sighed. "Some of the neighbors are trying to convince the mayor I should be run out of town on a rail."

Jackie's sisterhood gene kicked in. "The nerve," she sniffed. "I, for one, think this boarding house idea of yours is wonderful. In fact, if I wasn't chained to this display, I'd go straight over there myself and give the lot of them a piece of my mind."

"Well, it's nice to know I have some allies. In addition to Hackshaw, I mean. Anyway, we do have to run."

Now they were both looking expectantly at me. In a situation like this, you have to decide which option has the greater potential for future trouble—walking off arm in arm with Hester and thus infuriating Jackie, or staying behind and risking Hester's ire. On balance, Jackie Plummer was the more volatile and thus required special attention. Damage control, the pols call it.

"You know, it is getting late, Hester," I said. "But I did want to have a word with Jackie. Maybe you'd better go on ahead—I'll catch up in a minute."

She shrugged it off casually enough. "Okay. Just don't leave me hanging, Hackshaw. I'll need your input."

"I'll be along in two shakes."

With a parting wave, she moved off with the crowd, her hips rolling lasciviously beneath the billowy skirt. I couldn't help but notice, and neither could Jackie.

"I guess I can't blame you for ignoring my calls, Hackshaw," she said, into her martyr mode now. "She's even more attractive than I remembered."

"I wasn't *ignoring* you, dearheart. My phone was—"

"Dresses like a tart, unfortunately, but I suppose that's part of the attraction as far as you're concerned."

"Look, I've been hired to do a job for the woman—"

"Oh, you're getting a stud fee? How nice for you."

"Now, wait a damn minute—"

"Just out of curiosity, does she remove all that jewelry in bed? Because she must jingle like sleighbells—"

"*Shut. Up.*"

And she did, mouth agape, along with everyone else standing within a fifty-foot radius. I swept the crowd with a defiant glare, effectively turning all eyes back to whatever they'd been doing before my outburst—people like a scene until it threatens to include them—and pulled Jackie into a tighter orbit in front of her pottery display.

"Now listen, you," I said, teeth clenched. "Yes, Hester is paying me good money. To oversee renovations on her house. It's one of the ways I make a living, remember? The fact that she happens to be attractive isn't my fault."

"Next you'll tell me you and she aren't—" She began to pull away, but I wouldn't let loose.

"I'm not going to tell you what she and I are or are not doing, because it's none of your business. Just like it's none of my business what you and your real estate broker do or what you and that gallery director do when you get together"—two smarmy bastards if ever there were—"because, unlike you, I value the special relationship you and I have and I'm mature enough to understand that sex isn't as important as friendship and companionship."

It was working. Her eyes were turning sentimental.

"The fact is, I was looking for you to invite you out to

172

dinner tonight. At the Jameson House. Assuming one of your other 'friends' hasn't aced me out again."

"No, I'm free. Really, Hackshaw, I didn't mean to—"

"No apologies necessary," I said magnanimously. "Uh, would sevenish be too early?"

# 20

The mayor's office spanned the front half of the second floor of the town hall, a looming stone Romanesque building on North Main just across the canal bridge. It was sized more like a conference room than an office, which was a good thing, considering the number of irate Port Eriens who'd turned out for the lynching.

I was greeted at the open double doors by the backs of several buzzing people and the sound of a banging gavel.

"If everyone would just calm down and wait their turn, both sides will get their chance—"

"There isn't supposed to be any 'both sides,' dammit. Nobody invited *her* to this meeting—she crashed it!"

The first voice belonged to Port Erie's mayor, Larry Piper, an affable sort whose greatest political asset and worst character flaw was that he strived to please all of the people all of the time. The second voice belonged to good old Vern Murray, he of the violated lawn ornaments. The "her" was Hester, naturally, who stood alone on the far side of the room in front of a tall window, the bright sunshine backlighting her like a lunar eclipse.

"Be that as it may," Mayor Piper insisted, "this is a public meeting and it will be conducted as such."

He did a quarter turn and pointed the gavel at a gray, gourd-shaped man in a navy three-piece suit. Wesley Stanhouse of Silvertrees Retirement Community, I realized.

The mayor, standing behind his polished cherry desk, said, "I believe you had the floor, Wesley."

"Thank you." Stanhouse cleared his throat and held up a sheaf of papers. "As I started to say, we've presented you with the signatures of forty-three property owners, and/or their spouses, from the Virginia Street and Martha Street neighborhood. Basically we're asking—"

A voice in back—I couldn't help myself—called out, "Forty-three signatures out of what? A hundred fifty homes? Doesn't sound like much of a mandate."

Heads swiveled my way, followed by a few frowns and more groans than I like to admit. In addition to Stanhouse and the Murrays, I recognized the Costanzas and Jeff Jones, both of whom had had their garages defaced with satanic graffiti. Birdy Wade was there, too, standing patiently just off the mayor's left shoulder. Of the remaining mob, I could identify by name only two: Hester's immediate neighbor, Mrs. Mobley, whose head scarf didn't entirely disguise a crown of pink curlers, and old Miss Hobbes. Miss Hobbes was the only one sitting down and the only one who returned my smile in kind.

The mayor said, "If you're here to cover this meeting, Hackshaw, then save your remarks for the Q and A at the end."

"I'm not here to represent the *Advertiser*, Larry. More like a friend of the court."

"This isn't a court proceeding."

"What I mean is—"

175

"We know what you mean, Hackshaw." Vern. Pink as a salmon. "You're here to stick up for your girlfriend."

All heads swiveled toward Hester, giving me a moment to think. In truth, I wasn't sure exactly why I was there myself, but they didn't need to know that.

"I'm here to support my client, Ms. DelGado, true. But I'm also here as an expert witness on Victorian restorations and, uh—"

"And fornication." Doris Murray this time, who colored slightly at her own boldness.

When the tittering died out, Mayor Piper said, "Expert witness? I told you, this isn't a court proceeding."

Stanhouse harrumphed again. "I believe under Robert's Rules I still have the floor."

"Exactly right." Piper worked his little hammer some more. "Please, people, can we get on with this?"

A reasonable quietude settled over the room and Stanhouse, droning like a classical music deejay, read the petition's entreaty, which began, "We, the undersigned Port Erie property owners . . ."

No surprises in the text; the petitioners basically were saying that the Mott house was being used in a way that violated the zoning ordinances and if the town council didn't hold a special session and deal with the problem, the undersigned would have their heads in the fall elections. No specific mention of pregnant teens or the whimsical paint job or even Sue Krevin's murder—probably because the latter had occurred after the petition had circulated. But the formal petition was one thing; the follow-up free-for-all was another. The accusations began flying the minute Stanhouse finished reading the name of the final signatory.

Vern Murray got the ball rolling. "And we could've had plenty more names after that girl got killed."

"Plenty more," his wife echoed.

"Honestly, Mayor, have you *seen* what that woman's done to that house?" Mrs. Mobley whined. "I mean, the colors are just *hideous.*"

A man I didn't know, plump and self-satisfied, added, "Same color as Pepto Bismol, which is what I reach for every time I see the place." He picked up a few laughs, none more enthusiastic than his own.

"Fiddlesticks. The Mott house hasn't looked better in a hundred years, and anyone with eyes in their head and half a brain knows that."

That trenchant observation didn't come from me—fiddlesticks wasn't the F-word I had in mind—but from dear old Miss Hobbes. It appeared that Hester had a second ally, although you can't ever be sure with Miss Hobbes; she was a contrarian at heart, always eager to do battle with the powers that be. I inched around beside her chair anyway.

"We aren't here to argue about paint jobs," the mayor was saying. "It's still a free country and a person has a right to paint their own house any color they see fit."

"Not according to the code, they ain't." Another middle-aged geezer I didn't know. His eyes took on a look of manic myopia as he quoted from memory the town's code book. "Section three, subsection B, paragraph eye-eye-eye: 'Said structures, be they residential or commercial, shall not employ exterior finishes which can be shown to be disruptive of the general character of the Town of Port Erie. See subsection 3A.' " He grinned as if he'd just nailed *psilocybin* in a spelling bee.

"Oh, that!" Miss Hobbes cackled. "The late Mayor Hansen had that put in thirty years ago to get back at his next-door neighbors for painting their carriage barn lime green. Personally, I think what Miss DelGado has done with the Mott house deserves a commendation, not condemnation."

177

That didn't set too well with the room's majority, which began buzzing anew. Mayor Piper was quick to jump in. "We seem to be off the subject again. We're here to discuss an alleged nonapproved use of number 79 Virginia Street. Now, um, before I ask the property owner to give her side"—he nodded curtly in Hester's direction; she smiled serenely—"I'd like to hear if Wesley or his group have anything to add."

Stanhouse began to open his mouth, probably to deny responsibility for this bunch, but the Murrays and the Costanzas and the others superseded their nominal spokesman with a synchronous chorus of accusations.

"You bet I got something to add. Like a busted window I had to pay for out of my own pocket because of the deductible on my homeowner's policy—"

"A billy goat from hell sprayed on our garage—"

"Dead bodies lying around like cordwood—"

"Bad enough she's brought these immoral delinquents onto our street, now they're killing each other."

"I thought that drunk, Garris, did the murder."

"So? Who brought *him* into the neighborhood?"

"I hear the little tramp was askin' for it," said the pudgy one. "Isn't that so, Chief?"

To his credit, Birdy Wade gave the jerk a look that would frost a pumpkin. "Nobody *asks* to be strangled to death, Monty. Whatever the girl was up to, it pales compared to cold-blooded murder."

Monty moderated his smirk. "Well, sure. But I hear this Krevin kid was the one who was behind all the vandalism and break-ins and stuff."

"That's partly true and partly speculation." Birdy hitched up his tan double knits and launched into officialese. "Okay, as far as the status of my department's investigation, we uncovered substantial evidence linking the victim, Sue Krevin, to the satanic graffiti found on several properties on the west side." Giving no credit to yours truly, of course. "We'll continue to investigate, but if there are no similar incidents in the near term, we'll consider the case closed. As far as the break-ins, we have nothing *definitive* that would tie Krevin to any specific burglaries, but we haven't ruled it out." He straightened his shoulders and scanned the room. "I'd also like to point out that the town's population has increased by twenty percent in the past decade and my department's staffing and budget haven't kept pace. We just don't have the manpower to chase down every shoplifting incident and criminal mischief complaint that comes in—we have to prioritize. If I do say so myself, I think our swift results in arresting a suspect in the Krevin homicide shows just how effective the Port Erie PD can be when public safety is endangered."

That little set piece earned the chief a murmur of approval, followed almost immediately by the kind of what-have-you-done-for-me-lately carping that always makes me wonder why anyone would ever take a government job.

"All that's well and good, Birdy," said Vern, "but if your people had gone after that woman and her teen runaways in the first place, like we asked you to, there probably never would've been a murder."

"And even then, you put the killer right back on the street." Mrs. Mobley bobbed her head in Hester's direction. "I about had a stroke when I saw that nutcase out in her yard yesterday, free as a bird."

Birdy shrugged. "Nothing I can do about that. I guess the court thought fifty thousand dollars' bail would guarantee Garris stayed put. But all it took was a five thousand–dollar cash bond from Ms. DelGado there to spring him."

Now everybody was staring at Hester again.

"You mean *she* bailed him out?"

"That's right."

"I knew you were a strange one," Doris Murray said

darkly. "But why on earth would you help that murderous drunk get out of jail?"

"I had my reasons." Hester struck a defiant pose, hands on impressive hips, beautifully backlit by the window. Joan of Arc meets Max Factor. "Maybe because, unlike you people, I believe in fair play. Maybe because I believe a person is innocent until proved guilty." That last part came out *geel-ty*. I don't know if it was the stress of the situation or what, but suddenly a woman who normally showed only a lyrical trace of an Hispanic accent was sounding like Marlon Brando playing Pancho Villa.

"I thought we were here to debate my plan to rent rooms to young women at risk," she said, rolling her r's. "You did say I'd have a chance to speak my mind, Mayor."

"That's only fair. Go ahead."

Stanhouse protested. "I wasn't finished with—"

"We'll get back to you, Wesley," Piper said, nodding reassuringly. "Now. Miss DelGado?"

Hester took a step forward, very deliberately smoothed the folds in her skirt, exhaled, and said, "Actually, I didn't come here to try to convince any of you to give my halfway house a chance. I considered doing that, but I can see I'd be wasting my time. So I'm not going to beat around the bush." She crossed her arms, her eyes narrowing into slits. "I've put a lot of money into my house, believing I could make some of it up by renting out rooms. If I don't have that option, I can't make a go of it, it's that simple. So"—dramatic pause here—"I intend to go ahead with my plans, no matter what you people think." (Which came out *theenk*.)

The choir began grumbling immediately. Larry Piper, struggling to stay on top of things, said sternly, "What you don't seem to understand, Miss DelGado, is that the decision isn't yours to make. We have zoning procedures here and *we* intend to enforce them."

180

"Then you'd better be prepared for a court battle, Mr. Mayor. I've already spoken with my attorney and he assures me I've got precedent on my side."

"Precedent? What are you talking about?"

"Tell them, Hackshaw."

"Huh?" *Damn.* Helping Hester undermine the local authorities was one thing; taking the credit for it was something else again. Hadn't the woman ever heard of an unnamed source? But, in for a penny . . .

"Um, I guess you mean the late Mrs. Finney."

The mayor flinched at the mere mention of the name. Stanhouse closed his eyes. Old Mrs. Hobbes giggled asthmatically while the petition crowd observed a moment of anxious silence. The jig was up. Hester had bumped the ante, trumped the mayor's ace—and everyone knew it.

Piper tried to bluff anyway. "I don't see that Mrs. Finney is at all relevant to this situation."

Hester was unmoved. "My lawyer says otherwise. He says the fact that the town knew the previous owner of the Mott house was renting out rooms but chose to do nothing about it amounts to tacit approval. And everyone *did* know what Mrs. Finney was up to—Hackshaw can attest to that."

Mrs. Hobbes could, too. And did, intercepting a few of the hateful glares I was suffering.

"You know she's right, Larry," the old girl wheezed. "Why, your own cousin Alfred lived in one of Clara Finney's rooms for years."

"That was . . . an exception. Mrs. Finney's, uh, guests were like her extended family. This business about bringing in pregnant schoolgirls is a different matter entirely."

Hester said, "Tell it to the judge."

"Miss DelGado," Stanhouse said. "I can understand that you have a financial stake in the Mott house that you can't dismiss lightly. But it has to be clear to you that, even if the courts decide in your favor on a technicality—"

"Precedent, not technicality."

"Whichever. My point is, even if you prevail, you'd never feel completely comfortable with the situation, considering all the hard feelings."

Hester sniffed. "I'll just have to learn to make the best of it. And so will the rest of you."

"There may be a better way." Stanhouse surveyed the room a moment, picking up a few nods of encouragement from the others, then turned his gaze back to Hester. "Look, if we were able to find a buyer for the property, someone willing to pay you a fair profit above what you have invested, would you consider selling?"

I almost winced, preparing for Hester's outrage at the suggestion she give up her dream house, her plans, her ideals. But the storm never came.

"Well . . ." She gnawed her lower lip speculatively, then sighed. "Under the circumstances, I suppose I'd consider it. But it would have to be a good offer. I've gone to a lot of trouble, after all."

That, at long last, was when the penny dropped for me. Or at least, when it began its descent. I couldn't have told you just exactly what Hester was up to, but I'd seen that reluctant female gambit enough other times with enough other women to suspect what was happening. Like an undersized judo instructor, they let you throw your weight around until they've got you leaning in the direction they wanted you to go all along. Then they throw you for a loop.

While the petition crowd grumbled and threatened and cajoled the impassive Hester, I stared across the room at her, trying to think it through. But before I could get anywhere, Mayor Piper was back to gaveling.

182

"It's obvious we're not going to settle this today," he said. "So, unless anyone objects, I think we'll adjourn."

He banged things to a close and Stanhouse, the Costanzas, the Joneses, and the rest of us began to dribble out of the office. I lingered at the double doors long enough for Hester to come alongside. Also long enough to catch Vern and Doris Murray angling toward Larry Piper's desk.

"While we've got your attention, Mayor," I heard Vern say just as I guided Hester into the corridor, "I'd like to know when in hell you're going to get a handle on this damn deer epidemic . . ."

21

As soon as we descended the stairs to the main floor rotunda, I tugged Hester over to a private spot in a corridor leading to the cloak room.

"*Careful*, Hackshaw. You're yanking my *arm*."

"And you're jerking me around. I want to know why."

"Jerking you around?"

I let go of her wrist. "Very slick, the way you hammered those people, telling them just what you were going to do, defying them to do anything about it—"

"I was standing up for my rights."

"And with such panache! Strutting like a flamenco dancer, flashing your jewelry and clicking those stiletto heels. And the icing on the cake, that comic opera accent you put on."

She crossed her arms. "So now you're going to make fun of my Puerto Rican heritage? Just because my accent comes out more when I'm nervous—"

"You were about as nervous as an ice cube, honey. It was all part of the show."

"What *show?* Are you crazy?"

"No, but I'll cop to stupid. You know when it clicked? I'm standing there, taking in this little passion play of yours, wondering how a woman can pour all she's got into fixing up a place and then agree to give it up the minute the vigilantes show up—and I find myself staring at the code book lying there on the mayor's desk. All of a sudden, I remembered an old saying: If you want to hide a book, you put it on a bookshelf."

Now she was eyeing me as if I really were crazy.

"On the other hand," I went on, "if you want everyone to notice a book, you give it a splashy cover and leave it out on the coffee table. And if that doesn't get their attention, you rub their noses in it."

"Look, I'm not sure what's got into you, Hackshaw, but whatever's bothering you, I'm sure we can—"

"What's bothering me is how you *used* me in there today. Waved me like a red flag at a bullfight, me and the Finney thing both." I'll admit I was flying by the seat of my pants, impelled by anger and instinct, but the more I listened to myself, the more I realized I was onto something, the more I recognized what a chump I'd been.

"The whole thing was a setup right from the beginning, wasn't it? The splashy paint job, the boarding house for pregnant girls, hiring the town drunk. Hell, even seeking me out at the carnival and convincing me to go to bat for you. How'd that work, Hester? You found out I was disliked by half the old fogies in Port Erie and figured I'd fit right into your scheme? One more irritant to lay on the neighbors?"

She shook her head. "God, I don't believe any of this. Just what exactly are you accusing me of, Hackshaw?"

"Double-dealing. Sandbagging. Blowing into town like Auntie Mame's evil twin, buying a vacant fixer-upper cheap, and driving everyone nuts so they'd do anything to get rid of you—including pay you a premium for the Mott house."

"Right. I tore off all that old siding, refinished the floors, replaced the heating system, brought in expensive contractors—a couple of them are over there right now, at twenty-five dollars an hour—all on a gamble that I could get enough people pissed off at me to buy me out at a big profit. Does that really make sense to you, Hackshaw?"

I threw up my hands. "No! It doesn't make sense. But it's the only explanation I can think of that fits your crazy behavior. For Christ's sake, Hester, everything about you is calculated to upset the status quo—the way you look, your actions, the things you've said and done. At first I told myself you're just a little eccentric, but at least you've got guts and the courage of your convictions. Until today, that is. The minute Stanhouse bit, the minute he mentioned buying you out with a healthy profit—"

The sound of scuffling shoes swung my attention to the end of the short corridor. Birdy Wade, squinting into the shadows with that doleful expression of his.

"Thought I heard a cat fight down here. Figures you'd be in the middle of it, Hackshaw."

"We were just—working out a few things."

"Uh-huh." He hitched his pants. "Well, you better find someplace else to do it. The custodian wants everybody out so he can lock up."

"We were just getting ready to leave."

Birdy glanced at Hester, who was staring at the floor. "Just so you know."

As he began to turn, I said, "Heading home now, Chief?"

"Nope. Thought I'd do a walking tour of the festival activities before I hang it up for the day. Show the flag a little, if you know what I mean."

"No rest for the weary, huh?"

186

He shrugged. "Comes with the territory."

As soon as he was gone, Hester's head snapped up. "Why'd you wanna know where he'd be?"

"I was just making conversation—"

"Making trouble, you mean."

"Don't try to turn this thing back on me, lady. You're the reigning queen of trouble in these parts."

She started a retort, but nothing came out; just a tremor in her full, red lips.

I sighed. "Look, I've got a couple of things to do for the paper, but I'll come back to the house later to check on the men. Maybe afterward, once you've thought this thing through, you'll feel like telling me—"

"The only thing I feel like telling you, Hackshaw, is to go to hell. I expect you to use the advance I gave you to pay the men for work they've already done. I'll supervise the rest of the renovation myself. In other words, you're fired."

With that, she abruptly strode off, out of the narrow hallway and around the corner toward the entrance. I leaned back against the cool plaster wall and closed my eyes, half of me relieved to be rid of the woman, the other half—God help me—thinking, *Is there anything sexier than the sound of high heels clicking across a marble floor?*

I caught up to Birdy on the Main Street bridge.

"I was hoping I'd seen the last of you for one day, Hackshaw," he said without breaking stride.

"Afraid I'll cramp your style, Chief?"

"Let's just say it wouldn't help much if people thought you and I were friendly."

"Well, I'd hate to alienate the voters, but I've got a few questions. Maybe we could duck into the Village Diner for a cup of coffee or something."

He stopped abruptly and stuck his hands in his pockets

and stared down. Visible through the bridge's honeycombed steel deck, the Erie Canal flowed ten feet below us, green and slow as pea soup. Several powerboats were tethered to tie-ups along the canal's southside quay, their owners no doubt milling with the rest of the townsfolk at the festival's various venues along Main Street.

Presently Birdy looked up with an indulgent frown. "This is probably a mistake, but I suppose it's the only way I'm going to get rid of you."

We proceeded to the south end of the bridge and merged with the segmented crowds that moved languidly up and down the sidewalk, dipping into their cups of frozen yogurt and stopping every few feet to inspect tables piled with discounted clothing and used books and every manner of homemade knickknack known to man. Mixed with the boil of voices and traffic noises was the distant thump of a rock band banging out tunes in the Canal Park gazebo.

"Good weather for it, anyway," I said, taking a swipe at the perspiration beading on my forehead.

"Mmm. They say we might have thunderstorms moving in by Monday. That could screw up the raft race."

We weaved our way down the sidewalk, Birdy schmoozing expertly with passersby while I fended off the occasional glare with a fixed grin. Two blocks on we entered the relative cool of the Village Diner. Business was slow at that hour, mostly kids congregated around the old-fashioned soda bar up front. Birdy made a point of leading me to a corner booth along the back wall.

"You have questions," he said bluntly after settling in. "Another hatchet job for the *Trite?*"

I swallowed a tart reply. "Let's just say I'm curious about a few things. Strictly off the record."

"Taking a busman's holiday?"

"Something like that."

188

The waitress came, tapping her pad and snapping her gum and giving us a toothy grin that faded fast when we both ordered iced tea. We waited out in silence the two minutes it took her to bring the drinks. When she was back on a counter stool with her cigarette and magazine, Birdy said, "Now you've got me curious, Hackshaw. What's on your mind?"

"Something you said at the meeting today. About how you didn't have anything *specific* to tie Sue Krevin to any break-ins, but you weren't ruling it out, either."

"So?"

"So why haven't you ruled it out? I mean, were you just stroking the voters or do you actually have some reason to think the girl was a thief?"

He tapped his spoon on the table while his somber eyes studied me. "I don't know if you're working a story or not, but I guess it's no big deal. So long as nothing gets into print without my say-so. I'm giving you this on deep background only, right?"

Thanks to CNN and C-SPAN, every one-horse town in the country was getting media wise. Not that I minded in this case.

"I won't print a word without your say-so, Birdy."

He primed his vocal cords with a swallow of iced tea. "We've got no physical evidence tying Sue Krevin to any burglaries—but we've got something else." He checked the room before continuing. "She had almost a thousand dollars in a checking account at Port Erie Trust, most of it deposited in two transactions made within ten days of her murder— nearly four hundred the first time and four hundred thirty a week later. She'd also bought some new clothes and tapes and stuff over that same period."

"Was she working?"

"Part time at the ShopWise, taking home a hundred

bucks a week, most of that going for room and board at the Mott house, according to your lady friend."

"Maybe she was skimming from the supermarket till."

"Harv Stedman says no."

"But you think you know where the money came from."

"I know where it *could've* come from. You remember that break-in at the high school office just before classes let out for the summer?"

"Yeah." I'd written it up for the *Advertiser*'s police blotter. "Somebody stole the petty cash box."

"Four hundred and thirty-seven dollars, to be exact. And there were two separate residential break-ins after that. The Sandersons on Christian Avenue and a couple named Corley, got a ground-floor apartment over at Erie Court. Total cash taken, over five hundred dollars."

"Huh." I took a sip. "That's kind of unusual, isn't it? A girl, all alone, out knocking off houses?"

"Maybe she was the liberated type. Anyway, how else would you account for the money she was putting away?"

I couldn't, not just then. I fiddled with my glass a moment, trying to think of a good reason to avoid raising the next subject and not coming up with one.

"Your boy Ricky Reimer," I said, plunging ahead. "He and the Krevin girl were close—maybe closer than you know."

His bushy eyebrows rose. "What're you getting at, Hackshaw? I told you before, Ricky knew the girl in high school, probably even dated her. So what?"

This was the part I'd been worried about: how much I should tell Birdy. How much I should trust him. But if I didn't at least pass on my suspicions and give the system a chance to work, Step Garris was as good as convicted. Maybe he deserved to be—*probably* he deserved to be—but I didn't want to spend the next twenty years to life wondering about his guilt. And trying to suppress my own.

So I told him. About Sue's little rendezvous with a Port Erie cop—almost certainly Ricky Reimer—out at the secluded boat launch. And about Reimer's behavior toward me ever since my article on Hester had appeared; the bullying out in the annex parking lot when he'd ticketed my Jeep and his crude attempt to intimidate me out on Big Ridge Road. Before I'd even finished, a little blue vein began pulsating in the temporal region of Birdy's balding pate.

"It seems to me you're out to stir up something for no good reason, Hackshaw. Ricky ticketed you for a bald tire and you didn't like it. *Was* the tire bald?"

"Well, close enough, but—"

"As for 'stalking' you out on Big Ridge Road, I'll admit the kid can be a little overzealous sometimes when he thinks he's sticking up for me or my department. I took him in, recruited him, in fact, when he flunked out of Brockport State, and he figures he owes me. So maybe I need to have a word with Ricky, rein him in a little." He stuck out his index finger. "You wanna file a formal complaint, I can't stop you. But what really happened? You said yourself he didn't even try to pull you over until you committed a moving violation, pulling out into oncoming traffic the way you did. Seems to me you're lucky he didn't pursue you right on in to Chilton, which he could've done."

"Look, I understand you want to stick up for your men, Birdy, but you weren't there. I *know* Reimer had more than another citation on his mind. And when you put this harassment alongside his tie-in with Sue Krevin—"

"That's another thing. Who told you about this so-called rendezvous with the girl?"

"Step Garris," I said automatically; I get extra stupid when I'm riled.

"Oh, now there's a reliable source. I don't suppose it occurred to you that Garris just might be lying to divert attention from himself? Come on, Hackshaw."

"You're not taking into account the whole picture."

"Maybe you'd better draw it better," he said, his voice ferociously quiet. "What exactly are you saying?"

"Okay. Fine." I took a deep breath, then let it out with one great torrent of words. "I think it's at least conceivable that Ricky Reimer was trying to save your department from the budget cutters by creating a phony Satan scare, and that he got his girlfriend to help him, and that they decided they could get additional mileage if Sue attached herself to the growing controversy at the Mott house. Only something went wrong—things got out of hand somehow—and the girl ended up dead."

While I blathered, the chief's jaw gradually slackened. Now he leaned out over the table. "What in God's name has got into you—"

"Easy, Birdy."

"—that you'd want to destroy me and my department and everything I care about—"

"I'm talking about *one* bad apple here—"

"No!"

The sudden boom of Birdy's fist pounding down on the Formica drew the attention of everyone in the place—the counterman, the waitress, a couple of kids buying ice cream. But he was past caring.

"What you're talking about is torpedoing my life's work, just when I've made the biggest bust in my career. Accusing one of my own officers of conspiracy and—and maybe murder, for Christ's sake." He struggled out of the booth, his belly jostling the table, and glared down at me. "You're the one who said there wasn't a hidden agenda in any of this, Hackshaw, remember? Back when you were worried your girlfriend was under suspicion? Now you two have a falling out and suddenly you start sounding like Garris, hung up on some asinine conspiracy angle. Well, I don't know what you think you're doing, but I don't have to stand here and take it."

Just to prove the point, he spun on his heels and walked out of the diner.

22

It was just before three when Birdy stormed out, leaving me with the check and a couple of hours to kill. I hadn't been lying when I told Hester I had some newspapering to do that afternoon. I just failed to mention it wasn't until later in the afternoon—five o'clock, to be exact, when I was scheduled to cover a Boy Scout jamboree in South Chilton's Black Creek Park. In the interim I decided to wander around the Canal Days festivities with my notepad in hopes of gathering the odd tidbit for Ramblings.

At four-thirty I walked back to the Mott house. The workmen were gone for the day by then and so was Hester's little car, not that it mattered one whit to me. I retrieved my Jeep from the curb and headed south to watch two dozen khaki-clad adolescents pitch nylon tents and collect firewood and complain because the park wasn't wired for cable. It was after six before I managed to get out of there and drive back to Kirkville for a fast shower and a change of clothes.

All of which explains why I was a touch late picking up Jackie Plummer for our dinner date at the Jameson House.

None of which cut any ice with her.

"I still say you could've phoned, Hackshaw."

"Where from? A pup tent?"

"After you got back to your apartment."

"I was hurrying to get ready."

"So was I. I closed up my booth at the festival early and rushed home to make myself presentable, only to sit and wait on the porch for half an hour, wondering if I'd been stood up." She clucked as she fiddled with her chestnut bob. "I must look like a haystack."

And this was as we were finishing the entrees. You should have heard her on the walk over to the restaurant, or during drinks, appetizers, and salads—whining and dining, if you will.

"You look gorgeous," I said dutifully.

"I'll bet you say that to all the girls." She speared a brussels sprout. "As a matter of fact, I know you do."

Don't get the wrong idea. Jackie isn't always an insufferable bitch. Usually she's as warm and companionable as a terry cloth robe. It was the Hester thing that made her crazy. She was truly torn on the subject, wanting on the one hand to go into her attack dog phase, laboriously detailing why Hester was poison for me or any other man, and yet feeling restrained by the visceral allegiance she feels for same-gender social champions. Her ambivalence had caused her to studiously avoid the subject altogether up to that point in the meal, but the inner turmoil had to be directed somewhere, so it was vented on me and my alleged terminal tardiness. Anyway, I decided to put both of us out of our misery. After a little payback.

"Did I mention Ms. DelGado fired me today?"

"Fired you!" Her eyes grew wide with glee disguised as indignation.

"You were right about her." I sawed in half my last piece

195

of chicken whatever. "Flakier than a bowl of Post Toasties. You should've seen the little drama she staged at the mayor's office." I popped a slice into my mouth.

"Well—what happened?"

Sip of wine. "Oh, she basically ran the old badger game, conning her critics into buying her out. But you don't want to hear all this. Let's just enjoy our—"

"Hackshaw!"

"Well, if you're really interested . . ."

So I told her. What I knew for sure and what I suspected about Hester's perfidy. I left out the parts I didn't want to talk about—how Hester had used me, for example—and the parts I couldn't explain, like why she'd go to so much trouble to force an iffy sale on the Mott house. When I finished the litany, I ate the last morsel from my plate and waited for Jackie to deliver the first "I told you so."

"Didn't I tell you she was a phony? All that jewelry and glitz, the channeling mumbo jumbo, and the crystals."

"Actually," I said, "that's the one area where I think she was being herself. I get the impression she really believes in that supernatural stuff. Or wants to, anyway."

"Oh, come on, Hackshaw." She pushed aside her plate. "You're forgetting what the MacDennys told me about Hester being sued by one of her so-called clients. Honoria tells me the rumor was your ex-employer had to pay back thousands of dollars that she'd bilked from an old woman who thought she was Cleopatra or something in a past life."

"I don't remember you telling me that part," I said. "Besides, I thought the MacDennys believed in all that mumbo jumbo."

"Well, they do. But as Honoria says, just because Hester DelGado was a fraud doesn't mean the *concept* is flawed." She frowned. "What I really find unforgiveable is that she'd use those young women that way, just exploit their problems to

196

create a smoke screen for herself. Of course, maybe they were in on it with her.''

"Sue Krevin, maybe, but not the other boarder.'' Unless she was the world's greatest actress, or I was the greatest fool, poor bloated Jennifer had to be genuine. "Even in Sue's case, I think she may've had her own agenda.''

"Why would you say that? If the Krevin girl was behind the graffiti in the neighborhood, she had to be doing it for the sake of Hester's scheme. I mean, why else?''

I didn't feel like explaining my theory on the Port Erie Police Department just then. Instead I said, "You're probably right.''

"It always worries me when you're agreeable, Hackshaw.'' She plucked the napkin from her lap and dabbed at her mouth. "I'll tell you, the worst part about this will be having to admit to my mother that she was right all along.''

"Right about what?''

"That Hester DelGado and her girls were behind the vandalism. When I visited her at Silvertrees earlier in the week, Mother told me one of the other residents had seen the kid who was almost caught defacing the dining hall and that it was definitely a girl, and of course, to Mother and her friends, that meant it *had* to be one of the newcomers over at the Mott house. Well, you know the kind of eyesight most of those seniors have, and anyway, at the time I didn't know what we know now. So I scolded her for spreading gossip and jumping on the bandwagon, blaming everything on Hester and her boarders.'' She sighed. "God, will any of this be in the *Times-Democrat*? Because I'm picking up Mother tomorrow and I don't want to spend the afternoon listening to her say 'I told you so.' ''

Must be something hereditary. "I don't think the Rochester media is especially interested in a Port Erie crime; they have enough of their own to stay busy.'' The *T-D* hadn't even mentioned the graffiti angle in Friday's coverage of the murder, and there weren't any follow-up stories on Saturday—which probably didn't make Birdy Wade's day. "Besides, what I told you about the meeting today and Hester's con job is just my own speculation. I could be wrong." But I wasn't. I'd been had by a pretty face and a willing smile. Again.

Jackie reached across and patted my hand. "I know you hate losing out on a lucrative contract, Hackshaw, but look on the bright side. That woman did you a favor by firing you. Whatever she's up to, you don't have to worry about it anymore."

"Mmm." I poured the dregs of a bottle of chardonnay into Jackie's glass. "I suppose that's the silver lining."

"Careful with the wine, darling. You know how I am, liable to fall asleep on the ride over to your place."

This was the ultimate peace offering, her way of letting me know that all was forgiven and carnal pleasures awaited. I was grateful, of course, with one minor reservation. I had a scheduling conflict; the card game at Lou Edelman's place in Port Erie. I still wanted to talk with Lou. But once Jackie got settled in at my apartment . . .

"I was thinking, dear, that we might go to your place instead. Y'see, I've been, uh, spackling the bedroom and my only set of sheets is in the wash . . ."

"Well—" She consulted her watch. "I suppose we *could*. Krista's over at the Legion Hall for the teen dance, but it lets out at eleven-thirty. You'd have to be on your way no later."

"Then time's awastin'. I suggest we pass on dessert."

"Hmm," she purred. "Let's just say we'll defer it."

I made it over to Port Erie by a quarter to twelve, feeling thoroughly tired but in the most pleasant of ways. Lou's wife Jan greeted me at the door with a dirty look but allowed me to come in after I swore I was only there to have a word with her husband.

"They're in the rec room," she said, pointing me toward the basement stairs. "Tell Lou he's got fifteen minutes to get his playmates out of here—including you—or I invite my mother for *two* weeks next month."

I descended into a hell of cigar smoke and fake knotty pine paneling. The usual suspects were bellied up around a six-sided felt-covered poker table—all but the host, who was warming a stool at the wet bar, his hand wrapped around a bottle of Budweiser. I traded the standard insults with Buddy McCabe and a couple of the other players as I made my way to the bar.

"Tap out early, Lou?"

He grunted. "I know what they mean when they say charity begins at home. Ioletta took me for enough to keep his kid at Colgate for another week. Where you been, Hack? We missed your money."

"Now you know how I feel." Alas, the 10 percent I'd taken off the top of Hester's earnest money was down to a sliver. Whatever I'd hoped to risk at cards was now resting in the till at the Jameson House.

"Cash flow problems, huh?" Edelman grinned. "Those zaftig redheads require lots of upkeep, I hear."

"What I had going with Hester DelGado was strictly a business arrangement."

"Oh, I'm sure—hey, what d'ya mean *had*? The mayor didn't manage to run her out of town already, did he?"

"He's working on it. Why? Would it matter to you if he did?"

He shrugged. "I know people are worried about that kid's murder and everything, but I hate to see someone get tarred and feathered before all the facts are in, just because they're seen as an outsider."

"Your heritage is showing, Lou."

"Well, maybe I know how difficult it is to make a place for yourself in this burg, even when you've lived here for twenty years." He put his bottle on the bar. "You'll love this. I was at the ShopWise the other day, putting in an advance order for a couple cases of hot dogs for our Fourth of July family picnic, right? And the woman behind the counter, sweet as can be, says to me, 'I didn't know you people celebrated our holidays.' "

When we both finished chuckling, I said, "Listen, speaking of Hester DelGado, Buddy says you told him about some guy who tried to buy the Mott house before she came along. A doctor or something?"

"Yeah, kind of a snotty little guy. He wanted to convert the place into a health clinic and he needed a variance. Came into the meeting with this attitude, like he was doing the town a favor by showing up. I take it he figured he'd get approval no sweat under zoning's adaptive reuse policy, but that was never meant to be applied to purely residential areas like Virginia Street. Anyway, the neighbors around there put the kibosh on that idea, too, just like with your lady friend."

"You remember any of the details of this doctor's proposal?"

"Well, like I said, he wanted to open an outpatient clinic." He held up his palms. "It wasn't anything bad, like a drug rehab center. I think it was for something mainstream, like geriatrics or pediatrics—one of those 'atrics.' The only reason I knew about it at all is because the zoning board requires that a member of the planning commission sit in on all variance requests, and since I'm the new man on planning, I had to attend. Frankly, I didn't take a hard look at the guy's plan because by then zoning was passing the word it wasn't gonna fly anyway."

"Only because of neighborhood opposition?"

"That's the only reason I heard. Why so interested, anyway, Hack?"

"I don't know. The timing just seemed odd. What was this doctor's name, anyway?"

"Hmm. What the hell was it . . . something Greek . . ." He leaned back and stared up at the drop-in ceiling tiles. "Oh, yeah. Theophanis. Dr. Theophanis."

I took out my notepad and jotted it down. "I won't ask you to strain yourself for the first name. How many Dr. Theophanises can there be in the book, right?"

"True, but I remember the guy's first name all right. In fact, I almost laughed the first time I heard it, a Greek guy named after a Roman god. Janus. Janus Theophanis."

23

Lust puts blinders on a man, but you probably already knew that.

I should have known from the beginning something wasn't kosher about Hester DelGado. The money she was pouring into the Mott house, her near contempt for the young women she was supposedly dedicated to helping, the careless way she flaunted her eccentricities—every nagging detail a clue to the woman's duplicity, if only I'd had the brains to add it up.

Trouble is, even after coming to my senses, after seeing her flip-flop at the mayor's office, I couldn't put the *why* to any of it. Hester herself had stated it best: why would she put so much money and effort into the Mott house if she were planning to dump the place for a quick profit? It just didn't make sense.

Until I stumbled across the Janus connection. Dr. Janus Theophanis, an arrogant, impatient sort who apparently had expected the local bumpkins to roll over the moment he blew into town with a grand plan to convert a languishing old Victorian into professional office space. Only he didn't do his homework, and the bumpkins didn't roll, and his bid for the Mott house was history.

At least temporarily.

It explained a lot. The pink paint job, the pregnant girls, the drunken handyman. Why Hester insisted on an unnecessary upgrade of the electrical service—medical equipment draws a lot of juice, after all—and why she needed to "check with Janus" before having an expensive security system installed.

She was a Judas goat. A walking, talking worst-case scenario calculated to panic the neighbors and in the bargain make the good doctor's original proposal look heaven-sent by comparison. The Mott house had sat vacant for nearly two years after old Mrs. Finney's death, a victim of its own faded splendor and a moribund real estate market. There were just too few home buyers who needed a place that large, and too many vacant rental properties in the area for any potential landlords to risk the capital it would take to cut it up into apartments. So I ask you, is there any doubt who Stanhouse and his petitioners would call on in their search for a replacement buyer? And is there any doubt that Theophanis would answer the call like a white knight charging to the rescue?

Not in my mind there wasn't.

Very slick. And normally, bruised ego aside, none of my concern.

Unfortunately, there was a wild card in the deck: the late Sue Krevin. Horrible as her death was, it was easy to ignore when Step Garris was the obvious choice for killer. But then Ricky Reimer came into the picture and muddied things up. That was bad enough. Now there was Hester and Janus to think about as well. And the unexplained money in Sue's bank account. Payment for services rendered? Or, just maybe, a novice blackmailer's severance pay?

It was an unwanted new wrinkle, one that left fresh furrows in my brow. And one more question:

"Why me?" I muttered as I stared out through the Jeep's windshield.

On the drive over from Kirkville to Port Erie, I'd automatically taken the shortest route, a series of back roads that included that familiar, lonely stretch of Big Ridge Road paralleling the canal west of the village. But bad memories and the moonless night had convinced me to use a longer but more heavily traveled route for the ride home. After leaving Lou's house shortly after midnight, I headed south out of Port Erie on Union Street, planning to take it all the way into Chilton Center, where I'd take Buffalo Road back into Kirkville.

I was about halfway along the six-mile stretch between Port Erie and Chilton Center, almost to the intersection with Town Line Road, when flashing red-and-blue lights broke into my self-pitying reverie with sickening suddenness.

"Oh, *shit.*"

Despite the nearness of the Chilton town line, there wasn't any thought of a chase on that long, straight highway. If he wanted me, he'd have me. Better to pull off right there near the intersection and hope the intermittent night traffic whizzing by would be enough to protect me from the boy cop's worst inclinations.

I eased the Jeep to a stop on the wide shoulder and stared into the rearview mirror. Reimer climbed out of his unit, strolled around to the Jeep's right rear wheel well, and dropped out of sight for a moment. Just as I was beginning to wonder what he was up to, he stood again and came around to my window.

"What's the problem, Officer?" Trite, but under the circumstances I was lucky to croak out anything.

"You wanna step out of the vehicle."

No, I didn't wanna step out of the vehicle. I wanted to step on the accelerator and get the hell out of there.

"Sure thing." I switched off the ignition and climbed out. "Look, if this is about what happened over on Big Ridge Road—"

"You wanna step around to the back of the vehicle."

He led me to the right rear tire, the same one he'd cited me for earlier in the week. It had been bald then; now it was flat as my wallet. And the stem was missing, neatly sliced away by the look of it. Not that I intended to nitpick.

"I warned you about that bald tire."

"So you did. Well, it serves me right—"

"You got a spare?"

"Yes, indeed. No problem."

A car went by just then, slowing appreciably when the driver spotted the cruiser. I watched it disappear down the dark road, then turned my attention back to Reimer.

"Got something to show you," he said. He crooked his finger and once again I followed his lead, over to the left rear tire this time. He dug into his pants and pulled out a long pocket knife. There was a click and the blade sprang out. Instinctively I began to backpeddle, but Reimer merely knelt down beside the tire.

"See this here?" He tapped the knife blade along the edge. "You got serious sidewall wear. It's so thin in spots you can see the webbing. That's an unsafe condition." He looked at me, a lazy smile momentarily softening his square jaw—then he suddenly turned his wrist and plunged the blade into the tire. While I watched it deflate, he stood and pocketed the knife. That, at least, was an encouraging sign.

"You got two spares?" he said.

I shook my head.

"Looks like you're walking."

"Looks like it."

"Yeah, well, you could use the workout."

He didn't seem to know what to do next, like the villain in a high school play who forgets his lines. To compensate, he growls and glowers and prowls the stage until someone whispers a cue.

I didn't have anything else to do.

"Tell me, Ricky, what'd I ever do to you? Did I spell your name wrong back when you were running the ball for Port Erie High? Is that it?"

That drew a spark.

"You think I give a fuck about that stuff anymore? I got a whole book of press clippings at home, man. All-county, second-team all-state. Doesn't mean shit in the real world."

"People have short memories."

"Tell me about it. When I—dropped out of Brockport State I hit up every business in town for work. Nobody'd even give me the time of day."

"Except Birdy Wade."

"That's right." He took a step closer and pasted on the same hard stare he'd used in the annex parking lot. It wasn't as effective without the aviator shades, but close enough. "The chief called me into his office before I went on patrol tonight."

"Oh?"

"Reamed me out pretty good about that little pursuit on Big Ridge yesterday. He says you were scared shitless, that you were making all sorts of crazy accusations. He told me to stay away from you."

"You don't listen very well."

"Neither do you, Hackshaw, but that doesn't surprise me." Two more cars sped by, one after the other. Reimer paid them no heed. "I remember that story you wrote last fall, about the landfill deal over in Kirkville and the guy who got murdered. How you figured the whole thing out while the sheriff's investigator was tryin' to pull his head out of his ass."

"Dumb luck."

"Yeah, well—maybe." He began circling around to my left and I turned with him, holding eye contact, moving in sync but also moving away. Looking to distance myself, like a reluctant partner at the Saturday night dance.

"You think I killed Sue."

"I never said—"

"Yeah, you do. You've been pokin' around over there at the Mott house, just like I knew you would, and you think you know what went down."

"No, not really." My back bumped against the Jeep's liftgate. Nowhere to go. Reimer stepped forward, surrounding me with broad shoulders and steady gaze.

"I guess I fucked up a lot in my life and maybe I fucked up this time, too." The words hissed out like steam escaping a stew pot. "But I never killed anybody."

"Well, I'm glad we could clear that up—"

His right forearm slammed into my chest, driving me against the Jeep. "Don't bullshit me, man."

"I wasn't—"

Again the forearm pounded my chest, knocking me back as if I were one of the blocking sleds he used to train on at Port Erie High. When I rebounded, Reimer shoved the same meaty forearm up under my chin, his other arm snaking around to grab my shirt collar.

"Nothin' that went down on Virginia Street's got anything to do with Birdy or the department, you understand?"

I felt my face burning, only partly because he was slowly increasing the pressure, cutting off my air. It took my last breath to choke out, "You think this is helping Birdy, you *stupid bastard?*"

Reimer only pushed harder on my throat, forcing me almost onto my toes. I grabbed at his arm and simultaneously drove my knee upward, but he was ready for it, deflecting the impact with his thigh. He jerked me away from the Jeep with his left hand and used his right fist to pound my stomach with two quick blows. Then I was on all fours in the gravel, Reimer's measured voice filtering down from above.

"I don't give a shit anymore about me, Hackshaw, but I'm warnin' you. You mess things up for Birdy, I guarantee you'll be seein' me again."

I tried to mouth an answer, but the only thing that came out was my expensive Jameson House dinner.

You'd think someone would take pity on a lonely hitchhiker, but no. I walked a mile down Union, and then another, before coming to a building that showed any sign of life. It was a former gas station, metamorphosed into Perrini's Primo Pizza and Wings. Free delivery in the tritown area, the sign in the window said.

Ever the optimist, I first tried the pay phone mounted on the outside of the building. Naturally, someone had ripped off the handset. I stood there a few seconds, mumbling curses and gingerly rubbing at my sore belly. Then, resigned, I went inside.

There were just two people in the place. A heavy young guy in a once-white apron was behind the counter, fussing with the control on a pizza oven. Sitting at one of the tables and poring over a comic book was a bony teenager wearing an X cap and a varsity jacket in the familiar orange and purple of the Chil-Kirk High Fighting Spartans. Given the color scheme, I'd always thought the Fighting Nausea would've been a better nickname, but nobody consulted me.

"Help you?" the big kid asked.

I pointed to the phone sitting on the counter. "Car trouble. I'd like to make a call."

208

"There's a pay phone outside. This one's for business use only."

"The pay phone's broken."

He was unmoved.

"I'll give you the quarter—"

"Sorry. The boss says no personal calls. We gotta keep the line clear for customers. The customer always comes first, the boss says." As if to rub it in, the damn phone rang.

While he took the order, I fumed and paced and reconsidered my options. When he hung up, I rested my elbows on the counter and watched as he spread sauce on a circle of raw pizza dough.

"You deliver to Kirkville?" I asked.

He nodded without looking up. "Free delivery anyplace in the tritown area."

The boy at the table added, "In thirty minutes. Give or take."

"Great. I'd like to order a small pizza. Cheese and pepperoni, please."

The hefty one grabbed a handful of shredded mozzarella and began sprinkling it. "We don't have small pizzas, just medium and large."

"If you only have two sizes, wouldn't that mean—never mind. I'd like a *medium* cheese and pepperoni pizza. Delivered."

"Delivered?"

"Yeah."

"Well . . . okay." He shrugged—the customer always comes first—and went back to decorating the pie. When he was finished, he slid it into the oven and set the timer, then picked up his pad and pencil.

"Name and address, sir?"

As I gave him the information, the teenage delivery boy

piped up again. "I don't know Kirkville too good, Mike," he said. "You better like write down the directions to the house."

I said, "I have a better idea."

24

"Take a right up there by that Victorian."

"The what?"

"That gray-and-blue house there. After you turn, pull over in front of the carriage house."

"Huh?"

"The tall three-car garage," I yelled, struggling to be heard above the percussive racket pounding from the tape player. "You'll see it."

The kid barely slowed down, power sliding around onto the side road, then goosing the gas pedal to hurry us the remaining fifty yards and finishing with a sudden, sizzling stop on the apron of my gravel driveway.

He pointed to the travel clock propped on the dashboard and hollered, "Seven minutes. Didn't I tell ya?"

"Didn't I tell you there was no rush?"

He turned down the alleged music enough so the car stopped throbbing. "What'd you say?"

"I said what a rush. Dude." I climbed out of the low-slung Plymouth, placed the pizza carton on the roof, and fished a couple of dollars from my pocket. I leaned back inside and handed him the money. "Thanks for the adventure."

"Yeah. Happy trails."

I watched him make a three-point turn in the center of the road and roar off. Then I cut a diagonal for my front door. I was on the stoop, struggling to balance the pizza and retrieve my keys, when the gravel crunched again and headlights washed over me.

It took a couple of blinks before I could make out the car behind the lights and another heartbeat to make the association.

*Firebird . . . dark color . . . Jesus, what now?*

The driver's door was opening and a man was emerging. A very large man. When in doubt, follow your instincts. So I did, dropping the pizza carton on the stoop, hurdling the handrail, and tearing across the drive and out into the blackness of the broad lawn, destination the main house.

I made it about halfway before a pair of arms encircled my knees like a lariat and sent me sprawling into the cool grass. The body the arms were connected to followed me down, crashing onto the backs of my legs. The sudden pain from landing on my already-bruised stomach gave me enough strength to twist over to my back, but my attacker clamped fast to my ankles and began reeling me in even as I struggled to kick in his ugly face.

"Shut your damn hole or I'll shut it for you."

I didn't realize I'd been shouting, but it seemed like a fine idea, so I sucked in some more air and opened my mouth. The behemoth lunged, slapping a paw over my face and in the process plopping his bulk across my tender belly.

I boxed his ears and, when his hand pulled away from my mouth, screamed, *"My gut—Christ! Don't—"*

212

"Let him go, Teddy. Now."

The brute moved off, taking with him most of the pain in my abdomen.

"Didn't I specifically tell you not to hurt him?"

"Shit, I hardly touched the guy. What a pussy."

"Never mind." The pair of them were staring down at me—Teddy the Terrible and his keeper, a wisp by comparison. Both were wearing dark suits and ties, but only the wisp looked comfortable with the arrangement. Of course, his ensemble didn't include grass stains.

"I only wanted to have a word with you, Hackshaw," he said as if we'd just bumped into each other on the elevator. "Sorry about the little misunderstanding."

His features were indistinct in the darkness, and I wouldn't have known the face anyway. But the voice—that piercing New York borough bray—was immediately familiar.

I raised up on my elbow and panted, "Dr. Theophanis, I presume."

The anniversary clock on the bookshelf chimed the half hour: one-thirty. Another Saturday night I wouldn't want to relive, although not due to the usual sins.

"A little late to be making house calls, isn't it, Doc?" Never let 'em see you sweat. Anyway, now that it appeared that no one was planning to kill me immediately, I could afford to be glib.

The little man grimaced. "Please, anything but 'Doc.' "

"Okay, how about Janus?"

"At least you got the pronunciation right this time. You remember I had to straighten you out on that score when you called my house the other night."

I feigned ignorance, which comes easily, but Theophanis wasn't buying.

"I know it was you, Hackshaw. I have this handy little

feature on my phone. Caller ID. Gives me a readout of the caller's number. I had Teddy run down to the library the next day and look it up in the reverse directory. And here we are."

"Caller ID, huh? What'll Ma Bell think of next." And you thought call waiting was rude.

Theophanis cocked his head. "While we're on the subject, how did you know my surname? That number you reached me at is unlisted."

"I'm a professional journalist," I said, haughty as Dan Rather. "Whatever goes on in my paper's circulation area, I keep tabs. Zoning board meetings, for example."

"Ah. I see. I thought—well, that's unimportant." He saw me rub my stomach. "I'm sorry about Teddy's overzealousness. He didn't mean to hurt you."

I considered playing up his misconception, but then I remembered what the ox had called me out on the lawn and testosterone got the better of me. "I don't hurt that easy. All he did was aggravate a preexisting condition."

"Ulcers?"

"Not yet."

That brought a tight chuckle. He really was a sparrow of a man, small boned, almost delicate, with a narrow, beaky face and quick, sharp movements. Younger than I had expected— probably early thirties—and, if first impressions count, as casually arrogant as Lou Edelman had described him. The other one was his exact opposite: slab-sided, silent, and still, and tall enough that the crown of his curly black hair nearly brushed the apartment's low ceiling. Or so it seemed from my vantage point, looking up at them from my seat in the platform rocker.

"You want to sit down?"

"Why not."

Theophanis took the wicker love seat, but his stoic minion remained standing. I noticed the goon was wearing a

Mickey Mouse bandage on his right index finger and decided to lay on a little Sherlock F. Holmes. "So, Teddy, how're the wife and kids?"

"Real good, thanks—hey!" His nascent grin devolved into a scowl. "You know my family?"

"He's toying with you," Theophanis said. "Establishing his turf. Isn't that about right, Hackshaw?"

"You're the doctor. Geriatrics, wasn't it?"

He hesitated, then smiled. "I'm an internist, but the group practice I'm with specializes in geriatrics and preventative health care for the aging."

That was a definite clue to the whole Mott house conundrum, but at the time I was too fed up and sore to care.

"That's very interesting," I said. "But it's late and my pizza's getting cold. How about if you tell me what you're after."

"I thought you and I were due for a friendly chat."

"If it was a friendly chat you wanted, why sneak around in the middle of the night? And why bring him?"

He glanced over his shoulder. "Teddy, go wait in the car. I won't be long."

Teddy didn't seem to care either way, shuffling off toward the door without a word. As the sound of his heavy footsteps receded on the stairway, Theophanis stopped adjusting his rep tie and faxed me a smile.

"Teddy's my cousin. He drives for me sometimes. It's a skill I never bothered to acquire, having lived most of my life in the city." He meant New York City; like most of his fellow travelers, he didn't acknowledge there was more than one. "As for 'sneaking around,' I only wanted to have a private chat with you, Hackshaw, and you don't seem to keep regular hours."

"Yeah, I understand you cruised by the other day while I was out."

"That was merely a scouting expedition," he said, adding, "You *are* resourceful."

"That's the biggest difference between here and the metropolis. It's hard to hide anything in a small town."

"I'm beginning to realize that. It's the reason I decided to meet with you, in fact." He hooked one leg over the other and crossed his arms. "I came here to lay my cards on the table, Hackshaw. And to make you a business proposition. But before I do, I'd like to hear from you what you already know, or think you know, about me."

My first impulse was to tell him to go to hell—throw him out and lock the door, in case Teddy had any ideas. But I didn't. Because I wanted to see his cards. Curiosity and one dead young woman were reasons enough, but there was more. I wanted to know just how badly I'd been suckered, and I wanted to know whose idea it had been—this little geek's or Hester DelGado's.

After a decent pause, I said, "Fair enough. The way it scans, you wanted to buy the Mott house and convert it to a clinic, right? Only the neighbors and the town zoning board nixed the idea, which offended your finely tuned ego. To get even, you decided to create a crisis by arranging for Hester to buy the place and turn it into a sorority for 'disreputable' girls. You knew that would play on the neighbors' worst fears and, if things went right, they'd decide that maybe a doctor's office wouldn't be such a bad thing after all. Close enough?"

"Highly perceptive."

"A little Byzantine, though, isn't it? I mean, putting aside the revenge factor, wouldn't it have been a lot easier to find some other place to start a clinic?"

"Not when you consider everything that went into the decision to buy the Mott house in the first place—the size of the building, the relatively cheap asking price—and the demographics were perfect for our needs. I'll bet you didn't realize

216

that nearly a third of the population in Port Erie is over fifty."

He was right. I would've guessed over a hundred. "Still, weren't you taking a big gamble? That another buyer wouldn't come along and beat you out?"

"No, because I already own it. Or I should say, my partners and I own it through a corporation we control called Moonlight Properties. I'm the chief financial officer." Theophanis sighed. "I'm afraid I was a little too eager when I found out about the place. We'd been interested in expanding our practice with a satellite clinic on the west side of the county, and when I saw the Mott house, I knew it would be perfect. The owners insisted on a sizeable down payment up front—a buyout of one of the siblings who inherited the place, the realtor told me. So I paid it, fifty thousand dollars. Nonrefundable."

I said, "You forgot to look before you leaped."

"Mea culpa. When the local yokels turned down my variance request, I was stuck. Oh, I could've put our lawyers to work to try and get the deposit back, but that would've been expensive in itself; the money had been paid out, and all the heirs live out of state. Besides, I still wanted the property."

"That's when you decided to move Hester in as a front."

He nodded. "To drive the neighbors to distraction, as you said. I first considered something wilder—a third-generation welfare family, for instance, or a couple of hairy motorcycle enthusiasts. But I didn't want the place trashed, and, anyway, using Hester and the halfway house ruse gave me the cover I needed to proceed with the necessary renovations."

"Like a security system and an electrical upgrade."

"Yes. Anyway, to make a long story only slightly less long, I arranged a sale to Hester DelGado—legally speaking, a lease agreement."

"How'd you line up Hester? Look her up in the Yellow Pages under 'New Age Con Artists'?"

217

"As it happens, we—the partners in our group practice and I—also own the building she was living in. She'd been operating out of her apartment, holding readings and channeling sessions for the gullible. I knew she'd had some financial and legal setbacks. I offered to pay off her debt and my lawyers got a few minor charges against her dismissed." He smirked, taken with his own ingenuity. "She was perfect for what I had in mind. The Bohemian mystic, dropped like a chili pepper in the middle of the white bread and mayonnaise belt."

"And I was part of the setup."

"That wasn't one of my better ideas, as it turns out, but—" He shrugged. "You see, I'd heard about you, your reputation. A gadfly disliked by many of the more conservative elements in the community, a noisy advocate for architectural preservation, a notorious womanizer. And, I have to say, a man not excessively bound by ethics. I needed someone on hand to oversee the renovation work anyway, and I thought you'd also make a wonderful last straw, added to the pregnant girls and the drunken handyman and the rest. So now you know the whole story." He leaned back against the love seat and sighed, content. Confession, they say, is good for the soul. Assuming he had one.

"You know the best part, Hackshaw? Nothing I've done is even illegal. Anyone who wanted to bother could look up the title on the property at the county records office, and they'd find our corporation's name on the deed. All I did was lease a house. Not a thing criminal about any of it."

"You forgot to mention one thing. Your murdered tenant, Sue Krevin."

"That was terrible—but there's no way I can be held culpable. I mean, when I told Hester to hire a local derelict, I had no idea it would lead to such a tragedy. And I've never even met this Garris character. I have to admit, though, the, uh, incident certainly did speed up the timetable."

"It also makes you a prime suspect in her murder."

He frowned. "I don't see why. What motive could I have to—"

"Maybe Sue found out what you were up to and decided to try a little blackmail."

"Now who's being Byzantine, Hackshaw. I'm a doctor, for God's sake; I don't kill people, I cure them." He fluttered his hands. Looked away. Came back. "The fact is, the girl was in on the plan from the beginning, hired and paid for, just like Hester. Anyway, the police know who killed her and why."

The bit about Sue being a ringer threw me off stride a moment, but I recovered quickly.

"If you're so sure Step Garris killed the girl, why'd you have Hester bail him out of jail?"

"I didn't; that was her idea. I was upset about it at first, but then I decided, Why not? Garris will end up paying for what he did eventually, once he goes to trial. And in the meantime, bailing him out gave Hester another black mark with the locals."

"Is that the reason she did it?"

Once again he didn't answer immediately. "That's what she told me. But we're getting off the subject. I mentioned a business proposition. I'd like to hire you, Hackshaw, to act as a consultant on the Mott house—"

"Already been hired for that, Janus. And fired."

"Yes, I know about that. Hester called me this afternoon and told me you'd unraveled our little charade. You got her very upset; she wasn't sure how to handle it."

"Poor baby."

"You're bitter; I can understand that. But why not look on the bright side? There are worse ways to be used than by a beautiful woman, Hackshaw, and you even got paid for your, mmm, exertions—"

"I got paid for doing the job I was hired to do."

219

"Of course. And I'm here to ask you to continue doing that job. At a substantial increase in your fee." He reached inside the gray suit coat and pulled out an envelope and set it on the coffee table. My name was written on it.

"Go ahead," he said. "Take a look."

I picked up the envelope. It felt thick, and when I opened the flap I saw why. Crisp hundred-dollar bills, a couple dozen of them at least. And a folded sheet of paper.

I took out the sheet. "What's this?"

Theophanis leaned forward and hugged his knees. "Just a standard contract I had drawn up. It stipulates that, in exchange for continuing as my consultant on the Mott house renovations, you receive a fee of five thousand dollars, half now and half if and when a variance request is approved for the property."

"Uh-huh." I was scanning the contract. "This lists you as owner and gives a date from last January."

"That's when I closed on the place."

"And this last part? Where I agree to 'keep confidential any information regarding the purchase, renovation, and uses, both present and future, of the parcel described in paragraph one'?"

He grinned. "Standard boilerplate. The lawyers insisted on that."

"I'll bet." I laid the contract on the table. And stared at the bundle of bills peeking out of the envelope. Twenty-five hundred dollars. For doing what I do, overseeing restoration work on a Victorian. And for keeping my mouth shut about Theophanis's cynical little scam.

I looked him in the eye. "The last time you paid out a cash advance, you got burned."

"True, but I also found a way to get even. I always find a way to get even, Hackshaw."

"I'll keep that in mind." Then, "Got a pen?"

# 25

The money came in handy right off the bat.

At nine the next morning, I dragged my sore body out of bed and called Dwight Philby, who operates a garage in a converted barn on the outskirts of Kirkville. I told him about my disabled Jeep and that I needed it up and running ASAP. He sounded hung over, which explains why he refused to make a service call on a Sunday. But then I mentioned cash and he decided that, while he was far too pious to break the Sabbath himself, his brother Omar would happily risk eternal damnation if the price was right. After a bit of perfunctory haggling, he agreed to send Omar by my place to pick me up and chauffeur me over to Union Street.

One hundred twenty dollars and two new retreads later, the Jeep was roadworthy again and I was back behind the wheel, squinting against the brilliant morning sun as I headed into Port Erie. It was ten-thirty. Mass was letting out at St. Bartholemew's on South Main and a block down, near the entrance to the Catholic graveyard, a gnarled old woman was hunkered in a lawn chair, selling cut chrysanthemums. I pulled over and used a bit more of Theophanis's hush money to buy three bunches. As she pulled the flowers from the plastic bucket at her feet, I stared through the wrought iron fence behind her. Toward the back of the cemetery, a green canopy had been erected over a freshly dug hole in the ground.

I said, "Looks like you'll be busy soon."

She grunted as she took my ten-dollar bill. "If I can suffer this sun till this afternoon. They're puttin' down that girl got murdered t'other day."

"Sue Krevin?"

"If that's her. I seen it in the obits, but I don't remember names." She grinned, toothless as a newborn. "I just remember locations."

I wondered fleetingly if the Grim Reaper was married. The crone began rooting halfheartedly through the pockets of her windbreaker, looking for change.

"Keep it," I said and hurried back to the Jeep.

Now, about the money.

I'll confess, filthy lucre was one reason I signed on the dotted line—getting paid *not* to do a story was a new experience, one I could get used to. The fact that it was Theophanis's money I was taking made it all the sweeter, particularly since I hadn't planned to write a word about his little scam in the first place. No thank you. A second article on the Mott house would only remind people of the first article, where I made a fool of myself defending Hester DelGado's altruism. Better to let sleeping dogs lie, and, anyway, Theophanis and the Virginia Street vigilantes deserved each other. I mean, just because the good doctor was a sneaky rat didn't suddenly make the Murrays and the rest of the Port Erie xenophobes any less annoying, did it? A pox on both their houses, if you ask me.

Besides, I already had the specter of Ricky Reimer in my

rearview mirror; I didn't need Teddy the Terrible stalking me, too. So I'd stick with my end of the deal and not make any public utterances on Theophanis's plans for the Mott house.

On the other hand, that sheet of paper I signed didn't say anything about my looking into Sue Krevin's murder.

Silvertrees Retirement Community wasn't half as bad as it sounds. Not only didn't the place smell like the usual mix of boiled potatoes and disinfectant, it was actually very homey. The main building was a two-story white colonial, formerly a large single-family house that had been converted sometime in the sixties. It now had administrative offices, a central dining hall, and a common room on the first floor. As I recalled from previous visits, the second floor was used as a private residence by the owner and manager, Wesley Stanhouse. Two L-shaped one-story wings had been added to either side of the main house to accommodate twenty-eight residential suites. The els had the same colonial detailing as the original building and formed a private courtyard at the back of the property.

"Hackshaw? What are you doing here?"

Speaking of Wesley Stanhouse, he was strolling across the foyer when I came through the vestibule. He looked like a well-dressed bowling pin, decked out in a pinstriped navy three-piece number with a red carnation affixed to the lapel. He was frowning slightly, whether at my jeans and cord sportcoat or the bunch of white-and-orange mums, I couldn't say.

"Just back from church?" I asked him.

"No," he said. "I'm meeting with a prospective client this morning. One of our suites opened up this past week."

Somebody died, in other words. Or moved to Florida. I said, "I hope I'm not too early for visiting hours. I thought I'd drop in to say hello to Mrs. Devereaux."

His disapproving frown deepened. "This isn't a hospital ward, Hackshaw. We don't impose visiting hours. Our resi-

223

dents and their guests come and go as they please. Mrs. Devereaux is a friend of yours?"

"Yeah. Well, her daughter is, really."

"Ah, Mrs. Plummer." He nodded. "I should've guessed."

Before I could ask the self-righteous toad what that was supposed to mean, he peered over my right shoulder and said, "You'll have to excuse me. I think the couple I'm meeting with just pulled into the lot. You know Mrs. Devereaux's suite number, I take it?"

I guessed. "Seventeen."

He exhaled. "Twelve E, in the east wing." Then he brushed past me, making for the front door.

I cut across the foyer's oriental rug and started down a long, beige-carpeted hallway with windows along one side and a series of numbered doors opposite. About sixty feet along I came to a ninety-degree turn into an even longer corridor. The door I was looking for was third from the last, and open. I knocked anyway.

"Come on in."

The setup consisted of a small, windowless bedroom in front and a somewhat larger sitting room in back, overlooking the courtyard. Between the two rooms was a bath and a tiny kitchenette. The entire unit couldn't have been more than sixteen by thirty feet, but that made it only a tad smaller than my carriage house apartment. It was clean and comfy and cheery enough with the light from the courtyard streaming in.

"Why, hello, Hackshaw. What a surprise. Are those for me?" Jackie's mom was seated in an overstuffed chair by the picture window, a cup of tea on the table next to her.

I held out the bouquet. "I found them on your doorstep, Mrs. D. You must have a secret admirer."

"You're such a charming liar, Hackshaw. No wonder Jackie puts up with you."

224

Her smile reminded me of her daughter on a good day. She was a handsome old girl, somewhere in her seventies but eternally youthful in her outlook and her demeanor, as evidenced by the colorful jogging suit and tennis shoes she was wearing.

She popped out of the chair with enviable dexterity. "Let me find my vase. Would you like some tea?"

We spent the next half hour visiting about this and that— the weather, her cribbage partner down the hall, the sorry state of the world, the tasty meal Jackie had made the last time we were both over there for a Sunday dinner.

"She's picking me up soon, by the way," Mrs. Devereaux said. "I'm going to help her out with her display booth at the festival this afternoon. Provided it doesn't get hot as the devil out there," she added.

A perfect opening.

"That reminds me," I said. "Jackie says you were on top of this whole Satan scare thing right from the beginning. Saw the girl outside here or something?"

"Well, I didn't actually see her. It was John Sweet, over in 9W?" She gestured toward the window. "He saw her sneaking around at the back of the main building, outside the dining hall."

"He knew it was a female right off?"

"Oh, yes. A pretty little blond, he said. We figured it had to be something to do with the goings-on down at the Mott house, especially after Mr. Stanhouse told a few people about the petition. I tried to explain it to Jackie, but she wouldn't hear a word against that woman who bought the place. Not at first, anyway." She squinted at me. "Some of the older ones around here don't do much else but look out their windows. They keep a pretty good eye on the comings and goings on this street. I knew you were keeping company with that redhead even before Jackie found out."

"We weren't 'keeping company.' I was working on the house renovations—"

"I said you were a charming liar, Hackshaw, not a convincing one." She sighed. "I told Jackie it was her own fault. Nobody buys a cow when they can get the milk for free, I told her."

I'd like to have been a fly on the wall for that conversation.

"What'd you say your name was?"

"Hackshaw."

"Oh, right." He tapped the gray disk plugged into his ear. "This thing likes to whistle sometimes, like I'm hearin' everything in a wind tunnel. Hacksaw. That must be a nickname, huh?"

"Call me Hack," I said.

John Sweet looked as if he might've been a brawny young man, but that was long ago. Now he was sinewy and wizened and bent over like a question mark, as if he were imploding with age. Everything going but those sparkling, clear gray eyes.

He inched his wheelchair closer to the picture window and pointed. "Right there, she was. That piece of wall next to that door there, the outside door into the dining hall. Must've been after midnight. Shakin' her can." His laughter was like a barking dog. "The one she was holdin' in her hand, I mean. I tell it like that to the ladies around here, they think I'm a terrible old fart."

"They get a smile out of it, though, I'll bet." I swiveled around on the love seat for a better look. "It must've been awfully dark out there."

"Nah, there was a full moon, and some light comin' through the window there from the dining hall. They always keep a few overheads on in there. I could see her plain as day once I got focused in." He looked at me. "Now, I'm not sayin' I could tell it was a can of paint she had. I couldn't tell that at first. But then she started moving it around along the wall there, and I seen the marks start to take shape on those white clapboards."

"You're positive it was a girl you saw?"

"From the minute I spotted her." He grinned. "They don't move like us, Hacksaw. You ever notice that?"

"Every chance I get."

"Amen to that."

"I heard she was dressed all in black."

"Yeah. Well, dark clothes, anyway. Had on blue jeans and a dark-colored sweatshirt and one of those ski masks, like they use to rob banks."

"But if she had on a ski mask, how can you be sure she was a blond?"

" 'Cause her hair flopped down when he pulled off the mask, is how."

I frowned. "Wait a second—when *who* pulled off her mask?"

"Stanhouse," he said, like I should've known it all along—and maybe he was right. "Didn't I explain it? I'm watchin' the girl, and all of a sudden the dining hall door swings open and this arm reaches out and grabs her. Next thing you know, big old Stanhouse has her up against the wall. That's when he yanks off the mask."

"Stanhouse was right there, staring her in the face?"

"Yessir. Mad as hell, too. Wavin' his arm, pointin' a finger, yammerin' away. I couldn't hear what, but it was plain he was readin' her the riot act." John Sweet heaved his rounded shoulders. "Then he lets go of her, and he calms down, and that was about it. They talked back and forth a little, and then she took off back across the courtyard."

"She ran away?"

227

"No, he let her go." He shrugged again. "I guess Stan-house decided maybe she'd learned her lesson. Didn't wanna bring the police into it and make a fuss. Never figured him for a soft heart, but who knows? Pretty girl like that can talk a man into about anything."

# 26

Believe it or not, I wasn't all that surprised by what old John Sweet had told me; after all, my burgeoning suspicions had led me to Silvertrees in the first place. Initially I'd been intrigued by a comment Jackie had made at dinner Saturday night, about her mother insisting all along that it was one of Hester DelGado's girls behind the satanic shenanigans. That had started me thinking. But it was a couple of things Janus Theophanis said later that night that really set my cogs in motion.

First, there was his off-hand admission that it was his idea, not Hester's, to add me as one more irritant in the Mott house scam. Because of my tarnished reputation, he said, and I won't bother to debate the point. The question is, who told him about me in the first place?

That was the first thing. The second thing was this: if Sue Krevin was in on the scheme from the beginning, as Theophanis claimed, what was she doing the night I caught her rifling through Hester's desk? I mean, if she already knew what was going on at the Mott house . . . you see my point.

And on reflection, I'll add a third question to the list: why was Theophanis so confident his scam would work—that the hapless Virginia Street irregulars would, in the end, embrace his clinic proposal as the best alternative to Hester's halfway house?

The answers to questions one and three now seemed clear, or as clear as anything in this mess. Theophanis must have learned about me and my dicey reputation from a local source. Someone who had seen me at work up close—like when I'd campaigned against moving the Port Erie library and police department out to the new annex—and knew of my twin weaknesses for grand old architecture and lusty ladies. And this same local source was also the reason Theophanis was so sanguine about getting his way with the Mott house. Because he knew he had an ally on the inside, someone who at the critical moment could and would steer the others in his direction.

Wesley Stanhouse.

He probably favored the clinic idea from the outset. And why not? It could only help his occupancy and his rates at Silvertrees, having a bunch of geriatric specialists move in down the street. He may even have had some sort of kickback worked out with Theophanis for every referral Stanhouse managed to send his way.

The more I thought about it, it also may have explained question number two, why Sue Krevin was ferreting through Hester's papers at two in the morning.

Start with the assumption that Sue *wasn't* in on Theophanis's scam. She and her boyfriend, Ricky Reimer, had their own program, that is, creating a cult scare that would rile the citizenry and raise the profile of the embattled Port Erie PD.

So far, so good.

Now, while out one night doing her thing with a can of

spray paint, Sue gets nabbed by Stanhouse. He's angry at first, sure, but then what does he do? He sends the girl on her merry way and only later reports the incident to the police, claiming all the while that he never got a good look at the vandal. A flat-out lie, if John Sweet can be believed, and I believed him.

Which leads me back to the original assumption: Stanhouse was in cahoots with Theophanis. Therefore, he knew about the arrangement over at the Mott house—Hester and her phony halfway house. And when he caught one of Hester's girls outside the Silvertrees dining hall, he made an assumption of his own—that the girl must've been acting on behalf of Theophanis. So what does he do? He lets her go.

Maybe that in itself was enough to arouse Sue's curiosity. Or . . .

Maybe there was more; maybe Stanhouse let something slip when he was haranguing Sue. *You stupid little tramp, we're on the same team. Didn't Janus make that clear?*

A lot of what-ifs, I'll admit. But wouldn't it explain why Sue was going through Hester's chintzy desk? And how all that money ended up in her bank account?

She had to be blackmailing one, or all, of the schemers—Theophanis, Stanhouse, or even Hester. Which meant that any one of them could've had a motive to kill her. Of course, Ricky Reimer couldn't be discounted, either. If Sue was blackmailing anyone, it could as easily have been him.

And there was still Step Garris. He hated the girl for his own reasons. Whether he'd actually killed her in a drunken rage, I couldn't say. But then, neither could he.

*Damn.*

In effect, all I'd managed to do after three days of stirring the pot was to raise the number of suspects from one to five. And I had no solid proof against any of them.

Is it any wonder I hate mysteries?

\* \* \*

The cemetery was busier when I returned at one o'clock, but not much. Less than a dozen people were gathered under the green canopy. There was a thin woman in a black dress, weeping softly into a handkerchief while the priest recited the prayer. That had to be Mrs. Krevin. Holding her arm was another woman, a bit older, the facial resemblance suggesting they might be sisters. Then there was an old man in an old suit, head down, solemnly mumbling along with the priest, and several kids, all around Sue's age. Ricky Reimer wasn't among them, but Hester DelGado was, looking a little lost in her straw sunbonnet and simple blue shift.

The ceremony was mercifully short. The small congregation began to break up, Hester in the forefront of the exodus, moving quickly down the grassy incline and onto the narrow cemetery roadway. I was waiting next to the entrance. Not until she was an arm's length away did she stop and look up at me from under her wide-brim hat. I wondered if the distress I saw in her face was entirely due to the funeral.

"How'd you know I'd be here?" she asked. "Or am I being egotistical?"

"No, I was looking for you. I checked at the house first—Jennifer pointed me in the right direction."

"After what you said yesterday, I'm surprised you'd want to be seen with me."

"They say time heals all wounds," I said. "And speaking of heals, I met Theophanis last night."

"I heard."

"Did he tell you I was back on the payroll?"

She glanced around. "I don't want to talk here."

I took her arm and we started walking, through the open wrought iron gate and out onto the sidewalk near the spot where the old woman had been selling her flowers. She was gone now, probably disappointed at the low turnout for Sue

Krevin's interment. As we came alongside my Jeep, pulled in at the curb, Hester stopped and appraised me again.

"I'm walking—unless you want to give me a ride."

"That depends."

"On what?"

"On whether you're ready to level with me."

She frowned, puzzled. "Janus said he told you. You'd figured out most of it for yourself anyway."

"I know why Theophanis is doing what he's doing," I said. "I'm still not clear on why you're doing it."

The frown grew cynical. "Same as you, Hackshaw. I'm getting paid good money—"

"Why'd you bail out Step, Hester?"

It was the question that had brought me looking for her. I thought I knew the answer already, but I needed to hear it from her. Don't ask me why I even cared.

Long seconds ticked by as we stood there on the sidewalk, Hester staring at me from the shadow of her bonnet, her bright black eyes rimmed in blue. And red.

"You look tired, Hester. Not sleeping well?"

She sighed. "Why do this, Hackshaw? You said yourself, you're no private eye. Why can't you just take the money and leave well enough alone?"

"Why couldn't you?"

She began to raise her hands in supplication—no bracelets today—then dropped them to her sides. "All right. I'll answer your questions, if I can; maybe I owe you that much. But first there's something I want you to do for me."

As we came into the dining room, Hester went immediately to the cluttered desk in the corner and pulled open a drawer. When her hand came up, it was holding what appeared to be a slim packet of oversized playing cards.

"You know what these are?"

"A euchre deck for the visually impaired?"

She gave that wisecrack the snub it deserved and removed the rubber band from the pack. Then she fanned the cards expertly, showing me the backs—a medieval tapestry design—before deftly turning her wrist to expose the faces. "The Tarot trumps, twenty-two in all. I want you to let me do a spread, give you a reading."

"You wanna tell my fortune?"

"It isn't something to smirk at. Tarot is an ancient diviner's art, dating back to the Middle Ages."

"Along with leeches, sea monsters, and alchemy."

"You agreed to my terms, Hackshaw."

I shrugged. "Okay. What do I have to do?"

"Start by sitting down."

So I did, taking the place of honor at the end of the dining room table. She took the chair kitty-corner to mine and thumbed through the deck until she came to a card bearing the likeness of a man with Prince Valiant hair under a floppy hat. He was standing in front of a small table strewn with balls and cups and dice, and holding in his hand a short rod. Written in cursive script at the bottom of the card was "The Magician."

Hester centered it on the table. "This will be your significator, Hackshaw—the card that best suggests your personality and character."

"A magician?"

"Not literally. Some scholars say the figure represents Toth, the Egyptian god who invented writing."

"Ah . . ."

"Others claim it's actually Hermes, a messenger to the gods in Greek mythology. A patron of thieves and scoundrels and a notorious conjuror."

"Where do you come out on the controversy?"

"I'd say the magician is a little of both. A seeker of

234

knowledge, but also a manipulator when it suits him. And there's something else—the wand he's holding?" Her cheeks dimpled minutely. "That's said to signify an erect phallus."

"Really." It saved me from having to ask what the little balls signified.

She placed the rest of the deck facedown on the table and instructed me to cut the cards several times while occasionally turning the cut so that some of the cards would eventually be dealt upside down. When I finished, she had me randomly divide the deck into three piles.

"Good," she said. "Now clear your mind, let your intuitiveness take over, and choose one of the piles."

"Okay." I closed my eyes for show, did a mental eenie-meenie-minie-moe, and pointed to the middle stack.

She swept away the other stacks and scooped up the cards I'd indicated. Now she closed her eyes a moment and took two slow, deep breaths, then opened them again and quickly laid out the cards facedown in a cross pattern with my significator, the magician, as the axis. There were two cards each to the right, left, and below the magician, and a single card above it.

She pointed to the two cards on the right. "These represent events or influences leading up to your present situation." She turned them faceup. One was labeled "The Devil," a grinning ghoul with a pair of anguished acolytes chained at his feet; the other, depicting a man and woman apparently receiving some sort of benediction from on high, was titled "The Lovers." The latter card was upside down.

"Oh, wow," Hester mumbled.

"Bad news?"

"Well, the lovers obviously refer to me and you."

"Why are we standing on our heads?"

"Because there's been so much tension between us. Like our relationship's been upended."

True enough. "What about Lucifer there?"

"The devil—well, that's the adversary. Or it could simply indicate a negative circumstance or event."

"You mean like Sue's murder?"

She looked up from the table. "Yeah. I'd have to say that's what it's referencing."

"Or maybe it's supposed to be Theophanis—"

"It's meant to be symbolic, Hackshaw, not literal. The important thing is that it signals the need for caution in your future plans." I started to comment again, but she shook her head. "You're getting ahead of me. I need to see the whole spread to make any sense out of what the Tarot is trying to tell us."

With that, she flipped the two cards to the left of the magician. The first was obvious even without the legend at the bottom: "The Moon." I barely gave it a glance, my attention captured by the second card, a fearsome skeleton wielding a scythe. Skeptic or no, I have to admit it gave me a shiver even before the script at the bottom sunk in.

*"Death."*

27

Hester's shoulders slumped. "Wow."

"Wow again?"

"These two cards represent future trends if you make no change of course."

"Oh." I poked the death card. "More bad news, huh?"

"Not necessarily—not if you change course in time. The death card doesn't have to mean, y'know, *death*." She sighed. "There really aren't any set rules to this, Hackshaw. It's all a matter of interpretation."

"Uh-huh." That reminded me of a conversation I'd had with the *Advertiser*'s tax accountant just prior to our last IRS audit. "Look, how about if we move on to the question-and-answer portion of the program?"

"Not yet. I wanna see the rest of this."

She turned over the two cards lined up under the magician, explaining that they represented "adverse influences." The first picture reminded me of Diogenes—a stooped old man carrying a lantern. The legend read "The Hermit." The second, "The Woman Pope," featured a robed woman sitting on a throne. Like the lovers, it was upside down.

As Hester stared down at the cards, totally absorbed, I realized why all of this was so important to her. At first I'd assumed she wanted to scare me off, spin out a lot of mumbo-jumbo about death and doom in hopes I'd take the hint and run for the hills. Maybe that was her original intention. But she'd overlooked one thing: I didn't believe in the power of the Tarot, but *she* did. And what she was seeing spread out on the table made her uneasy—not so much because of what the cards prophesied for me, I suspected, but because of what they told her about herself. And I thought, *Advantage, Hackshaw.*

She looked up, her brow furrowed, and shook her head. Then she flipped the last card, the one positioned above the magician. A jester hefting a hobo's sack.

" 'The Fool,' " I read. "What's that supposed to tell us?"

"I'm not sure," she murmured. "It's the positioning of the cards that dictates the message. The one above the significator indicates your future course of action." She went to the bookcase, bringing back to the table a slim book titled *The Tarot Revealed.* Instruction manual, apparently.

After reclaiming her chair and absently hooking a lock of dark red hair behind her ear, she leafed through page after page of colorfully illustrated text, unaware that I was reading along over her shoulder. Every so often she'd glance at the spread of cards, mutter ominously, and then continue perusing the Tarot interpretations. After a couple of minutes, I couldn't resist the urge to prod things along.

"That hermit card sounds like Step Garris." I began reading, " 'The Hermit represents an escape from the responsibilities of daily life, but also the inexorable march of time . . .' "

Hester wrapped an arm protectively around the book.

"Who's the reader here, Hackshaw, you or me? It isn't proper for a subject to do his own interpretations."

"I'm only saying, it's there in black and white—"

"I know what it says; that isn't the point."

"So you don't think the hermit represents Step?"

"I didn't say that. It probably does, okay? Now stop being a backseat driver and let me do my thing. God."

She went back to the book for another thirty seconds, then said, "I think I've got it. The lovers, that's me and you. And the devil, that represents all the outside pressures that have come between us—Sue's murder and everything. Right?"

"If by 'everything' you mean the scam you and the doctor have been running."

She pursed her lips. "Just so you understand, it doesn't necessarily mean Janus's plans for this place and what happened to Sue are related."

I decided to let that go for the time being. Hester went back to her cards.

"The two on the left, the moon and death, those are the future trends, if you keep doing the things you've been doing. Now, the moon card means powerful unseen forces that push and pull you where they want you to go, instead of where *you* want to go—like the way the moon affects the ocean tides. That's why it's also a water sign, you see?"

"I guess." Not.

"And death—like I said, that doesn't always have to mean literal death. But it could. Anyway, taken together, the two cards make a powerful statement of danger."

"They do, huh?"

"It's obvious." She indicated the two cards under the magician, the hermit and the woman pope. "The course you're following now—whatever that is—is pulling you deeper into trouble. And it's because of the adverse influences

239

put on you by Step Garris and, frankly"—she picked up the card bearing the woman pope—"by your knack for creating your own bad luck."

"Wait a minute. I can maybe buy the part about Step causing adversity—as much as I can buy any of it. But how do you figure some topsy-turvy female in a mitred hat represents my penchant for getting into trouble—assuming I actually had a penchant for trouble, which I don't."

"Well . . . because the woman pope symbolizes Lady Luck. And being reversed, well, that clearly indicates *bad* luck . . ." She was dissembling like mad—it takes one to know one—but I wasn't about to let her get away with it.

"That's not what your little book says, dearheart. According to what I read, the woman pope represents hidden knowledge and also the undermining of established order, which I find very interesting. It's also the only card besides the lovers that was dealt upside down, which I also find very interesting."

"Five minutes ago you were snickering and now you're an expert on the Tarot. Is that it?"

"I'm a fast study." I leaned out over the spread. "The way I see it, you and I may be the lovers, but you're also the woman pope." She began to sputter, but I kept on talking. "And since the lovers and the woman pope are both inverted, I'd say that means if I'm in danger, you're in it twice as deep."

Bull's-eye. Suddenly the cool facade, as carefully applied as her makeup, began to break down.

"Don't you think I know that? *Shit!*" She buried her face in her hands. "Jesus, I wish I'd never heard of this godforsaken town."

"Yeah, well, I'm sure the feeling's mutual, but like it or not, we're both stuck in the middle of this thing."

But she was still resisting. She dropped her hands and desperately scanned the spread again. "That's why we need this guidance. The fool is key. Positioned where it is, it's supposed to indicate a safe course of action. Only I don't know what it's trying to tell us, because I don't know where you're coming from."

"That makes us even then. Forget about the cards, Hester. The Tarot isn't going to get you out of whatever mess you're in, but maybe I can. But only if you're straight with me for a change."

She searched my face, nibbling her lower lip. "If I only knew I could trust you, Hackshaw . . ."

"*You* trust *me?*" Talk about hutzpah.

"What do you expect, after the way you snapped up Janus's offer? For all I know, he sent you here to test me, see if I'd talk."

"You don't really believe I'd do that."

"Like hell. You work for him now, don't you? You'll end up doing whatever he wants you to."

"You work for him. Do you always do what he wants?"

"Unlike you, I never had any choice."

"Oh, yeah? What about bailing out Garris—he didn't want you to do that, did he?"

The question caught her off guard, which may explain why she answered so readily. "No, he didn't like that. He was really pissed off about it at first. Until he decided it could work to his advantage."

"So why did you do it? Never mind, I'll tell you. You spent five thousand dollars of Janus's money to bail out Step because your conscience was eating you up. Because you *knew* he didn't kill the girl—"

She shook her head, adamant. "No, that's not true! I mean, I don't know if Step did it or not. That's the problem, don't you get it?"

I'd been inching forward on my chair, pressing her hard.

Now I leaned back. "I want to get it, Hester. If you'd just explain it to me."

And finally she did. Halting at first, talking around the edges when it suited her, but giving me enough of an outline that I could fill in the blank spaces on my own.

She'd gotten into trouble a few months back while holding seances and channeling sessions at her apartment on South Plymouth Avenue. One of her clients, a well-off suburbanite named Louise, paid Hester a tidy sum—she wouldn't say how much—to channel for her. Louise was convinced she'd led numerous past lives, including stints as Helen of Troy and Betsy Ross, and she wanted to contact a spirit guide who could confirm everything for her.

"Why is it," I said, "that nobody ever thinks they were an indentured servant or a scullery maid? So, anyway, you cooked up a spirit guide for her?"

"Nothing was 'cooked up.' I was able to make contact with a real spirit, a sixteenth-century theologian named Roger."

"Roger?" I couldn't help it. "You conjured up a monk named Roger?"

"He wasn't a monk—do you wanna hear this or not?"

"Sorry."

Roger, it seems, was indeed familiar with the many incarnations of Louise. Alas, he was also a scrupulously honest puff of ether who kept informing her, through Hester, that she had been at various times a Frankish pig farmer, a slave on a Jamaican plantation, a prostitute in a Chinese brothel, and so on. Well, Louise wasn't at all pleased. She told Hester there had to be a mistake; maybe Roger was an evil spirit, or maybe Hester should invest in a new Ouija board. For her part, Hester was worried she was about to lose her best customer. So when Louise offered to double her fees if only she'd double her efforts to contact Louise's "true spirit guide," Hester—

who wasn't nearly as encumbered by scruples as Roger—agreed.

"In other words," I said, "you eighty-sixed Roger and just told your client whatever she wanted to hear."

Hester's jaw jutted defiantly. "It served her right, the silly cow. She wasn't interested in honest self-discovery—wasn't worthy of Roger. So I invented Zena."

"Zena?"

She shrugged. "I told her Zena was a Persian princess at the court of Darius."

Naturally, Zena spewed forth everything Louise wanted to hear. And Louise was thrilled, so thrilled she started showing up three times a week and handing over cash like an ATM. Which is when the source of the money—Louise's husband—came into the picture.

"Hubby wasn't a believer," I said.

"He went ballistic when he found out. Sicced the cops and a whole law firm on me. I was looking at half a dozen fraud charges and a civil suit that I couldn't have paid off in a hundred years."

"I take it this is when Janus Theophanis came riding in like a white knight and offered to help you out?"

"White knight?" Hester snapped off a curse straight out of the marine corps manual. "Janus is Louise's husband."

"Aahhh."

You can guess the rest. A few weeks after Theophanis brought the law down on Hester, he came by with a settlement offer of sorts: *Front my little Mott house scam and all will be forgiven. We'll even put it in writing.*

"The way he explained it, it seemed pretty harmless," Hester said quietly.

"Until Sue Krevin ended up dead on your doorstep."

"God." She closed her eyes and shuddered. "I didn't

243

know what to do. I tried calling Janus at his private number, but he wasn't there. So I called you."

"What about later, when Birdy was interrogating us?" I prompted. "You seemed to agree then, along with everybody else, that Step was the likely killer."

"Yes. I mean, it was shocking and stupid, but it made sense because I knew how much they hated each other." She exhaled. "But then I started to wonder. When I found out Sue was behind the graffiti? I thought that was spooky—why would she do that? So I told Janus about it, but he was, like, real calm. Like he already knew."

"Maybe he did," I said, casually adding, "Maybe she was working for him all along."

"No, I don't think so. We agreed at the beginning that it was up to me to find boarders, and, anyway, he was up front with me about the other ringer—" She broke off suddenly and shifted her eyes away.

"The other ringer," I said. "You mean he had somebody else working on the inside?"

She struggled with it a moment. Then, much to my relief, she admitted what I already had surmised.

"Stanhouse," she said. "The guy who runs that old folks home down the block? He's been in it with Janus from the start. Supposed to agitate the neighbors against me and at the same time push the idea that Janus's original plans for the house would make a reasonable compromise. That's how I knew about the closed meeting at the mayor's office yesterday—Stanhouse told me in advance."

"So maybe that's why Janus wasn't surprised when you told him about Sue's nocturnal artistry. He already knew about it, because Stanhouse had filled him in."

Hester cocked her head to one side. "But how could Stanhouse know, unless—you think he put Sue up to it in the first place?"

244

"No, but I think he caught her at it."

Since she seemed to be leveling with me at long last, I decided to return it in kind. I told her what I'd learned about the incident at Silvertrees. For good measure, I also told her about Sue and Ricky Reimer, then explained about the money in Sue's account and the Port Erie PD's budget woes. Her face fell farther with each revelation.

"Jeez, Hackshaw, you know what all that means? Any one of them could've killed Sue—Step, Janus, Stanhouse . . . even that kid cop."

"Exactly."

"Still," she said, "if I had to bet money on it, I'd go with Janus. He's a mean little prick, believe me. He wouldn't take kindly to anyone blackmailing him. And he's desperate to save this Mott house deal."

"Why does it mean so much to him?"

She laughed. "I guess he didn't tell you that part, did he? He likes to come off like he's his own man, but the truth is, he's only one of five or six doctors operating a group practice in the city. Janus is like the managing partner of this real estate group they've put together—they own the building I used to live in—and from what I can tell, he spends more time working on their investment portfolio than he does working on patients. Anyway, I found out from Louise that Janus went ahead with the purchase of this place without running it by his other partners. Now, if he doesn't bring it off, he not only has to pay back the kitty out of his own pocket, he might even get pushed out of the group practice."

"That explains a lot," I said. "But I'll tell you what bugs me. If Theophanis was willing to throw five thousand my way to keep me in line, why would he kill Sue to save a few hundred?"

"I don't know. Maybe she asked for more, maybe she changed her mind and threatened to go public—"

Hester was interrupted by the sound of a door banging shut somewhere in the house. Seconds later the door from the kitchen swung open and Reggie, the latest and youngest of Hester's boarders, walked through, bobbing and weaving to the private sounds of her Walkman.

She pulled off the earphones and, between snaps of gum, announced, "There's some weird old guy out back friggin' around by the garage. I think it's that strangler Jen told me about."

"Step Garris?"

The girl tossed her tiny shoulders. "I guess. Anyway, just so you know." She slipped the headphones back on and danced her way out to the foyer and up the stairs like it was all in a day's work. Killers on the prowl. Cool.

## 28

"Kids," Hester said. "Nothing fazes 'em. They grow up so fast these days."

I was ready to forgive Hester a lot, even the way she'd used and manipulated me—I was, after all, my own worst enemy on that score. But the girls were another story.

"What happens to her and Jennifer when Theophanis 'buys' this place from you?"

"Jennifer's leaving in a few days. Bobby's mom wants her to move in with her so she can keep an eye on her impending grandchild. And maybe shame her son into doing the right thing." She smiled.

I didn't. "And Reggie? What's her fate? Back to juvie hall?"

"She'll go back home." The rouge on Hester's cheeks seemed to spread to the rest of her face. "She lives at my old apartment building. Her mother's a friend of mine. She wanted to go out west for a few weeks to look for work, and I needed to line up another boarder, so . . ."

"So Reggie was a pawn, too. All that stuff about shoplifting and sexual abuse was just part of the con, huh?"

"Would you rather it was true? Jesus, Hackshaw, stop looking at me that way." She swept her arm across the Tarot spread, knocking several cards onto the floor. Then she got up and stared out the bay window overlooking the side yard.

"It was a shitty deal all the way, okay? I'm sorry I let Janus talk me into it and I'm sorry I suckered you and I'm sorry about the girls. And Sue." Her shoulders trembled inside the blue shift. "Nobody was supposed to get hurt; it was just a business arrangement. I come in and annoy the hell out of everybody, the town reverses itself on the zoning thing to get rid of me, Janus gets his office space, one two three. And for that I get out from under the lawsuit that he filed on me, maybe with a few dollars left in my purse to boot. Then I'm gone. Not just out of this place, but right out of the state. Someplace where a tie-dyed shirt doesn't get you burned at the stake."

"So if that's your plan, why didn't you just take off in the first place? Tell Janus to stuff his lawsuit and his wife and everything?"

She whirled around. "Because I spent all the money Louise was paying me and I didn't have much more coming in. When Janus offered me his deal, with a bonus at the end if everything came off as planned, I figured it was the best way. Plus he locked me out of my apartment and threatened to sell off all my things. So I went along, even signed a damn lease agreement with his name all over it—a little insurance in case I tried to back out on him, he said. He got you to sign something, too, didn't he?"

"Yeah. For what it's worth."

"Don't kid yourself, Hackshaw. It'll be worth plenty if you cross him. You think his lawyers won't drag us both into it if Janus gets nailed for fraud? Or maybe murder? Christ, I'd probably be indicted as an accessory."

I got up and paced alongside the battered dining table, hashing things out as I went. "The way I see it, we've got two ways to get out of this clean," I said. "The first way, we do absolutely nothing. Keep our mouths shut and let Step Garris take the fall for Sue's murder."

Another test, but Hester passed this one, too.

"I thought you said clean. That sounds pretty dirty to me, Hackshaw. I don't know if Step is guilty or not, but if I didn't care either way, I wouldn't have bailed him out of jail in the first place."

"And I wouldn't be here wearing a trench in your floor. So it looks like we agree on one thing: we want the real murderer caught, whoever it turns out to be."

"Yeah," she said ruefully. "Only how do we manage that—and without sticking our own necks out too far?"

"That brings me to our second option. We've got to find a way to convince the police to expand their investigation beyond Step Garris. The problem is, Birdy Wade has jurisdiction, and he's not about to reopen the case on my say-so. Even if we went to him with everything we know—"

"That's another problem. If we take away his prime suspect, that puts me back on his list. And don't forget Janus. If he goes down, he'll take me with him."

"Not if we work out an immunity deal with Birdy first. I'm sure he'd go for it, if the information we give him pans out." I threw up my hands. "But we're still stuck on square one. Birdy thinks he has his man. The only way we can get him to investigate Janus and the others is if we can somehow prove Step didn't do it. Or at least cast some serious doubt. And how in hell do we do that when Step isn't even sure himself what happened?"

"You know, I've been thinking about that—Step's blackouts? There's a chance we could help him remember what he did, or didn't do, that night."

"Yeah?"

"It isn't foolproof, but . . . I have a girlfriend who's on staff at the Alternative Health And Biofeedback Project in Rochester—"

I grimaced. "Just what we need, some New Age bunco queen—"

"She's not a 'fortune teller,' you idiot! She's a certified hypnotherapist."

"A hypnotist?"

"Hypnosis is a legitimate tool for restoring memory loss. If you've got any better ideas—"

"Not a one. I apologize, okay?" I began pacing again. "Hypnosis. It might tell us *something* useful. Worth a try anyway . . . You think you could get your girlfriend out here, set up a session?"

"Sure. She'd love a challenge like this; give her a break from chronic bedwetters."

"Let's do it, then. The sooner the better."

"I'll see if I can put it together for tomorrow. I'll take time off from work if I have to." She paused. "There's just one thing, though. I think we have to have somebody from law enforcement there in a situation like this, to make it official."

I mulled that over for a moment. "I don't know . . . I might be able to get Birdy to go along."

"How? You just said he won't listen to you."

This time I did allow myself a smile. "It involves the carrot-and-stick principle—but you let me worry about that. Concentrate on lining up your friend."

"Okay. But I just thought of something else. Step would have to agree to do it."

"So? Why wouldn't he?"

"Well, sometimes people lose their memories because there's something they don't want to remember."

"Mmm. Like maybe subconsciously he knows he actually did kill Sue?"

She nodded, then tapped the side of her head. "He might not want someone poking around in there."

"There's one way to find out," I said. "Let's go out back and ask him."

Garris was in the same spot I'd found him on Friday afternoon, staring impassively at the back entry porch, as if he hadn't moved in two days.

I let Hester talk him down this time.

"What are you doing out here, Step? Step?"

His lips moved—at least, the bushy black hair surrounding them did—but that was it.

She gently touched his sleeve. "Are you okay, Step? It's me—Hester DelGado."

His shoulders slumped as he turned toward us. "Hello, Miz Hester. Hackshaw. Didn't see you come up."

All we had done was walk right down the porch stairs he'd been eyeballing. I leaned in cautiously and took a sniff, but I didn't smell anything nearly as pleasant as stale booze.

"I ain't had any today," he said without rancor. "Though it ain't for lack of tryin'." His shock of gray hair was tangled and dirty, his eyes sunken and cold, like two steel marbles dropped in a snowbank. I've seen cadavers with more color.

"You shouldn't put yourself through this," Hester told him. "Standing out here in the hot sun—"

"There's nothin' else to do, ma'am. I guess I burned all my bridges in this town. People had enough of me, and the Lord's give up tryin'. Now they're gonna put me away for stranglin' that girl."

"You don't know that for certain."

"Oh, yeah. Got me for sure, old Birdy Wade says. Gonna lock my sorry ass up and throw the key away." He glanced back at the porch. "I just wish I could remember what it was I done."

"Maybe we can help you remember, Step."

He chilled me with a look I hadn't seen outside of the late show—Raymond Massey playing abolitionist John Brown. Same righteous fervor, same mad desperation.

"You could do that, Hackshaw?"

"It's a possibility." I nodded to Hester. "Tell him what you had in mind."

She told him, all right, slow and patient, like a mother explaining a child's first visit to the dentist. A nice lady will sit you in a chair and put you into a deep sleep and gently probe your brain. Won't hurt a bit and you'll wake up nice and refreshed. I half expected her to tell him there'd be a lollipop in it for him if he was a good boy.

Garris wasn't overly taken with the presentation, either. When Hester finished, he scowled at her and said, "You wanna hypnotize me, why didn't you just say so? I ain't dumb, y'know. I seen 'em do that on TV lots of times."

"Oh." Hester blinked. "You'll do it then?"

"Well . . . This gal of yours, she wouldn't go askin' me about my childhood or other times I maybe got in a little trouble, things like that?"

"Nothing like that. She'd just try to help you remember what happened last Wednesday."

"Sounds okay. Only I guess I'd have to run it by my lawyer first. He don't want me doin' nothin' on my own."

"Good advice," I said. "What's the lawyer's name?"

"Uh, Dickey somethin'. Or somethin' Dickey, I guess it is. We only talked that one time so far, after the judge give him to me."

Step tugged his billfold from the pocket of his olive drab

Sears work pants and thumbed through the odd bits of paper stuck in where the currency would've been if he had any. "Got his business card here someplace with his home phone number on the back. Call any time of the day or night, he tells me."

"That's encouraging," Hester said. "Sounds like he's engaged, anyway."

"Oh, he's a real go-getter, if that's what you mean. No older'n my youngest boy Chucky, but got a whole lot more on the ball. Here it is."

Garris held the card at arm's length and read it: " 'Dwight T. Dickey, associate, Graves and Fike, attorneys at law.' Betcha he took some grief in school, a name like Dwight Dickey."

I told Hester, "That's a two-man law firm over in Chilton—Graves and Fike. I didn't know they had any associates."

"Says he's been with 'em almost a year. Says I'm his first felony case." Step grinned like an idiot, if you'll excuse the redundancy. "Eager as a pup. I figure that's the one thing I got goin' for me right now—the boy's itchin' to make a name for himself."

"Uh-huh. Great." A sacrificial virgin appointed by the court. "Well, why don't we go inside and have you give him a buzz?"

We entered through the back, Garris moving warily around the spot where Sue's body had been found. While he placed the call on the kitchen phone, Hester edged over beside me.

"I think the lawyer'll go for it, don't you?"

"I don't see why not," I said. "Look, if Step gets the okay, why don't you send him home and then see if you can make the arrangements with the hypnotist, okay? Call me at my place later and let me know where we stand."

"I thought . . . you might stick around awhile. For Sunday dinner."

"I don't think so, Hester."

The high heels put her eyes almost level with mine. She searched my face, just inches away.

"I want you to know, Hackshaw. Bringing you into this was Janus's idea, but the other part was up to me. I really felt like we had this synergy going for us. I . . . I'm really going to miss that."

"Yeah, well, you'll get over it," I said. "I did."

29

There were no problems with the lawyer or with Hester's hypnotherapist friend. She called me at my apartment a couple of hours later and gave me the tentative details. The session would be at her place the following afternoon at three. My job was to pick up Step in Muletown and see that he made it to the Mott house with no detours to Cap's Liquor Store along the way.

But that was only part of my job, and the easiest part at that. I also needed to find a cop, preferably one with jurisdiction, to act as an official witness to the proceedings. It wasn't a mandated requirement, the freshman lawyer told Hester, but without it the court was liable to rule inadmissible anything that came out of the session.

It took me two bowls of pipe tobacco in my cozy platform rocker to decide that I had no choice but to call Birdy. For a second there I toyed with the notion of bringing in Mel Stoneman, the sheriff's investigator for our corner of the county. But I was kidding myself. Birdy Wade didn't like me too much these days, but Stoneman hated my guts, these and all other days.

So I dug out my address book, picked up the phone, and tapped out the digits for Birdy's place. He answered on the second ring.

"It's Hackshaw," I said. Sounding very Sam Spade, if I do say so myself. "We need to talk."

"About what?"

"About the Krevin murder case and whether you come out of it looking like a first-class investigator or a world-class fool."

"Are you threatening me, Hackshaw?" Apparently Birdy likes the late show, too.

"Yeah. I'm threatening to help you sew up your case, if you'll give me a fair hearing. If you don't, I'll have to find some other outlet for my story."

I listened to his steady breathing for the next ten seconds. Then: "Okay."

"Okay?" I hadn't expected that.

"I'll hear what you have to say. My office, tomorrow morning—"

"This won't wait until tomorrow, Birdy. And I don't want to meet in your office."

"Where'd you have in mind?"

"Someplace neutral would be nice."

"Hypnosis, huh?" Birdy's lip curled. "I'm surprised Garris and his lawyer would even agree to it. On second thought, no, I'm not. That lawyer's greener than a St. Paddy's Day parade."

"Why shouldn't they agree?"

"You ever hear of self-incrimination, for Christ's—" He broke off to check our flank. We were at Norb's Nook, seated in a quiet booth tucked into an alcove just off the taproom. It was crowded and almost as loud as the Hawaiian shirt Birdy

256

was wearing. And that was the point. The Nook was out of his jurisdiction and too public for him to make much of a scene.

"Forget it, Hackshaw. I don't see why I should waste my time on this. It's like that old football coach used to say about the forward pass: there's only three things that can happen, and two of 'em are bad."

I had to take a second to work that one out. "By bad outcomes you mean either the hypnosis doesn't reveal anything at all, or it does work and Step remembers something that might prove his innocence."

"Not prove his innocence," he said, shaking his balding head. "But maybe give his lawyer some little thing that would create doubt in the jurors. Look, I've got Garris on motive, on method, and on opportunity. He's guilty as hell and I can prove it. I got absolutely no incentive to cooperate with you on this hypnosis deal."

"We can go ahead without you, you know."

"Be my guest."

I hate it when they call your bluff. "You're putting an awful lot of faith into a two-foot length of clothesline, aren't you?"

"It's how the girl was killed. We've got tissue samples. And fiber evidence we took off Garris's clothes shows he'd been handling the stuff—"

"Of course he'd been handling the stuff. Because Hester told him to string a new clothesline that day. It doesn't prove anything."

"Yeah? Well, I've got a near-empty bottle of Jim Beam that will."

The puzzled frown on my face spoke for itself. Birdy let me hang for a moment while he sipped the head off his beer and decided how much to tell me. Then he shrugged.

"What the hell. It'll come out in discovery, anyway. Garris must've been feeling his oats Wednesday night. Bought himself a fifth at the liquor store, but not his usual rotgut. Cap told me Garris only buys Beam once in a blue moon, when he's on a serious toot." He smiled. "So guess where we found the bottle?"

"At Hester's?"

"In the garage, tucked inside a bag of lawn fertilizer."

I felt like crying in my beer, but I took a sip instead. "Motive, method, and opportunity. Christ, maybe the crazy bastard *did* do it."

I waited for Birdy to start crowing, but he surprised me again. He leaned forward onto his elbows and said, almost collegially, "Answer something for me, Hackshaw. Why're you so set on helping Garris in the first place?"

"I'm not. The truth is, I don't care much about Step one way or the other. I just want to see Sue Krevin's killer put away—and I'm still not completely satisfied you've got the right man. So let me ask you one: if you're so damn sure Garris did it, why'd you agree to meet me?"

He mulled that one over for awhile, too, protracting things further with a long swallow of beer.

"I'm surprised you haven't mentioned Ricky Reimer yet," he said. "You had another run-in with him, didn't you?"

"He ambushed me out on Union Street last night." I gave him the details, with heavy emphasis on the slashed tires and the unprovoked battering I'd suffered. "Of course," I concluded, "I'll bet Reimer's version was a little different."

Birdy responded by taking a folded sheet of paper from his shirt pocket and sliding it across the table. I spread it open. A note comprised of six handwritten lines, done in an over-sized, childlike scrawl and signed at the bottom: "Ricky R." I read it through.

*"You'll probably hear from Hackshaw before you get this, Chief, and I'm sorry I didn't leave him alone like you*

*said but I get too mad sometimes and don't listen too good. No
matter what he tells you, I didn't do anything except for trying
to save the department some grief. I owe you a lot and maybe
this is the only way I can pay you back.*"

I looked up, straight into Birdy's doleful brown eyes.
"God, this sounds like . . . he didn't—"
"No. At least, we haven't found a body." He reclaimed
the note and tucked it back in his pocket. "Ricky must've left
this on my desk when he came off shift last night. Along with
his shield and ID."
"What about his gun?"
He shook his head. "My officers pay for their own side-
arms. He didn't have to turn it in."
"But you don't think he was planning to use it on himself."
"I can't say, but it doesn't look that way. I don't usually
go into the office on Sunday, but I needed to get some data for
a report I'm working on—a response I'm putting together for
the citizens group that wants to abolish my department. Anyway, when I found the note and everything, I went over to
Ricky's house. He still lives with his parents over on DelMar
Drive. His mother heard him come in in the middle of the
night, but he went out again. When we checked his room, she
told me a bunch of his clothes and personal things were
gone."
"So he might've just cleared out of town."
"Looks like it."
"Are you still looking for him?"
"You think I should be?"
The question wasn't a rebuke, but an invitation. Now I
knew why he had agreed to meet with me so readily. Reimer
was a loose cannon, and Birdy wanted to know which direction it was pointed.

"Give me five minutes," I said. "Then you tell me."

I know what you're thinking, but the hell with Janus Theophanis and his hush money and his crummy contract. I've been sued by better men than him, and besides, all he could really hope to accomplish with that piece of paper I'd signed was to embarrass me in the community. And I've done that on my own so often it hardly warranted consideration.

So I laid out every fact and every conjecture I had; everything I'd tried to explain to Birdy at the village diner the day before and everything I'd found out in the tumultuous twenty-four hours since. What I'd learned about Theophanis and his Mott house scam, Hester's role in it, Stanhouse's duplicity and his lying about the graffiti incident at Silvertrees. Then I weaved in Sue Krevin and the time I'd caught her rifling Hester's desk, restating my suspicions about her relationship with Reimer, and reminding the chief of Reimer's open hostility toward me ever since I first mentioned Sue's name to him.

Two conspiracies for the price of one, I told Birdy. The Theophanis-DelGado-Stanhouse trifecta, angling to con the locals into granting a variance on the Mott house—that one was definite. And the Krevin-Reimer duo, cooking up an adolescent scheme to create a minor crime wave to provide the Port Erie PD with a raison d'être—a definite maybe.

"Then an already confusing situation got even more so when the two conspiracies became enmeshed somehow," I said. "Probably because Sue Krevin decided to add blackmail to her resume."

Birdy was drawing little circles on the tabletop with his index finger. "Let's say you're right about all this, Hackshaw."

"Lets."

"First thing"—he pointed the index finger at me—"it doesn't lessen the evidence against Garris."

"No, but it surely presents alternatives."

He granted me that much. "But here's the other thing: you're assuming the girl was extorting money from someone—most likely this doctor—and that the doctor got tired of it and killed her."

"Or had her killed," I said. "One or the other."

"You caught the girl going through the desk on Tuesday night, looking for this doctor's name."

"Looking for information she could exploit. I'm guessing she found Janus's name and number, just like I did."

"Uh-huh. So she made the connection to Janus Tuesday night, and by Wednesday night she was dead."

"Right."

"There's only one problem, Hackshaw. That money we found in the girl's bank account? She made two deposits—one on Tuesday, hours before you ran across her rifling through the desk, and the other even earlier, the previous Thursday." He folded his bare arms over his chest. "In other words, she had the money *before* she found whatever she was looking for in the desk."

"Oh. That's right." I told you I wasn't any good at this sort of thing. "But she still could've been blackmailing someone."

"Yeah, someone. Like your girlfriend, Hester."

"What about Stanhouse? Or even Reimer? Sue could've been pressuring him—"

"*If* your theory about him being involved in that half-baked Satan scare is true. And even then, I don't see Ricky strangling that girl."

"Well, I don't see Hester doing it."

"Me neither. We checked her alibi; she really was in the city late that night, doing an inventory at the place she works and stopping after for drinks with the girl she works with." He drank down his beer and pushed aside the empty glass.

"But that doesn't mean she didn't arrange to have one of her admirers do the murder for her."

"Now wait a minute, Chief. I have an alibi, too—"

"I'm talking about Step Garris. If anybody thought he owed Hester DelGado, it was Garris. She gave him a job, treated him with respect—"

"You're trying awfully hard to make this fit the hole you cut, aren't you? If Ricky Reimer had ever put you in a choke hold, maybe you'd know what he's capable of. And how about Stanhouse? You conveniently forgot him." I shook my head in disgust. "Protect the home boys, is that it, Birdy? The voters? Meanwhile, the outsiders and the town drunk are expendable."

His face went crimson and he came halfway across the table after me. But then, mindful of the crowd milling in the taproom behind him, he dropped back into his seat.

"You're one to question my motives, Hackshaw. You're about as pure as shit in all this. Give me one reason I shouldn't lock your ass up right now for withholding evidence and obstructing justice."

"Leaving aside the First Amendment," I said, cocky as I could manage, "I'll give you two reasons. Because you're worried that I might be right about Reimer—that he and the girl fabricated a crime spree to make your department look good. And because you know that if I tell the whole story in the *Advertiser*, you can kiss the Port Erie Police Department good-bye."

He immediately seized on the operative phrase. "If you tell the *whole* story?"

"Our news hole isn't that big. As editor in chief, I have to make critical judgments all the time—what to put into a story and what to leave out. Now, if Reimer's role in all this proves not to be directly connected to the girl's murder, I could decide it isn't relevant . . ."

262

I left it there and gave Birdy time to think about it. He didn't take long.

"And in exchange for your, uh, editorial discretion?"

"Well, for starters," I said, "you could agree to cooperate on this hypnosis thing."

# 30

I woke up the next morning thinking about the guys who paint the Golden Gate Bridge. I read somewhere that the job is so big, by the time they finish, they have to go back and start all over again. It never ends, in other words. And on that particular rainy gray Monday, I could relate.

So what if I'd lined up Birdy Wade for the hypnosis session? What were the chances it would add up to anything, that Step Garris would utter something that would clear up the Krevin murder once and for all and let me get back to my normal pursuits? Using Birdy's analysis as my guide, the best odds I could hope for were one in three.

Not great, I thought as I climbed out of bed, but a long shot was better than no shot at all.

A hot shower brought me halfway to life and a hot mug of coffee would do the rest. But no sooner had the coffee maker stopped its gurgle than the telephone burped.

"I see your phone's still working, Hackshaw." Mr. Johnson, my erstwhile tenant, sounding far too pleased with himself. I decided to sit down.

"When you plug 'em in, they stay plugged," I told him. "Count yourself lucky it didn't turn out to be a faulty microchip."

"Amen." It was like talking to a wall.

"You run into an IC problem, you might as well chuck the whole thing in the trash. Same with everything nowadays. You know that dishwasher Mrs. J. had you put in?"

"I'm still making the payments."

"That touch-pad control panel? Nothing but integrated circuits. I'll tell you, gone are the days of the do-it-yourselfer with his trusty soldering iron."

"You're not having problems with it already—"

"No, runs like a top." He chuckled. "My only problem is she thinks it's a damn china cabinet. You think I can find a clean dish in the cupboard anymore?"

I lapped up some coffee. "Listen, Mr. J., I'm running a little late for work . . ."

"Reason I called, it looks like I was right about that stalker I told you about. The one in the black Firebird?"

"Yeah, you were right about that."

"Only it wasn't a black Firebird after all. It's a brown Celica. I don't know how I could've confused the two, but like I said, my night vision is getting pitiful."

"Wait a minute. A brown Celica?"

"Uh-huh. Followed you home last night. I was sitting out on the front porch, trying to catch a breeze—we need to talk about air-conditioning this place, Hackshaw."

"Bad for your sinusitis. What about the car?"

"I got a good look at it this time, under the street light on the corner there. Your Jeep made the turn, then a few seconds later this other car did, too. Maybe fifteen more seconds and I see the same car come back this way."

"Well . . . maybe he was just lost."

"Yeah. And maybe he wasn't."

* * *

I'd forgotten all about it by the time I made it to the office a little past noon. Most of my morning had been spent in Kirkville, interviewing the highway superintendent about his new grader and picking up ad copy at Ridgeway Chevrolet and the IGA and half a dozen other small businesses whose advertising dollars help keep our own small business afloat.

My sister was in the reception area, hunkered over Mrs. Hobarth's desk, when I walked in.

"There you are, Elias."

She should have T-shirts made up.

I waved the portfolio I was carrying. "I collected all the display material from the Kirkville regulars *and* I got the interview you wanted with Cy Burke and his new toy."

"And still found time to stop off at the Nook."

Don't ask me how she always knows; something to do with that second X chromosome they all have. "I grabbed an early lunch. It was on the way."

"Hmmph. Seems that place is on the way no matter where you go." Mrs. Hobarth, slipping in her two cents.

Ruth said, "Well, I'm glad you followed through with Cy. Did you remember to get pictures of the new machine?"

The camera was hanging around my neck, for pity's sake. "Yes, I did."

"Good. And speaking of pictures, don't forget about the Canal Days' closing festivities today in Port Erie. We'll need some good art, probably the raft race would be best. And interviews with some of the merchants and artists for your feature—"

"I picked up all the quotes and color I'll need when I was over there on Saturday," I said. "How 'bout having Alan do the photos? He's got a better eye than me."

"Well, if you think so." She gave me the once-over while

266

nibbling her pencil eraser. "I take it you have other plans this afternoon?"

"I do have a conflict."

"Hah!" Mrs. H. was grinning ear to ear, a rare and always troubling sight. "You're going to that seance over there, I'll bet."

I stared at the old witch. She'd gotten it wrong, but the question was how had she gotten it at all.

"Where'd you hear about that?"

"Wouldn't you like to know."

"You're going to a seance, Elias?"

"A hypnosis session." I still hadn't taken my eyes off Mrs. H.

"Hypnosis?" Ruth frowned with sisterly concern. "Are you having trouble sleeping again?"

"Not him," Mrs. Hobarth said. "It's for that killer. The one strangled that girl."

"Oh, the Mott house tragedy?" I wasn't sure if Ruth meant the murder or my flattering article on Hester, but her next comment settled the issue. "I had hoped you'd learned your lesson, Elias. My advice—not that you'll listen—is to stay away from anything connected to that place or that woman. The last thing we need is another story on her; it would only remind people of the last one."

"I couldn't agree more, Sis. Only there's a small chance this hypnosis deal could yield some surprising results. Maybe even lead to an *Advertiser* exclusive."

I was mostly bluffing, of course, but Ruth's attitude ticked me off and it was the best comeback I could think of. She used to hate running crime stories; not the sort of thing our readers look for in a weekly, she'd say. But that was before last fall, when we managed to scoop the world on a sensational murder over in Kirkville. Our subscriber base jumped 20 percent as a result.

Her big brown eyes grew bigger. "I thought that case was supposed to be open and shut."

"Not necessarily. There's a possibility Step Garris may remember something that could clear him, maybe even point the finger at somebody else. Now, I've got an inside track with Birdy Wade on this, so who knows? If the rest of the media doesn't get wind of anything—"

"Hah!" Mrs. Hobarth nodded toward the tinny little radio she keeps on her desk. "Too late for that, Hackshaw. Mike Morten already reported the whole shebang on his midday show not twenty minutes ago."

"You're kidding." Morten had a talk show on WCPE, the tiny community radio station that operated out of the former telephone company office on Chilton–Port Erie Town Line Road. Local news and call-in programs sandwiched around country and gospel music. "He couldn't have picked up on this already. Unless—" I was about to say unless Birdy Wade was out drumming up publicity again. But as usual, I had the right motive, wrong culprit.

"He had an interview with that Garris fella's lawyer," Mrs. H. said. "Dicky something or other. Sounded sorta like Doogie Howser, if you ask me."

"Well, there goes any chance to scoop the daily press, Elias. It's probably just as well. Anyway, now you're free to get those photos we'll need—"

"No, I'm not. I promised I'd drive Step to the Mott house for the session."

Ruth's next salvo was interrupted when Liz Fleegle and Alan Harvey strolled through the front door, not quite arm in arm but chattering away like long-lost sorority sisters.

"I *warned* you she was a sow."

"*God.* I didn't know there was that much spandex in the universe."

Alan had abandoned the preemie ponytail for his old

brunette Veronica Lake look, left eye hidden behind one long wavy lock of hair. Liz was only slightly less feminine in a chichi white jumpsuity thing and matching heels. Picture a blond Q-Tip.

"Greetings, everybody," she said, all teeth. "We got our interview with that Della Ward, Ruthie." For my edification she added, "The hausfrau in South Chilton who collects Elvis memorabilia. We'll have to go back later for pix—we didn't have the Minolta because *somebody* failed to show up for work this morning."

"That's because *somebody* was out shooting an earth mover," I said.

Alan glanced sidelong at Liz. "Gee, maybe we could substitute one of those." Whereupon they both tittered.

Ruth said, "I'll need you to run over to the Canal Days Festival later, Alan, so maybe you should head right back to South Chilton now and shoot Mrs. Ward—"

"With an elephant gun," Liz quipped, with predictable results from her soul mate.

I slipped the camera strap over my head and handed the Minolta to Alan, who was trembling with mirth. "Don't be cruel," I said.

He blushed. "What?"

"My favorite Elvis tune. Say hi to Della for me."

The rain had cleared by the time I broke away from the office a bit after two and drove north up Union, then west on Town Line until it connected with Big Ridge Road. After crossing the old canal bridge into Port Erie, I took a hard left onto Sandpit Road and followed it as it meandered in rough parallel to the Erie Canal and the towpath.

The Jeep's radio hadn't worked since Reagan's first term and I knew the scenery by heart, so I passed the time reviewing the call I'd received from Step's lawyer.

269

"Mr. Hackshaw? Dwight Dickey." I'm not sure if it was the phone line or his voice that kept cracking. "Just wanted to touch base, make sure we're on the same page. You're the one who'll be picking up my client at his place?"

"That's the plan."

"Super. I'd do it myself, but I've got a one-thirty closing at Chilton Home Savings and I understand the sellers had a couple of liens on the house, so there could be complications. I should still be able to make the session in Port Erie by three, though."

"Just so long as we're not inconveniencing you."

"No problem. I thrive on the pressure." He paused to reinflate his ego. "One request, Mr. Hackshaw. If possible, I'd like you to pick him up early enough to see that he's, uh, presentable. You know what I mean—sober, groomed, dressed halfway decent. If you have any influence with him, you might try convincing him to shave off that beard, too. Anything you can do to get him there looking like a normal, nonthreatening, guy-next-door type."

"This is just a hypnotherapy session, Dwight, not a dress rehearsal for the trial."

"Don't be so sure. With any luck, I may have swung it so a TV crew shows up for my press conference afterward. Look, between you and me, my client's probably toast, okay? Sure, most of the evidence against him is circumstantial, but there's an awful lot of it to refute. I'm thinking my best chance is to force a plea bargain, maybe get the charge reduced to manslaughter."

"Force a plea bargain?"

"Exactly. I keep pushing the ADA on how soft this prima facie case of his is, while at the same time I try to build a little public sympathy for my client. Talk up his tragic past to the media. Play up the alcoholism and the blackouts, the lack of education. Possibly some childhood abuse in there somewhere—that's where this hypnotherapy angle could help. Anyway, it makes him look cooperative and remorseful, which couldn't hurt."

"If it did, you wouldn't feel it anyway," I said. "I don't suppose you've even considered the possibility that Step Garris may be innocent?"

"Innocent? Right." He chuckled. "Tell me another one."

"Okay. Did you hear the one about the lawyer who frantically phoned nine-one-one when his office caught fire?"

"No. What happened?"

I hung up on him.

Now, as I passed by the entrance to the public boat launch and began to slow down for the turnoff to Muletown, I wondered if I hadn't been a tad holier than thou with the little parasite. Only a few days earlier, I'd been as ready as everyone else to see Step Garris take the fall. Maybe Dickey was right. Maybe a manslaughter conviction was the best Step could hope for—and a better fate than he deserved.

I pulled in next to the heating oil tank in Step's hard-packed yard and got out of the Jeep, pausing a moment to pan the dozen ramshackle houses scattered up and down the dusty dirt street. Discounting the barking dogs, the place was quiet as a church. Three doors down a woman in a baggy house-dress was sitting out on her stoop, smoking a cigarette. When she saw me looking at her, she tossed the butt away and, rising one weary bone at a time, disappeared back inside her house.

I fortified myself with a deep breath, walked up to Step's front porch, and swung open the old wooden screen door. *Better than a doorbell,* I thought as it slammed shut behind me. I rapped twice on the interior door and waited. And waited. Then I rapped again, harder and longer this time. And still no response.

"Step. Come on," I called out, leaning in and cupping my

271

hands around my eyes, the better to see through the grimy glass panes. "It's Hackshaw. Time to go—"

That's when I spied a pair of legs stretched across the floor beside the battered sofa, bare toes pointing down.

I fumbled with the knob and the door swung inward. I rushed inside and knelt beside the body.

It was Garris. Facedown on a faded hook rug, illuminated by a rectangle of sunlight streaming through a side window, as still as the musty air around us.

"*Jesus.*" I took his wrist, hoping to find a pulse, but my hands were trembling so badly I gave it up and instead grabbed onto the back of his shirt and slowly rolled him over. His eyes were wide open but opaque, staring at the ceiling, seeing nothing. Just two lifeless black pits . . .

But then he blinked.

And moaned.

And finally let go a bubbling, fetid belch.

# 31

Dead drunk.

His breath stank of booze, and now that my initial panic had subsided, I was able to register the empty bottle of Dewar's discarded under the end table.

"Ahhhnnngh."

Garris's head lolled to the side, sending a stream of drool coursing down into his matted beard. God knows what else he had in there.

"So much for the guy-next-door look." I pulled him into a sitting position, hooked my arms under his, and hoisted him onto the end of the sofa. "I oughta walk out of here right now and leave you to whatever Birdy and the DA and that cold-blooded lawyer of yours come up with. If I didn't think there was half a chance you're innocent, that's exactly what I'd do, too."

"Ahhnngh." His eyelids slowly closed and his chin began to droop onto his chest. Then his head snapped back up and he blinked at me again. "Hackshaw?"

"Christ, look at you! We're supposed to meet with the hypnotist in forty minutes and—what the hell good will it do now, you stupid brain-dead son of a bitch?"

Pretty cold, I know. But I was furious. I mean, it's no wonder people refuse to get involved these days. Anyway, I figured a little shock therapy was the best thing for him just then. And it seemed to work.

Step wiggled into a more or less upright position.

"Only wanted to settle m'self down some," he muttered sheepishly. "Lord, I was hurtin'. Didn't see how a few nips could hurt either way."

"A few nips?" I rubbed a hand across my eyes and groaned. "I thought you were supposed to be broke. Where'd you get the money to buy the scotch?"

"Huh?" His face scrunched up into a fur ball. "I didn't buy nothin'. He did."

"*Who* did?"

"Him." Step's arm came up and pointed unsteadily over my shoulder. I turned my head—and damn near fainted.

"Don't move, Hackshaw."

He was standing in the doorway to the kitchen, wearing a baseball cap, tennis shoes, and a gray jogging suit. And holding in his hand a nasty little chrome-plated pistol.

Wesley Stanhouse.

All I could think to say was, "Where's Theophanis?"

"Shut up." He waggled the pistol. "Sit on the couch."

I sat, as far from Garris as I could get.

"Hey," he said, staring across at Stanhouse. "What's the gun for?"

I said, "What d'ya think it's for, you—"

"I told you to *shut up*, Hackshaw." Stanhouse took two halting steps into the room. "Give me a chance to think."

I gave us both a chance to think. It was obvious that Stanhouse was on his own and almost as scared as I was. He'd

274

come there with a bottle for Garris, and a gun if he needed it. But that was just an insurance policy. The idea had to be to get Garris drunk—simple enough—and then to . . .

Step broke the silence with, "Somebody wanna tell me what's goin' on?"

"Suicide," I said.

"Huh? Somebody gonna kill hisself?"

"Yeah. You are." I was watching Stanhouse, watching me. "That was the plan, right? Get him loaded, and when he blacks out, kill him and arrange it to look like he'd done himself in." I stole a glance at Garris. "I saw a couple of propane tanks along the side of the house, Step. You have a gas stove?"

"A gas—yeah. In the kitchen." He still didn't have a clue. "Why's Mr. Stanhouse got a gun, Hack? Last I recall, we were havin' a friendly drink."

"How about it, Stanhouse?"

He ran his tongue around his lips, shook his head. "I didn't mean for anyone else to get hurt. Just—him."

"Hurt? Let's can the polite euphemisms. You mean dead, don't you? Like Sue Krevin."

*"That was an accident!"*

I resisted the urge to ask him how you accidentally strangle somebody with a clothesline, but he told me anyway.

"It wasn't premeditated. I didn't—" He broke off and looked up imploringly at the water-stained ceiling. Then, moving ponderously, he lowered his pear-shaped frame into the beat-up recliner.

"There's no point in talking about it now, Hackshaw," he said quietly. The hand with the gun was propped on the armrest, the gun still aimed in my direction. "Nobody would understand, anyway."

"Un'erstand what?"

"Shut up, Step," I growled out the side of my mouth.

275

"Look, maybe I do understand. I'm sure it wasn't premeditated. You just snapped, right? The girl was blackmailing you, wasn't that it? And you couldn't take it anymore?"

"Yes! Ever since that night I caught her defacing my property. I let her go because I thought—" He smiled sadly. "You know about that, now, too, don't you? Janus's plan to convert the Mott house to medical offices? He told me you knew."

I nodded. "Did he put you up to this?"

"No. I called him the night I caught the girl. That's when I found out she wasn't working for him. But I never told him about the blackmail or—what happened later. I was too afraid and ashamed to tell anyone." His eyes misted. "That night I caught her, I let too much slip—about Janus and the DelGado woman and everything. Anyway, I let her go. Next day she called me, said she needed five hundred dollars. She made it clear she'd go to the police about the Mott house if she didn't get it." He shrugged. "I decided to give it to her and hope for the best."

"But she came back for more."

"A few days later. Another five hundred. I left it for her in the same place as before, tucked into a niche in the public phone kiosk down on the corner of Virginia and Main. I was still hoping—but I knew she'd call again. She was hard as steel, that little slut."

"And she did call again."

"Last Wednesday afternoon. This time she knew more; she had Janus's private number and she threatened to call him for money. She wanted a thousand dollars this time." He wiped the perspiration from his face with the sleeve of his sweatshirt. "I agreed to leave the money, same place, just after dark, like before. I was going to let her keep it, too, but this was going to be the last time. I decided to put the fear of God into her, make her realize what a dangerous game she was playing.

"So while she was out picking up the payment, I snuck over to the Mott house, through the hedge in the backyard. I hid behind that yew next to the porch steps and waited for her to come back. There was a piece of rope lying on the ground there, and I picked it up. Not consciously or anything. I mean, I just . . . picked it up and began fooling with it while I waited."

And now I waited as Stanhouse seemed to drift away for a moment, caught up in the memory, the pistol's short barrel angling toward the floor. I checked Step out of the corner of my eye. He looked to be half asleep, breathing raggedly through his mouth. For some reason I thought of an old joke: Two guys in a jungle come face to face with a man-eating tiger. The first guy says, "Run for it." The second guy says, "You can't outrun a tiger." The first one answers, "I only have to outrun you."

But before I could talk myself into a headlong dive through the window, Stanhouse came alert.

"Forget it, Hackshaw," he said, bringing the gun up.

"Forget what?"

"Don't underestimate me. Don't condescend—I can't stand it!" He hopped to his feet with surprising agility. "She underestimated me, too. Laughed in my face when I came out of the bushes after her, called me a fat old man."

"Calm down, okay?" The gun was shaking so bad I hardly noticed my own tremors. "We can sort this out—"

"Don't patronize me. I strangled her, there on the porch, and took back my money. She didn't give me any choice." His shouting revived Garris, who sat up straighter. Stanhouse swung his aim toward him. "Don't stare at me, you bastard! I try to sleep and all I see is that night, and you! Standing there in the garage door like a devil, staring at me with those horrible black eyes—"

Step belched. "What the hell is he talkin' about?"

"You don't remember—that's what saved me. That's what saved *you!*" Back to me. "I ran, Hackshaw, like a rabbit. Out of there and back to Silvertrees, shaking like a leaf and waiting for the police to come. Only they didn't, and then I heard about Garris and the arrest and the blackouts. I thought I was home free."

"Until today, when you heard on the radio about the hypnosis session."

"I couldn't let that happen, could I? He'd tell everyone what I did."

Step finally caught up with the program. "Why you dirty, sneakin' bastard." He struggled up from the sofa—I tried to pull him back, but too late. "It was you all the time—"

"Stay away!"

The shot sounded like the snap of a tree branch. I wasn't even sure what had happened. Until Step fell back onto the sofa beside me, mouth agape, eyes rolled back in their sockets, as if he was looking up at his own forehead, amazed as I was at the blood oozing from the little round hole in his brow.

Now I really felt bad about that brain-dead crack.

"It just . . . went off." Stanhouse was staring at the pistol in his hand. "It was an accident."

"I'll show you an accident—"

I lunged at him, stupid with rage and fear. He brought the gun around again, but too late—the sound of the shot roared in my ear just as his forearm banged against my shoulder. I grabbed a handful of sweatshirt and took a swing, my fist glancing off the side of his head and knocking off the baseball cap. His elbow smashed down on my shoulder, sending a bolt of pain through my arm. I managed to clamp his wrist between my side and my arm, but the arm was starting to go

278

numb and he was pounding at me with his left and I began lose my grip on his gun hand . . .

Then, simultaneously, a cannon went off and chunks of plaster rained down on us and a voice was shouting. Stanhouse pushed me away and began to turn, and I saw him then—Ricky Reimer, charging through the front door, his revolver pointed toward the ceiling, hollering—and suddenly tripping, sprawling across the ratty hook rug.

That's when Stanhouse shot him, too.

What came next I couldn't say. I only know I dove behind the sofa even as I heard more shouts and a second explosion from Reimer's revolver and an answering crack from Stanhouse's pistol.

Then there was silence—total, but for a steady ringing in my left ear, the residue of Stanhouse's stray shot. I lay unmoving, straining to hear and terrified at what waited for me on the other side of that sofa.

"Hackshaw?" A hoarse whisper, off to my left, broke the spell.

"Reimer?"

"Over here."

I inched forward on my elbows and cautiously peeked around the side of my upholstered fortress. He was sitting in a corner of the room, shielded by the bulky recliner, the gun hugged to his chest, his right leg stretched out straight. There was blood on his pants.

"Is it bad?"

"No. Creased my thigh. You hit?"

"No." We were still whispering. "Did you get him?"

"I don't know how I missed."

I muttered a curse. "Where is he?"

Reimer pointed the gun in the general direction of the kitchen. "In there. I think. He killed Sue?"

I nodded. "She was blackmailing him. He killed poor Step, too."

"I can see Garris. He's bleeding heavy."

"Of course he's bleeding—he's got a bullet hole in his head."

"Dead men don't bleed. He's still alive."

I started to get up to look, then thought better of it. "We have to get him an ambulance."

"All this firing, somebody probably already called the emergency—"

"In Muletown?" I snorted. "Don't count on it. Are you sure Stanhouse didn't take off? I don't hear anything."

"Let's find out." Reimer reached up and rested the butt of his revolver on the top of the chair and without looking fired twice toward the kitchen. "Heavy loads. Those'll punch holes right through the drywall—"

He curled up fast as two answering holes appeared in the plaster above his head in concert with the snap-snap of Stanhouse's little chrome pistol.

"Son of a bitch." Reimer stared across at me. "It's a stand-off. He doesn't know what to do, either."

"Yeah, but he's not bleeding to death." Then I noticed something. I leaned out as far as I dared and whispered, "There's a phone on the stand, other side of your chair."

While he maneuvered around to try for the phone, I decided to distract Stanhouse. I called out, "This is crazy, Stanhouse. Even if you kill us, where you gonna go? People will figure it out—"

"Shut up, Hackshaw!" His voice was on the edge of hysteria. "Just—shut up!"

"Fuck." Reimer had the phone to his ear now, but he threw it aside. "No tone. The old rummy probably didn't pay his bill."

I bristled for some reason. "Maybe it's the wiring or a bad chip or something."

"Who the hell cares?" He grimaced and put his head back against the wall. "Jesus, this is startin' to sting. We're gonna have to rush him."

"I hope that's the royal 'we' you're using."

That's when we heard heavy footsteps pounding across the kitchen, followed by a slamming door.

"He's running!"

The first thing I saw as we worked our way down off Garris's front porch was a brown Celica parked beside my Jeep.

"You've been following me."

"Yeah. Lucky for you I was."

"I'm not the one who's limping."

"Screw you. I'm okay." Reimer took his arm from around my shoulders and gingerly tested the leg. "Damn."

I helped him over to the Toyota and leaned him against the driver's door.

"First we need a phone."

"I've got a two-way in the car," he said, his square jaw rigid. "I'll call in the medivan for Garris and alert Birdy to the situation. He can meet me down the road at the boat launch—"

"The boat launch?"

"Stanhouse had to walk in here from somewhere—there's no cars but yours and mine. I figure he parked down at the boat launch and hiked over along the towpath. Now he's heading back the same way. Only I'll be there to greet him." He yanked open the door and gingerly folded himself behind the wheel. Then he handed me the revolver. "You better take this. I've got a backup piece in the glove compartment. There's only two rounds left, so make 'em count."

281

I cradled the gun in both hands. "I don't mind riding shotgun, but what do I need this for?"

"You're not coming with me." He leaned in and grabbed the hand mike dangling from the dash. Then he looked up at me. "Look, I can't run on this leg, so it's up to you. I want you to work your way east on the towpath, make sure Stanhouse doesn't try doubling back."

"Wait a minute. Why don't we let the police—"

"We've got this son of a bitch in a box, Hackshaw, and we're gonna keep him there. Now *move*."

 32

Don't ask me why I did it.

Maybe it was the challenge I saw in Reimer's face—the same contemptuous sneer I remembered from my high school days whenever the jocks swaggered down the halls in their letter jackets. Maybe I was just tired of looking away.

Or maybe it was a fresher memory—Step Garris lying on that sofa with a bloody hole in his head like some tragic Fearless Fosdick, hanging onto life by a thread and not even knowing it.

Anyway, I ran to the house three doors down and banged on the door until the woman came out. After I blurted an explanation, she promised she'd do what she could for Step until help arrived. I thanked her on the fly and took off up the high berm, past the stone remnants of the old lock and onto the towpath.

The midafternoon sun was hot and the revolver was heavy. Off in the distance came the first reassuring sound of a siren—the medivan was coming. I stayed to the left side of the macadam path, where the overgrowth of sumac and elders and field grass offered instant cover if the need arose. To my right was the Erie Canal, pea soup green and placid, the far bank too symmetrical and true for anything but a man-made river.

I moved slowly the first hundred yards, flinching every time a bird flushed from a tree or a squirrel thrashed in the bushes. Gradually I picked up the pace, shuffling, then jogging as I followed a long, gentle bend in the towpath. I'd gone little more than half a mile, encountering no one, when the wall of brush off my left shoulder petered out and I could see the boat launch inlet and its makeshift parking area just ahead and below me.

I paused to catch my breath, hands on knees. The parking lot was crowded with cars and empty trailers—the Canal Days raft race, I remembered. Most of the participants and spectators would already be out on the water; only two boats were in the ramp area, a powerful-looking inboard and a smaller open-bow outboard. The brown Celica was blocking the near end of the parking area's center aisle, Reimer standing alongside with his arms extended across its roof, gripping an automatic with both hands. Birdy Wade's big Ford was just coming in from the main road, followed by two cruisers, all with lights flashing but no sirens.

Reimer spotted me and hollered, "Where is he?"

I threw my arms out in an elaborate shrug and shook my head. "He must've veered off into the woods."

While he occupied himself banging the top of his car, I started down the grassy berm along a steep, rutted footpath. I was almost to the bottom, moving around an old storm-damaged willow tree, when an arm snaked around my neck.

"Drop the gun, Hackshaw."

"I already did." The damn thing had slipped from my sweaty hand the instant Stanhouse grabbed me.

"All right, I see it. Move ahead two steps and kneel down. Slowly."

Reimer was shouting at us by then, but I was concentrating on the pistol jabbing my back. I followed instructions and kneeled awkwardly on the slope. Moments later the pistol went away, replaced by the weightier feel of the revolver.

Stanhouse hissed in my ear. "Do exactly what I tell you or I'll blow out your spine."

Something was different. All the blubber was gone from his voice, replaced by a calm fatalistic resolve. I knew then that Stanhouse had crossed a threshold somewhere in the desperate journey from Step's kitchen to this bolt hole in the weeds. There would be no plea bargains.

"Move down to the edge of the lot, then to the right."

He prodded me along like a calf he was taking to market, careful to keep me between him and the array of pointed guns that were now bunched around Reimer's Toyota and Birdy's Ford. Everyone stock still, staring, including the two elderly men standing in their boats at the launch ramp. We were moving in their direction.

Birdy had it figured, too.

"There's no point in this, Wesley," he called. "The canal can't take you anyplace we can't find you. Put down the gun and let's talk about this."

Stanhouse ignored him, kept moving us along.

Birdy tried again. "You know me, Wesley. I'll do everything I can for you, if you'll just stop this now."

We stepped onto the wooden dock that paralleled the launch ramp. The large inboard was already running, its owner standing in the stern with his hands up like a B-movie cowboy. Stanhouse waved the gun, motioning the old man to get out. When he was up on the dock, Stanhouse had him stand in front of us while we climbed into the boat.

He pushed me into the seat behind the steering wheel and

hunkered down next to me, then told the old man to untie us. When the bow drifted free of the dock, Stanhouse said, "Take us out of here."

I stared at the throttle control. "I'm not sure—"

The revolver dug into my belly. "I could've exchanged you for the old man, Hackshaw, but this is all your doing—if I go down, you're going down with me. So unless you want it to end right now, get us *out of here.*"

"Okay, okay." I put my hand on the control. Simple enough—up for reverse, down for forward, the farther down, the faster you go. I took a breath and eased the lever down a notch. The engine's warble raised pitch slightly and the boat slowly pulled away from the dock. Ahead was the arched towpath footbridge and below it the channel into the canal. I aimed for the center of the channel.

Stanhouse scrambled onto the passenger seat, his legs hanging in the aisle that separated us. "Wade's going for the other boat." He brought the revolver up and steadied the barrel on the back of the seat.

"There's no need for that! They'll never catch up to us in that little—"

He fired just as we passed under the footbridge, the single shot reverberating like a twenty-one gun salute.

"*Jesus.*" We cleared the inlet and were now out onto the canal. I looked back over my shoulder; as if framed by the footbridge, I could see Birdy and two of his uniforms zigzagging across the inlet in the small outboard.

Stanhouse yelled, "Never mind them! Bear left and give it some gas!"

"Not left! We'll get into—"

"You want the next bullet?"

I grabbed the throttle and pulled. The sudden surge threw us both back against our seats and the bow of the boat rose up like a wall of fiberglass.

"I can't see where we're going!" My hand instinctively reached for the control, but Stanhouse slapped it away.

"Stand up and steer!"

I pulled myself up with my left hand and peered out over the top of the windshield and the bucking bow, squinting from the glare of the sun on the water. We had just passed under the old Big Ridge Road canal bridge and were heading due east. There was nothing immediately in our path, and despite the situation, I started to relax a bit as the cool wind washed over my face. But the respite was short-lived. After we'd covered about a mile, the scenery began to change; a few hundred yards ahead, the canal's flat profile suddenly broke up into a low, irregular horizon. The Great Port Erie Raft Race was, you should pardon the expression, dead ahead.

I tried to point out our dilemma to Stanhouse, but he shook it off.

"That's the idea, Hackshaw," he shouted over the throbbing of the engine. "An obstacle course of innocent bystanders for the police to worry about. You just worry about holding speed and taking us through."

"How'm I supposed to take us through all that?"

"Serpentine. Serpentine!" And he started to laugh like the maniac he was.

I rested one knee on the seat to steady myself and glued my eyes to the scene ahead. We were closing fast—I had no idea how fast, but it felt like we were skimming the surface at mach one. The makeshift flotilla was only fifty yards out now. The center of the canal was swollen with homemade rafts, most of them powered by bedsheet sails or oars, most of them dressed up with painted cardboard superstructures. There were floating six-packs and miniature Mississippi paddle-wheelers and ersatz Volkswagens and a score of other whimsical shapes bobbing and weaving their way toward the finish line, the Main Street lift bridge.

And there was precious little room to maneuver on the flanks, either. Dozens of powerboats had dropped anchor along both banks of the canal, their decks crowded with spectators cheering on the raftsmen.

I flinched as the revolver roared again—Stanhouse firing another wild shot to discourage our pursuers. His last, as it turned out. I glanced to my right just as he angrily tossed the empty gun over the side. I thought about throwing myself over with it, but in the instant it took me to decide, he pulled the little chrome pistol out of his waistband and leveled it on me.

"Full speed ahead, Hackshaw."

I computed my options and decided to angle to the left, hoping to find a seam between the pleasure craft along the north bank and the outer fringe of the rafts. I almost clipped a straggler piloting a sheet of plywood lashed to old tires, his sunburned face stared up at me in horror as we flashed by, and then we were in the clear and speeding down a narrow, shifting alley of water.

Ahead on my right, alerted by the whine of the inboard, some raft crews were struggling to alter course toward the center of the canal, while others simply dove over the side and swam for it. On my left I could see the angry faces of the spectators on the anchored boats and up on the canal bank, a blur of shaking fists and open mouths.

I checked Stanhouse. He was sitting up on the back of the passenger seat, his free hand clasping the top of the windshield, his eyes narrowed to slits as the wind and spray hit his face. Staring straight out over the bow, uncaring about— maybe even unaware of—the chaos and panic around us.

Again I considered diving overboard, but it was too late by then. The boat was running flat out; if I gave up the wheel, it would surely careen out of control and either cut a swath through the helpless rafts or smash into one of the pleasure crafts sitting at anchor.

Fifty feet ahead a bearded man in a floating bathtub suddenly broke away from the pack and paddled furiously for the left bank of the canal. He was too late and too slow, succeeding only in blocking my way. I cut the wheel right, then left again, somehow missing both the man in the tub and two kids on a log raft. I risked a quick look back; my backwash had swamped the bathtub, but its former occupant was all right, doggedly stroking toward the shore. The two kids, still seaworthy, were giving me the bird.

Stanhouse hadn't moved a muscle.

Eyes front again.

We were almost home free—the main convoy of racers was falling away on my right—but there was one last obstacle. Just ahead were the serious contenders, five rafts in all, strung out across the canal like sculling crews sprinting for the finish line. Oblivious to the juggernaut at their backs, each intent on crossing under the Main Street lift bridge in the lead, believing that the screaming spectators on the banks and crowding the top of the bridge were merely rooting them on the last hundred feet.

My best chance was to split the two rafts on the end of the line, directly ahead of me—a giant cardboard shoe on the left and, to its right, a catamaran-style raft with oil-barrel pontoons. There was no margin for error; if either raft drifted off course . . .

I gripped the wheel with both hands and hunched my shoulders and began mumbling a prayer. Twenty yards, fifteen yards, ten . . .

The two-man crew in the catamaran spotted the danger at the last moment and panicked, throwing themselves over the far side. Their momentum pushed the catamaran into my path. I reacted instinctively, cutting the wheel hard left, then frantically whipping it back, but it was too late—I couldn't correct in time to miss the shoe raft. I registered the bump and scrape against the fiberglass bow at the same time I caught a glimpse of what was left of the sign painted onto the side of the now-listing loafer: FINAPOLIA SHOE RE . . .

"Damn!" I craned my neck to check our wake. Two men were bobbing in the water beside the wreckage of cardboard, one of them managing to wave a familiar fist in the air.

I couldn't resist. "Who's all wet now, Finapolia?"

But my giddiness didn't last. We were clear of racers, with no serious harm done. But there was still Stanhouse.

"Cut your speed to a quarter." He was all business again, the pistol back at the ready. "We're riding too high. Wouldn't want to shear off the windshield, would we?"

I jerked my head around. The steel lift bridge loomed not sixty feet ahead. He was right; there wasn't much clearance with the bridge down, but we'd make it if we took it slow. My trembling hand found the throttle control and inched it upward. The bow began to lower.

That's when the windshield exploded.

Stanhouse shouted a curse and dropped into his seat, his lap sprinkled with broken glass. Then he screamed—"*Bastard!*"—raised the gun above the shattered windshield, and fired toward the bridge.

I looked up. The crowd of spectators had scattered, leaving the center of the walkway to one man. He was leaning out over the railing, both hands gripping a large automatic, lining up a second shot.

Ricky Reimer, still trying to be a hero.

In the next split second I decided I'd rather risk being shot by the nut with the little gun than by the nut with the big gun.

I let go of the wheel and brought both feet up onto the seat, preparing to leap. I heard Stanhouse scream again and felt his fingers clawing at me. His arm must've come down on the throttle control; the boat accelerated again and veered wildly to the left, and suddenly I was somersaulting through the air.

The cool canal waters and the horrific sound of fiberglass meeting steel reached my ears simultaneously.

After that, everything turned wet and blurry.

Then there were all these hands, reaching down like pall bearers and hoisting me over the concrete breakwall and dropping me none too gently on a strip of grass. And a circle of faces overhead—ugly, angry, buzzing faces.

"It's that bum from the *Advertiser*."

"Lucky he didn't kill half the town, a stunt like that."

"Shoulda let him drown."

I somehow struggled to my feet, one dripping, bedraggled limb at a time. "Not my fault," I panted. "Stanhouse . . . he was the one."

"Oh, sure, blame it on the dead guy."

"You were the one behind the wheel, Hackshaw."

I pushed past two of my accusers and staggered to the edge of the quay and stared at the base of the lift bridge, twenty feet away. The big inboard was splintered nearly in two, its bow sandwiched into a four-foot gap between the bridge's steel and concrete supports, the rest of it half sunk into the canal. A slick of oil and gas floated on the calm water.

"Where's Stanhouse? I don't see him—"

"And you don't want to, either."

An all-too-familiar voice. I turned. Reimer was limping toward me on his injured leg, the automatic shoved in his belt. Trying not to look too pleased with himself.

"He caught that second pier with his face," he said, pointing like a goddamn tour guide. "Very messy."

"That stunt of yours almost got me killed."

The bastard shrugged. "Like my old football coach used to say, all's well that ends well."

I worked up a smile and took a step closer—"Here's something else he used to say"—and rammed my knee between his legs.

"Always wear your cup."

# Epilogue

It's a historical fact that in good times and bad, the people in small towns tend to band together—barn raisings, quilting bees, bucket brigades. The occasional lynching.

Fortunately, things never went quite that far. But sentiment was strongly against me for a while there, particularly after two dozen already angry Port Eriens witnessed my sneak attack on Ricky Reimer. Even when Birdy Wade showed up to sort things out, he didn't have an easy time convincing the mob that it was Wesley Stanhouse, and not I, who was responsible for ruining their precious raft race.

Stanhouse was one of their own, you see, and it's always easier to blame the outsider.

But cooler heads did prevail, and eventually most folks were willing to concede that I hadn't done all that badly, given the circumstances. Everyone except Vern and Doris Murray, who kept insisting I had to be guilty of *something*. And of course little Luigi Finapolia, who claimed I'd plotted the whole mess just to screw up his chance to be a winner once in his miserable life. He cursed me up, down, and sideways there on the quay, then vowed on all the saints never to speak to me again, which was the best news I heard all day.

Callous as it may sound, Stanhouse's death saved a good deal of trouble and expense. Rather than a trial, there was a simple inquest, at which the obvious conclusion was reached—that the deceased had died of massive head trauma while attempting to avoid arrest for the murder of Sue Krevin. There were the predictable grumbles when the public learned of the motive behind the murder—lots of I told you sos regarding Hester DelGado and Janus Theophanis and the elaborate Mott house hoodwink. But for the most part, people seemed eager to put the matter behind them and to return to what passes for normalcy in Port Erie. Again, I suspect the citizenry's outrage was mitigated by the knowledge that it was one of their own well-regarded neighbors who had actually committed all of the violence.

And speaking of violence, I'm pleased to report that Step Garris not only survived a .25-caliber bullet between the eyes, he seemed much improved for the ordeal. Born again is how he put it, and who can argue with the results? He gave up the booze, got his wife to move back home, and even landed semisteady work, recounting his personal salvation to Evangelical groups at two hundred dollars a pop. Dr. Ramathan was so impressed with Step's miraculous recovery that he wrote up the case and submitted it to the *New England Journal of Medicine*. When they rejected the piece, he ended up placing it with *Reader's Digest*.

Step eventually did undergo hypnotherapy, by the way, at the request of the district attorney's office. Wouldn't you know, he still couldn't remember a blessed thing about the murder.

Anyway, no one was happier to see the case closed than Birdy Wade—and with good reason. He and I had a nice chat with Ricky Reimer that afternoon, just as soon as the punk stopped vomiting.

It was quite a performance, Reimer sitting there in the backseat of Birdy's Ford with a bandaged thigh and a wounded expression. He swore Sue Krevin had been nothing to him but casual sex, and that he hadn't known about the fake pregnancy or the satanic graffiti business until after the fact. When Sue finally came to him and confessed what she'd been doing and why—to pay him back for taking her for granted, he claimed—Reimer was afraid he'd look foolish in the eyes of Birdy and the other men. Worse, he feared someone like me might jump to the wrong conclusion and decide he himself had concocted the whole vandalism episode to make the police department look useful.

So he had done his clumsy best to cover things up, first by making the girl promise to retire her paint can and, after she was killed, by trying to harass me into leaving well enough alone.

I didn't believe more than half of his story, but I couldn't prove otherwise. Besides, Birdy strongly hinted we'd all be better off if the matter were dropped. I suppose I could've forced the issue by filing a formal complaint of police brutality, but I didn't. It's Chief Wade's town, after all, and I still have to work in it.

Which was more than Reimer could say. At its next meeting the Port Erie Town Council decided to keep the police department but to cut its budget by 7 percent. That meant Birdy had to permanently eliminate one slot, and that slot turned out to be Reimer's. Not that he had a prayer of being reinstated, anyway; that boy just had too much cowboy in him to be a good law enforcement officer, Birdy told me, and I heartily agreed.

Apparently Reimer wasn't convinced, however. Last anyone heard, he'd packed everything he owned into that little Celica and was headed west, buoyed by a rumor that the LAPD was hiring.

Now for the bad news–good news bit.

The bad news is I never got to file an exclusive on the murder for the *Advertiser* because the damn story broke on a Monday. As a weekly we publish only on Thursday, and by then the Rochester *Times-Democrat* had already reported everything worth reporting. C'est la vie.

But the good news is Janus Theophanis never got a chance to embarrass me with that paper I signed. It seems his partners at the downtown clinic had been left in the dark about the little bloodsucker's Machiavellian maneuverings out at the Mott house—until they read about it in the *T-D*. It took them about ten minutes of media queries to decide they needed more bad publicity about as much as they needed an internist who spent most of his time making bad real estate deals. So they dumped Theophanis from the partnership, although I think "severed their ties" was the phrase they used in the press release.

Perhaps the greatest irony of all was the fate of the Mott house itself. Theophanis's former partners tried selling the place, but when no decent offers came in, they decided to resubmit their geriatric clinic plan to the Port Erie Zoning Board. And guess what happened? The neighbors, having seen they could do much worse, agreed to drop their opposition to the variance change, with one stipulation: that the vibrant polychrome paint job be replaced with a pristine coat of New England white.

To this day, I wince every time I have to drive up Virginia Street.

And then there was that other painted lady, Hester Del-Gado. She beat it out of town the minute the DA gave her the green light. Where she ended up is anyone's guess—the speculation ranged from Taos, New Mexico, to the Planet Zevon.

The only thing I can say for sure is she was never seen again in our corner of upstate New York.

I'll admit she still crosses my mind from time to time, like the twinges a reformed drunk feels whenever New Year's Eve rolls around. But I'm getting better, one day at a time.

Oh, and one last thing. Jennifer Hadley? She waddled up the aisle with her boyfriend about a week before delivering a healthy, screaming baby girl. Last I knew they were all living happily ever after at his mother's house—Mom, Jennifer, Bobby, and, of course, little Bobby Sue.